THE SPEAR OF VENGEANCE

THE SPEAR OF VENGEANCE

A MODERN-DAY THRILLER

F. DAVID SMITH

Charleston, SC
www.PalmettoPublishing.com

The Spear of Vengeance
Copyright © 2021 by F. David Smith

All rights reserved

Hardcover ISBN: 978-1-68515-437-0
Paperback ISBN: 978-1-68515-436-3
eBook ISBN: 978-1-68515-438-7

To Zachary—for your story ideas, critiques, and our character John. I could never have written this without you.

And to Amanda, Reci, Mike, Marc, and Connie—you read, encouraged, critiqued, and offered brilliant suggestions when I needed them the most.

Truly I say to you, there are some standing here who will not taste death…

—Jesus the Nazarene

PROLOGUE

Twenty Years Earlier

Dan burst through the door into the lingering daylight of a warm summer's evening and ran for the convertible. Billy had the car idling at the curb by Mall Door Six with a big grin plastered across his dumb seventeen-year-old face. Mark sat in the back seat and waved Dan on with a laugh.

As he neared the car, Dan shouted, "Go! Go!" Behind him, the mall door banged open, and he heard his brother shout an obscenity. Dan laughed, jumped onto the car's trunk, slid forward, and dropped into the back seat. Billy hit the gas, and the tires screeched as the car sped away. Dan twisted around to watch as his brother sprinted after them. The look on his face was priceless.

"What did you tell him?" Billy called back from the front.

"That we were getting something for Mom," Dan said. "For her birthday tomorrow." His brother ran harder as Billy turned right and headed toward the exit. "That I'd give him some money so he could buy it for her."

Dan watched his brother give up and slow to a stop in the middle of the street. A loud honk from a car horn made his brother jump like a startled cat. Laughter filled their car again, but Dan thought he saw tears on his brother's face. His smile faded a little, and he slid around in the seat to face forward.

A second later, Mark tapped Dan on the shoulder and pointed out the rear of the car. "I think he pissed those guys off," Mark said. "Maybe we should go back."

Dan took a quick look. His brother still stood in the middle of the lane, now flanked by two men in suits—but they seemed to be just talking. "Nah, he'll be fine," Dan said. "Besides, he's too big to mess with, especially when he's mad." His smile returned. "He might just beat the crap out of them. Then it'd be Mom that's pissed."

———

Three hours later, Dan led his friends out of the movie theater. They lingered around a poster for the movie, adrenaline still pumping from the final action scene.

"Man, I did not see that coming," Billy said.

Dan agreed and gave Mark a shove. "I thought you were going to puke when the alien exploded."

"Yeah, well, at least I wasn't crying like your brother," Mark said. "Did you see him back at the mall?"

Dan felt flushed, but he did not know why. He turned his back on Mark and exhaled hard. "Just shut up, dumbass," Dan said. "You don't know anything." A moment of silence stretched out as Dan stared across the parking lot.

"Come on, you idiots. Let's roll," Billy said. "I've got to get home. My dad's going to kill me if I'm late for curfew."

Mark and Billy headed off down the sidewalk. "You still have a curfew? Your parents are so…" Mark's voice trailed off as they rounded the corner of the building, never noticing that Dan had not followed. He looked up at the movie poster again. His brother would have liked it.

His friends' stupid conversation dominated the ride as they drove on into the night. Dan rode in the back and remained silent, as a cold knot had formed in his gut. The top was down, and the wind helped drown out their chattering—and the feeling that maybe he had gone too far this time.

I'll make it up to him.

Dan slouched a little lower into the seat. They turned onto his cul-de-sac just after 10:30 p.m.

"What the hell?" Mark asked.

Dan grabbed the seat in front of him and pulled himself forward. Emergency lights strobed into the night. Two police cruisers and a black SUV sat in front of Dan's house. The closest car had its lights flashing, and two officers sat in the front seat. As one talked on the cruiser's radio, the other stepped out at their approach. Billy stopped his car two houses away, and Dan jumped out.

"You guys better get out of here," Dan said softly. Billy turned the car and rolled into the night. Without waiting, Dan headed down the sidewalk.

"Hold it right there. Let me see some ID," the officer said.

Dan fumbled with his wallet and handed the man his driver's license. "I'm Dan Alexander. I live here. What's happened?"

The policeman keyed his shoulder mic. "The brother is here. He's safe."

Dan's head snapped toward his house. "What do you mean *safe*? What's happened?"

The policeman stepped forward and took his arm. "Come with me, young man."

Dan jerked his arm free. He stood about an inch taller than the cop and outweighed him by about thirty pounds. Dan's hands balled into fists. "What the crap is going on?"

The officer's hand rested on the top of his sidearm. The man's eyes blazed.

His mom's warnings echoed through his thoughts. *You boys are getting so big. You've got to learn to be careful. How to act. How to stay calm. Always follow the rules.*

Dan exhaled a quick breath. "I'm sorry, sir. But please, is my mom okay?"

The policeman's gaze softened, and his arm relaxed away from his weapon. "She's fine, son. It's your brother."

Dan stumbled back a step. "Is he hurt?"

The man looked at the house and then back to Dan but said nothing.

This time, it was Dan who grabbed the man's arm. "Is he dead?"

"No, son. He's missing."

A light breeze brushed Dan's face. He wiped cold sweat from his forehead. "Missing?"

"There were witnesses. He was abducted."

Dan stared at the man and tried to make sense of the words, but they seemed out of order. Wrong. He shoved past the man and sprinted for his porch.

"Mom!"

As Dan leaped up the porch steps, three uniformed officers and a woman in a suit filed out the front door. His mother stopped at the threshold. Tears glistened on her cheek. He froze on the top step, suddenly afraid to move any closer.

The woman handed his mom a business card. She clutched it like a precious stone. "Call me anytime, day or night, if you need me or hear something," the woman said. "I'll leave a patrol car out front tonight in case he returns, and we'll monitor your line for any calls. We'll find him, Mrs. Alexander."

And then they were gone, and it was just Dan standing on the steps and his mom filling the doorway. She straightened and made a quick swipe at the moisture on her cheek. Her voice hardened with each word that followed. "They said people saw it. At the mall. Some woman called 911. They took him in the parking lot." Her voice broke, and she choked back a sob. "Oh God, Dan, what if they hurt him?"

Dan's gaze fell to the wooden planks of the porch. His face burned.

"Why did you leave him?" she demanded.

Dan lifted his eyes to meet her stare. His heart hammered. "It was just a joke."

Her eyes hardened like they always did when he disappointed her. "If they hurt him, just remember, it's you that put him there. I'll never forgive you, boy. Never."

She faded back into the house and slammed the door. He stood staring at the doorknob until he heard the click of the deadbolt. With an ache in his chest, Dan slumped down onto the top porch step.

What have I done?

CHAPTER ONE

Present Day

The *ding* of the elevator caused Dan to glance up. Except for the small FBI logo etched in the glass, the window by his door gave Dan an unobstructed view of the corridor. The other agents hated this office. Too many distractions, they all said. But he liked distractions. He waited for the soft *swoosh* of the opening doors and hoped it might be Molly from Accounting. But no, it was just "the Intern."

Dan watched the criminal justice major sprint into the hallway only to slide to a stop in front of the office across from Dan's. The young man raised his hand to knock but hesitated. Dan smiled at his distress and waited. The Intern peeked right and then left, hand still poised before the door. He slowly rotated toward Dan. Relief washed across his face when he took in Dan's smile and burst through his door.

"Agent Alexander, the Special Agent in Charge Thompson, *um*, I mean, SAC Thompson said to rush this to Agent Reid," the Intern said. He thrust a sealed red folder forward. His eyes pleaded for Dan to take it.

Dan kept his hands folded on his desk and raised his left eyebrow. The young man cringed.

"Please, sir. Agent Reid is so busy." The folder began to tremble. The newbies always believed the stories about Reid.

Dan glanced past the Intern and into the office across the hall. The narrow window next to the door allowed him to see his partner, the famous Zachary Reid. He sat behind a well-organized desk with an array of awards on the wall—the ones they required him to display. Reid had done it all, except take any promotion that moved him out of fieldwork.

Dan knew Reid liked to lecture at the Academy but only to ensure that the trainees knew how to do it *by the book*. The graying at his temples provided the only clue to his actual age of fifty-five. Otherwise, Reid's trim physique and polished appearance made most think of him as fifteen years younger. And like the Intern, many avoided those steel-colored eyes and the steel-trap mind behind them.

A Reid-ism from Dan's days at Quantico floated through his mind. "The FBI does not torture detainees." He suppressed a chuckle and took the folder.

"Thank you, sir," the Intern said just above a whisper. The young man backed into the hall and rushed toward the elevator. He jabbed the down button five times in rapid succession like a woodpecker after a prized beetle. As the doors slid open, he called back, "Oh, and SAC Thompson said to meet him in Conference Room Two in ten minutes."

Dan smiled, shook his head, and opened the folder. As he read, the world faded into the background.

Holy crap!

———

Dan plopped the dark-red folder in the center of his partner's desk and sent a neat stack of Reid's papers fluttering off the edge like a flock of birds disturbed from their roost. Reid looked up from the case file in his hand and frowned. Though thirty-seven years old, at six foot two, Dan still had the physique of a linebacker. But he understood the boyish look of his face made it hard for Reid to take him seriously. Given Dan's time as a Navy SEAL, the folks in the Bureau had expected a polished professional. But his suit jacket always looked rumpled next to Reid's, and how did the man get his tie so straight? Seven months of that perfectly straight tie.

"N-S-A priority alert," Dan said. A grin flashed across his face, and he ran a hand through his light-brown hair. "Looks like the nerds at the National Security Agency are on to something, and we're on deck. Thompson wants us in Two ASAP. Wait till you read it."

Dan hesitated as Reid laid the case file in his hand into a tray with similar files. Reid straightened the corners of the stack before turning his attention to the red hard-cover folder Dan had tossed onto his desk. He focused on the black letters embossed into the cover. *National Security Agency—Top Secret—Eyes Only*. Dan knew Reid had seen six of these red folders during his personal twenty-year war on terrorism—all of them bad. Three assassination plots, two dirty bombs, one anthrax exposure. All Reid's cases. No lives lost.

Except for the perps'.

Reid took a deep breath and opened the file. His fingers brushed over a black-and-white photo of a middle-aged man wearing a white medical jacket. The picture sat atop the neatly bound thirty-two-page briefing. Dan glanced again at the name, printed in bold letters, that rested above a simple but telling phrase. *Dr. Kevin Restor: Cause of death: Aneurysm.*

Dan rounded the desk and peered over his partner's shoulder as Reid flipped past the photo with professional disinterest. The next page led with the clipped phrasing of the data analysts at the NSA. Columns of dates and times, locations, and names. More photos. More doctors. All dead.

Reid studied the summary page, absorbing the same facts that had excited Dan. Twenty-two doctors and scientists in the United States and Europe. All leaders in their fields—mRNA, rapid vaccine production, infectious diseases, microbiology, immunology, virology, and a few other "ologies" that Dan had not recognized. Accidental death or natural causes listed in every case. All died within the last thirty-six hours. The NSA nerds correlated the probability of a simple coincidence at less than 0.15 percent. Conclusion: Coordinated activity, intent unknown.

Like they needed a supercomputer to figure that out.

Reid let the folder rest back on the desk and turned to stare out the window at the downtown Atlanta skyline for a long moment. Dan slid into the chair across the desk from Reid. His partner's gaze shifted back to Dan, and Reid seemed to measure him—as if weighing him for what was to come. A small frown creased Reid's brow. He rose from the desk, straightened his already straight tie, buttoned the top button of his suit jacket, and picked up the red summary of death. "Let's go," Reid said, and they headed out of the office together.

———

After a quick stop at his office and the break room, Dan hurried down the hallway toward the conference room with a notepad pinned in an armpit and a cup of coffee in each hand. A doughnut perched on the top of each cup. The standard see-through glass of the conference room radiated the opaque sheen of the privacy setting. Two vague outlines stood near the back of the room.

The door swung wide and banged against the strategically placed door stop on the wall as Dan backed into the room. He pushed the door closed with his left foot and let the notepad drop onto the table. Special Agent in Charge Gregory Thompson stood gazing out the window, hands resting on the rail designed for that very purpose. Reid stood next to him. Silence provided the only clue to the SAC's mood. Reid's frown was much easier to read.

Dan mumbled, "Sorry I'm late," around the yellow wooden pencil clenched in his teeth. "Coffee?" he asked his partner. Reid just shook his head. Dan shrugged and glanced toward the still silent SAC. He sighed, set both cups down by his notepad, and slid into the nearest chair.

A neat stack of photos rested in the center of the table. Dan downed half a doughnut in a single bite, wiped the back of his hand across his mouth, and reached for the photos.

"Suspects?" Dan asked.

"No," the SAC said. His attention never left the windows. "If the analysis is correct, we believe these are the next targets."

The first picture featured an older man, sixties, frazzled gray hair, unkempt lab coat. He stood near a whiteboard with a marker in hand. Dan leafed through the next four in rapid succession—all of the same man in different locations. Photo number five made his head snap back a little, and his breath caught. It framed an attractive woman, late thirties, raven-black hair, on the steps of a large, curved glass office building. A twin structure stood to its right. Farther on, a black wrought-iron security fence separated the building from a surrounding wooded landscape. Dan thought he might have seen the buildings.

But he knew the woman.

Dan exhaled a measured breath that ended in a low whistle. He set the pictures down on the table in front of him and rubbed his forehead.

Reid moved to sit in the chair opposite his partner and pointed to the picture on the top of the stack. "Who is she?"

Thompson wheeled around to face them. "*They* are the only two mRNA experts left in North America. The NSA took its own sweet time to share the intel, but it appears that all of the other leading scientists in the field have died."

"Died?" Dan asked. He pried his eyes from the photo and focused on the SAC.

Thompson began pacing across the back of the room. "Regardless of what the autopsies say, we're sure that they were well-disguised murders. How? The nerds don't even have a guess. Whoever is behind this and what they intend has the brass sweating bullets."

"And you want us to find the bad guys," Dan said.

"That's not your assignment," the SAC said. Thompson paused by the window again, scanning the horizon like a lookout searching for some hidden enemy. "You're to find and secure the two remaining doctors. If something bad hits the fan, the White House thinks we'll need them."

Dan glanced back at the photo of the woman. "Why us?"

"The luck of the draw," SAC Thompson said. "Seems they are both in Atlanta today. Attending some conference at the CDC at one-thirty this afternoon. I want you on-site ASAP, and I want the good doctors back here by two." The SAC turned back to the table. "Reid, make it happen, and, Dan, no shortcuts. By the book this time."

Dan sank a little deeper into his chair. He caught his partner's icy stare and heaved a sigh.

"There won't be any issues, sir," Reid said. He stood, straightened his still straight tie, nodded to the SAC, and headed for the door.

Dan sat a moment longer. His thoughts raced as he stared at the photo of the woman.

"Is there a problem with this assignment, Agent Alexander?" the SAC asked.

Dan straightened in his chair. "No, sir," he said. He met Thompson's gaze as he stood. "No problem at all."

Unless she kills me.

CHAPTER TWO

Fifteen minutes later, Dan rounded the corner and spotted Reid by the elevator with his hands folded behind his ever-straight back. Dan had his suit jacket hung over his left forearm, and he carried a large duffel bag in his right. He smiled at his partner. Reid only raised his eyebrows, glanced at his watch, and pressed the down button on the elevator. The door opened with an immediate *ding*.

"I hustled down to Provisions and grabbed some must-haves in case we find ourselves having to track these scientists down," Dan said. "Did I keep you waiting long?"

Reid ignored the question and stepped into the empty car. With a forced smile, Dan tossed the duffel in the elevator and took his spot at Reid's three o'clock. Reid pressed the "B" button, and silence filled the elevator car as they progressed down.

Dan checked his watch. "I also pulled up the schedule at the CDC. Looks like both the docs are speaking as part of some panel discussion at one-thirty this afternoon. They won't be happy when we yank them out of there. Maybe we should just let them do their presentation, and then we can swing them back here to HQ."

As the door slid open, Reid said, "The SAC said two. We'll have them here by one fifty-five. Early is always on time."

They angled across the garage to their assigned black SUV. Dan threw the duffel into the back alongside their standard tactical gear. He withdrew a file folder from the top of the bag and headed for the passenger door. Reid slid into the driver's side, buckled his seat belt under his tie, and fixed Dan with a stare.

"How do you know her?" Reid asked in an ice-cold voice.

Dan gave a start. He turned to look out the side window and remained silent.

"Thought so," Reid said. He pulled out of the parking garage and merged into the traffic on Flowers Road. The faint *click, click, click* of the turn signals provided the only interruption of the silence in the SUV.

After a few moments, Dan cleared his throat, opened the folder, and picked out the photos. He studied the first one and read the attached bio. "This guy is Dr. Alan Brown. It says he's the head of the molecular virology department at Yale and a leader in the field of rapid mRNA vaccine creation. Was on the COVID team for one of the big pharmaceuticals. Looks like a really smart guy." He switched pictures and paused while he took in the photo. "And she is Dr. Amelia Cranford. Her friends call her Ames. Still single. Has invested her whole life into her career. Specializes in virology, infectious diseases, and vaccines. She's got an mRNA lab at Stanford and has worked closely with the CDC on several projects."

"And you got all of that from just a picture?" Reid asked.

Dan stuffed the photos back into the folder. "No, Reid. She and I knew each other a long time ago. Before I went into the Navy. I've checked on her a few times since I've been back, but we haven't spoken since college."

"And I take it she won't exactly be happy to see you?"

Dan stared out the front window and shook his head. "Let's just say she might doubt my commitment to protecting her."

Reid gave his partner a hard look. "These two doctors are our only priority. Don't let your past get in the way of the mission."

Dan nodded his agreement. He flipped the folder back open. But as he studied the picture, he only saw trouble in the woman's green eyes.

———

Dan slumped in his seat as Reid flashed his badge at the CDC guard station and then drove into the east parking lot. A sour taste had formed in Dan's mouth. He exited the SUV as soon as Reid parked. As Dan marched across the parking lot, he thought back to the last time he had seen Ames. He sighed and peered up into the clear blue sky.

It's Dr. Cranford now.

Reid caught up with him as Dan rounded the CDC marquee in front of the building about one hundred and fifty feet from the front doors. "Hold up a second," Reid said. "You go find Dr. Brown. I'll search out and retrieve your lady friend. We're going to avoid any undue notice or incidents."

Dan's face flushed, and he spun toward his partner. "She's not my lady friend." Over Reid's shoulder, he caught sight of a woman rushing across the parking lot—tall, about five eight, jet-black hair, athletic build, attractive but stern face, conservative dark business attire.

Ames.

Dan pointed across the lot. "Or how about we just stop Dr. Cranford before she enters the building?"

Reid rotated to his left, spotted her, and headed off on an intercept course with Dan trailing along behind him. As they approached, Reid called out, "Dr. Cranford, can we have a word?"

She glanced at Reid but did not slow down. "I'm sorry, but I'm late," she said. "Perhaps we can chat at the doctors' reception this afternoon."

Reid continued to close in on his target. With precision, he reached into his coat, pulled out his badge, and held it up in her direction. "Dr. Cranford, I must insist. I'm Special Agent Zachary Reid with the FBI."

She pulled up and turned to Reid. Her gaze focused first on his badge and then his face.

"And I believe you may know my associate, Special Agent Daniel Alexander."

Her eyes darted to Dan and widened in a moment of surprise. A frown creased her brow, and she returned her attention to Reid. "What's this about? I'm giving a lecture in five minutes, and I'm late. Can't this wait?"

"I'm afraid you'll need to miss your presentation. We'll send word while we're en route. We have reason to believe that you and Dr. Alan Brown are in imminent danger. You need to come with us. We'll collect Dr. Brown and debrief you both on the way to our offices."

"In danger?" She studied the courtyard for a moment before locking her eyes back on Reid. "How can I be in danger here? This is a very secure facility. You are free to come along, but I must insist—"

A low, loud *wumph* interrupted her, and Dan felt a tremor in the ground.

"Get down!" Dan shouted and launched himself at Ames. Bright white light and a deafening roar erupted from the main building. He wrapped his arms around her shoulders and dove for the ground. Ames gasped as they landed hard on the pavement. A second later, a hailstorm of hot glass pelted Dan's back like shards from an exploding volcano.

He released Ames, rolled to his right, and sat up to take in the scene. The left side of the upper half of the building had disappeared, and flames engulfed the bottom three floors. He raised a hand to ward off the heat rolling out from the blazing building and staggered to his feet. Debris littered the parking lot. Thick black smoke poured over the area. He spotted his partner lying on his side.

"Reid!" he called out. "Are you injured?"

Reid rolled onto his back and coughed. "I'm fine. Check the doctor."

Dan put a hand on her back. "You okay, Ames?"

She raised her head and pushed herself up onto her hands and knees. "No, Agent Alexander, I am not *okay*. And don't call me that." She ignored his offered hand as she rose to stand by his side. "My God, what happened?" she asked.

A man caught Ames's attention. He writhed on the ground, his leg pinned under the remains of the decorative stone column that had supported the CDC marquee. She started forward, but Dan grabbed her arm.

"We need to move. We're not safe here," Dan said.

She glared at him, shook her arm free, and pointed at the man. "There are injured people. We have to help them."

Reid moved to stand at her side and withdrew his cell phone. "He's right, Doctor. I'll call for emergency services, but we have to get you to a secure location."

Reid punched a four-digit short code into his phone. The connection took only a second. "This is Special Agent Zachary Reid. I'm at the CDC main campus in Atlanta, and there has been an explosion. Possible terrorist activity. Expect many casualties. Notify SAC Thompson. Dispatch local fire and emergency services to this location, and deploy the on-call tactical team ASAP."

The wail of a distant siren added its agreement to the agents' demands. Shouts filled the air. A man ran past with a smear of blood on his face, headed for the parking lot. Ames's face hardened as she scanned across the scene, and she strode off toward the man with the trapped leg.

Dan started to follow her, but the roar of an engine and the screech of tires from the far side of the parking lot caused him and Reid to turn. They watched a black Mercedes enter the parking lot and race toward them down the rows of parked cars.

Reid took a step toward the approaching vehicle. "Stay with the doctor, Dan."

Glass crunched underfoot as Dan caught up with Ames. The cries of the injured drifted across the area as black smoke continued to swirl from the blazing inferno. He stopped next to where she knelt by the man.

"Lie still," she ordered the man. "Dan, give me your tie."

Dan's attention remained on the car, even as he loosened his tie and slid it from around his neck. He glanced down as she took it and saw the bloody mess of what remained of the man's leg.

"What's your name?" she asked the man in a calm voice.

"Henry," the man replied through gritted teeth.

"Well, Henry, your leg's in pretty bad shape, but I'm—" she continued, but Dan tuned out the remainder. Instead, he focused on his partner as Reid took up a position about twenty-five feet from them. With his badge in his raised left hand, he stood next to a line of parked cars. His right hand hung casually near his holstered weapon.

The car skidded to a stop two rows away from where Reid stood. Three men exited the vehicle while the driver remained behind the wheel. Dressed in dark suits and white shirts, the three looked like every private security team Dan had ever seen—tall, square shoulders, short-cropped hair, straight backs, nice suits, but loose jackets. They paused in a line next to their vehicle and surveyed the area. Tinted windows prevented

Dan from having a clear view of the driver, but something about him seemed familiar.

"I'm with the FBI," Reid said. "Identify yourselves, and state your business."

"We were passing by and saw the explosion. We stopped to render possible assistance," big guy number one said. The three started forward in confident strides.

"Stop!" Reid shouted. He slid his Glock 22 from its holster. "This area is not safe. I will have to ask you to wait for the emergency services."

Big guys number two and number three both looked to big guy number one. Dan saw the smallest of nods. He stepped in front of Ames and drew his weapon.

Like a choreographed dance, the three drew submachine guns from inside their jackets. Dan fired four rounds at the closest target. The man recoiled and dropped to his knees as at least some of the bullets found their mark.

Reid fired three quick rounds and hurried for cover as the two remaining assailants fired short bursts from their automatic weapons in his direction. The glass in the nearest car exploded under a hail of bullets. Reid ran further to his left, drawing their attention away from Dan and the doctor.

Startled by the gunfire, Ames tried to stand, but Dan placed a hand on her shoulder and forced her to the ground behind the remains of the column.

Reid fired again but quickly became pinned down by the alternating fire from the gunmen. Dan watched as the two moved in a coordinated fashion to flank Reid and distance themselves from Dan's position. Dan fired two more rounds, but the parked cars blocked any clear shot. His combat training ran to a quick conclusion of the tactical situation.

Reid's got maybe ninety seconds before he becomes the next casualty. Then it's our turn.

Dan glanced down at Ames. She crouched low—afraid but still in control. He would have to trust her. With his voice void of any emotion,

Dan said, "Ames, I've got to go help him. I want you to run to the other side of the building and hide until I come back."

"But what about Henry?" she said in a soft voice. "He'll die if I don't help him."

He pulled her up by her arm. "We are all dead if we don't move now." He pointed her in the other direction. "Now go!"

Ames jerked her arm free, glanced at the men firing at Reid, and then ran as directed without another word. She had only taken three strides when the squeal of tires forced Dan to realize his mistake. The driver in the Mercedes must have been waiting for this opportunity. The car sped down the row of vehicles in the direction Ames had run. Dan glanced at Reid, still pinned down with only moments left. Indecision froze him for the briefest of moments.

Damn.

As he turned to pursue Ames, he saw a dark-gray four-door Jeep Rubicon with large off-road tires bound over the curb outside the security fence at high speed. Its oversized metal bumper struck the wrought-iron fence and tore an eight-foot section from the posts just as the Mercedes made its turn at the end of the row of cars. The Mercedes fishtailed to avoid the piece of fencing that rocketed across the parking lot. With a loud crash, the Jeep plowed into the side of the Mercedes and smashed it into the parked cars. The Jeep quickly backed up and shot forward, hitting the car a second time. With a *pop*, the airbags deployed in the Mercedes. After reversing again, the Jeep sped around the disabled vehicle and raced toward Ames. She ran harder, angling away from the approaching Rubicon.

Dan sprinted after her but could only catch up as the Jeep slid to a stop just in front of them. The passenger-side door popped open. Dan forced himself in front of Ames—gun leveled at the driver. The man wore dark aviator sunglasses and a brown duster and had unruly black hair with a full beard. His olive complexion hinted of a Middle Eastern origin.

"Get in!" the man shouted.

"Like hell," Dan yelled back. "Identify yourself."

Gunfire echoed from across the lot. Ames gazed up at Dan for direction as he hesitated.

The man shook his head and heaved a sigh. "Look. Either shoot me and take my Rubicon, or get in. There's still time to save your friend if we move fast."

Ames decided for them. She pushed past Dan and jumped into the front seat. Dan frowned and followed but did not lower his weapon. He jerked open the rear door and grabbed the frame as the Jeep accelerated.

The parked cars flashed by as they sped toward Reid. "You can thank me later," the man said. He caught Dan's eye in the mirror. "Ditch your pistol. There's something better in the back."

Dan glanced behind the seat. His eyes widened as he surveyed an array of weapons and tactical gear.

They sped around a pile of rubble and swerved to avoid Henry. "Make it fast," the man said.

Dan grabbed the closest rifle, an M4 carbine, checked the magazine, and chambered a round. One of the gunmen spun at their approach. He sprayed bullets in their direction. Ames screamed as several struck the windshield and more thudded into her side of the Jeep. But the rounds only produced small cracks in the windows.

The Rubicon lurched to a stop about fifteen feet from Reid. Dan slid to the far side of the Jeep and leaped out. With the weapon pulled tight to his shoulder, he rounded the back of the Jeep and opened fire on the nearest man. The M4 delivered a half dozen rounds, and the man went down with several wounds to his chest and neck.

Across the parking lot, another Mercedes turned in from the street. Its engine roared as the car sped in their direction.

"We've got to go!" the man in the Jeep shouted.

Dan did not have a clear shot on the final gunman, but he took one step forward and began firing to pin the man down. He yelled, "Reid, let's move."

Reid fired two more quick rounds, turned, and sprinted to the Jeep. Dan just made it back to his door as the Jeep sped forward. He craned his neck to peer out the rear window for any pursuit. To his surprise, the man he had downed with the M4 sat up, rolled to his feet, and began firing at them. Dan could see the red stains on the front of the man's shirt.

What the hell?

———

"Hold on!" their driver shouted as the Rubicon bounded over the curb and smashed through the security fence. Dan bounced off the back of the seat in front of him, and the man glared at him in the mirror. They plowed through a ditch on the west side of the building, hopped another curb, and swerved through the traffic to join the flow heading toward I-85.

Ames released her death grip on the grab handle above the door and secured her seat belt with a loud *click*. She stared out the side window at the billowing smoke from the CDC.

Dan leaned forward and asked, "Ames, are you okay?"

"Of course she's not okay, you idiot," the man replied for her. "They just tried to blow her up, shoot her full of holes, and run her down."

Ames flinched after each declaration and twisted around to see if anyone had followed them. She clutched the seat belt like a desperate climber who had slipped from a cliff face.

"Everyone calm down," Reid ordered from the back. "Who are you, and what is going on?"

The man glanced to either side as they sped through a red light at an intersection. Horns blared all around them. The Jeep skidded around a corner and headed up the on-ramp for the freeway. Dan bounced off his door and caught a view of the dash, not surprised to see that they hit eighty by the time they reached the top of the ramp. The Jeep swam into the flow of traffic only to take to the shoulder and pass a semi on the right.

Dan checked behind them and saw no pursuit. "Jesus, man, slow down. We're safe now. There's no one following."

"Jesus?" the man asked. He checked both ways. "Did you see him? Do you think he's here to help you?" the man said. He laughed a mirthless laugh as his face darkened. "And you are far from safe. You have no idea who is behind this. You must leave Atlanta right away."

"Look," Reid said, "we are federal agents. I need you to identify yourself and exit the freeway *immediately*. We will arrange for transport to the FBI field office."

"Sit tight, G-man. I'll drop you *agents* off," the man said. He turned to Ames and took off his sunglasses. "But, Doctor, you should stick with me. You're not safe in Atlanta."

Ames peered at him and waited for more. But the man offered nothing. She said, "I don't even know who you are. And how do you know who I am?"

"I'm just a very interested party," he replied. He met her gaze with his dark-brown eyes for a long moment and then swerved the Rubicon the next second to miss the back of a pickup truck by mere millimeters.

"Dr. Cranford stays with us," Reid stated flatly. "She is now in federal protective custody, and her safety is our responsibility."

Ames touched the man's arm. "Please, tell me your name."

The man locked his eyes forward again. In the mirror, Dan saw a small tick begin under the man's right eye. Silence filled the Rubicon for a long moment.

With a sigh, the man's face softened. "I've been called many things, but you can call me John."

"Who talks like that?" Dan demanded. "What are you, CIA?"

Ames shot Dan a withering glare but smiled at the man and said, "Then thank you, John, for saving us...for saving me."

John slid his sunglasses back on. They exited the freeway at Chamblee Tucker Road and turned right toward the FBI field office. He eased the Rubicon into the parking lot. It rolled to a slow stop across the asphalt from the security gate.

John said, "You should come with me, Doctor." He gestured toward the building. "I know what's coming, and I can protect you more than these."

"She's not going anywhere, and neither are you," Reid said. "I need both of you to come with us while we sort this out."

John let out another sigh and lowered his head. With his lips pressed into a tight line, John turned toward the rear seat. A gun just appeared in his left hand—pointed at Reid's chest. He locked eyes with Dan and simply said, "Don't." A tense moment passed, and then he added, "I have more important things that require my attention. The doctor can go with you, but I warn you, do not feel safe here. Leave right away. Now get out of my Jeep."

Reid kept his hands in view and reached for the door. Dan waited for Ames to open her door and followed in a slow exit. As soon as Ames closed her door, the Jeep sped away and left the three standing in silence.

Ames spoke first. "Please tell me you have some idea what is going on?"

"We need to get you inside, Doctor. We'll tell you what we know once you're safe," Reid replied. As he turned to lead the way to the security station, he called back, "Dan, I'm sure you got the Jeep's license plate. See to the all-points bulletin as soon as we get the doctor settled. I want him back for questioning today. I'll brief the SAC on the attack."

"APB. On it," Dan said. He began repeating the plate numbers in his head.

Ames followed Reid but continued to stare after the Jeep. "What do you think he meant? About knowing what's coming?"

Dan shook his head and fell in behind her. He was confident they would find some answers once they brought John back for questioning.

And whatever it is, next time, I'll be ready.

CHAPTER THREE

Dan sat alone in Conference Room Two. They had handed Ames off to a female agent who escorted her to the locker room to get her cleaned up. Reid had disappeared into SAC Thompson's office, but the muffled sounds of raised voices and a couple of slammed doors made it clear how the conversation had gone. After he provided a brief statement to another agent, Dan found himself deposited in the conference room to wait. And wait he had—for the last forty-five minutes.

Dan stood and began pacing in front of the south-facing window. He glanced toward downtown and rubbed the back of his neck. East of the city, a dark smudge of a reminder hung in the air. He replayed the events at the CDC over in his mind and came to the same conclusions and questions.

We know nothing about them, but they seemed very prepared for us.

And who is this John guy?

And what about Ames?

It had been less than three hours since they had met in this room to get their assignment and learned that Ames was their charge to protect. But seeing her in the parking lot and then almost failing to defend her had left his stomach churning.

But I did fail.

His mind drifted back to those last days at UCLA fifteen years ago, and the small sting of regret surprised him. He supposed that she had a right to be angry still.

Dan ran his hand over his face. He returned to the table and dropped back into his chair just as the door opened. SAC Thompson entered at the head of a small parade of agents—three men from the antiterror team, a woman in an ATF jacket, and Reid. Reid took the chair across from Dan and met his partner's gaze with a small shake of his head. The other agents spread out and took seats, but Thompson stood at the head of the table.

"Could this be any worse? Preliminary counts have the number of casualties at over five hundred," the SAC began. His glare shifted between Dan and Reid as he continued. "Not only did we lose Dr. Brown, but there were over one hundred and fifty of the top medical minds in attendance at the conference. All dead."

Several of the agents shifted in their chairs. Dan felt their stares. He kept his hands folded together and let them rest on the table, but he wanted to wave them above his head and shout, "It wasn't my fault." With a deep breath, he kept his gaze on his hands.

Thompson turned to look out the south window. "Henderson, what do we know from your review of the security cams?"

Henderson cleared his throat. "Not much, sir. None of the internal feeds survived the blasts. We have some decent footage of the action in the parking lot from the cameras on the garage, but nothing yet of the actual placement of the explosives. We are still waiting for the download of the last two weeks from the CDC cloud backups."

"Put some heat on them, man. How long does it take to get a download? Johnson, what about forensics from the abandoned car?"

Johnson flipped through a few pages of notes. "High-end Mercedes. Smashed up pretty good. No prints. Really clean. We're having it towed to the lab for a detailed look, but I'm not optimistic. Registered to some shell corporation. The address was fake."

Thompson cracked his knuckles and continued to stare out the window. "So, we don't have squat. Anything on the explosives yet?"

"Site's still too hot for much of a search," the ATF agent replied. "But based on our preliminary review and Agent Alexander's initial description," she said with a nod toward Dan, "this is not a car bomb or some lone wolf with a bunch of ammonium nitrate. Much more precision and detonated within the structures. Likely military-grade explosives. We'll know more by the end of the week."

The SAC began pacing, gesturing with his hands as he spoke. "That's not good enough. Washington thinks this is just a prelude to something else, and I agree. We need to identify this group fast if we're going to have any hope of knowing what's coming."

Something the man, John, had said echoed in Dan's mind. *I know what's coming.* His heart beat a little faster, and he leaned forward. Dan looked up at Reid for support, but his partner gave him another slight shake of his head.

Thompson continued, his voice growing louder with each word. "This is a terrorist attack on my watch, and I'm not—"

"Sir," Dan interrupted. Reid put his head in his hand and rubbed his forehead. Dan looked up at Thompson and plowed ahead. "I think we need to focus our efforts on the civilian that assisted us. He seemed to be well informed and—"

The SAC whirled on him. "You mean the armed individual that you allowed to flee the scene? The one with the vehicle using stolen plates? The man who you think might be Middle Eastern, but you didn't get his real name?"

Dan swallowed hard but continued to meet the SAC's glare. "With all due respect, sir, the situation unfolded rapidly, and our choices were limited. The man did provide valuable assistance. I'd like—"

The SAC cut him off a final time. "Agent Alexander, what you'd like is not a part of the tactical plan at this point. You are on desk assignment pending further review of your actions in protection of Dr. Cranford and your support of Agent Reid."

Dan's face reddened, and he turned to Reid. They locked eyes. This time, Reid gave him a small nod and mouthed, *"Just wait."*

Thompson moved back to the head of the table. "I need ATF's evaluation by end of day tomorrow. Henderson, you and James take point on the fieldwork at the CDC. Johnson, you're with Reid. Crack that shell corporation. I want a name ASAP. Dismissed."

The other agents rose and filed out. Reid motioned for Dan to wait as the agents left, and then he approached the SAC.

"Sir, I'd like Agent Alexander's assistance in pursuing the civilian. Johnson can get the Intern to help him with the computer work on the shell company. But I think this guy should be a high-value target for the investigation. With your permission, I'll take full responsibility for locating and apprehending him."

"I've seen the surveillance videos, Reid. Are you sure you can count on Agent Alexander having your back next time?" the SAC asked.

Dan's breath caught, and he looked down.

"He saved my life, sir," Reid replied.

"That's one way to look at it," Thompson said. He moved to stand behind Dan. "Others might think he was forced to abandon you after making a *stupid* decision as to how to protect the doctor." The SAC paused. Dan knew the SAC waited for him to launch into some defense of his actions.

But he's got it exactly right.

When Dan remained silent, the SAC said, "Okay. This is on you, Reid. You have twenty-four hours to locate your mystery man." Thompson turned to leave.

"What about Dr. Cranford?" Dan asked softly.

Thompson paused by the door. "She stays here for now. I've asked the Marshal's Service to send a protection detail for her transport to a secure location. They'll be here in six hours, and then she's their responsibility." The SAC pulled the door closed as he left.

Dan turned to Reid and said, "Thanks."

"We've lost a lot of time already. Just make sure you prove me right," his partner replied.

——

Dan sat at his desk, reviewing the security footage. It contained several long-range views of the action in the parking lot. The techs had already applied their enhancement magic, and the images revealed a surprising level of detail. Facial recognition had not yielded any hits on the three gunmen, and there was no image of the driver of the Mercedes. They had one clear view of their rescuer, John, but the techs said his picture caused the facial recognition software to malfunction, whatever that meant.

Dan kept replaying the sequence of the Jeep crashing through the fence at just the right moment to save Ames, picking them up, and racing to Reid.

Who are you, John?

He concentrated on details of the vehicle and what they might reveal about the man. Did the bulletproof glass and doors show preparation for this attack, or did people regularly shoot at him? The Jeep was well equipped for traveling off-road but showed no signs of any recent adventures off the pavement.

After twenty run-throughs focused on the Jeep, Dan restarted the video at the point where he and Reid arrived and let it run until after their exit. He leaned forward as the second Mercedes entered the lot, and the Jeep rammed through the fence to escape. Two assailants continued to fire at the retreating Jeep. With the Jeep out of range, they hurried to the man Dan had downed first. The two lifted the man by his arms and pulled him clear of the cars. The second Mercedes slid to a stop, and they loaded the man in the trunk before piling into the back seat and sped away.

But Dan knew he had shot two of the men, not just the one. He thought back to the final seconds of their escape and recalled his confusion. He reset the video back to the moment he stepped out of the Jeep with the M4 to help Reid. Dan zoomed the image in on his target and watched as the man recoiled four times from direct hits—three to the chest and one to the neck. Even if he was wearing body armor, the neck wound appeared fatal. The man tumbled out of view behind a car.

Dan continued to watch as he moved to support his partner, and Reid ran to the Jeep. As Dan's image rounded the back of the Jeep, the man he had just downed rolled out from behind the car and sat up. Dan paused the video and stared at the single frame. Red stains covered the man's white shirt, but nothing remained of the gaping neck wound. Dan replayed the sequence again and rubbed his chin. He ran through the video in slow motion and tried to make sense of the images. With a shake of his head, he decided that the wounds must have been superficial and not as bad as they appeared.

Must be a glitch in the enhancement software.

———

"Find anything?" Reid asked from the doorway.

With a start, Dan rocked back from the desk. "Jesus, man, you could knock, you know." He glanced at his watch. *8:42 p.m.* Four hours had passed. Four hours of watching more video, listing out features of the vehicles, itemizing weapons used, compiling a detailed description of John. None brought him closer to knowing anything useful. Reid raised his eyebrows to reemphasize his question.

Dan rubbed his temples and offered a dejected, "Nope."

"You should eat," Reid said. He turned and headed back to his office.

"What about you?" Dan called after him. "Anything from the plates?"

"It took a while, but I found traffic cam footage of him lifting the plates from a Prius. Not very useful," Reid said. "I'm trying to backtrack from there to see if we can get his starting location. But it feels like a waste of time. He seems very aware of possible surveillance and took many precautions."

Dan's stomach growled its agreement with Reid's suggestion regarding food. He logged off his computer and headed down the hall, calling out, "Want anything?" as he passed Reid's office.

"Maybe later," came the expected reply.

Dan took the elevator down two floors, strolled into the cafeteria, and spotted Ames. His hunger forgotten, he made his way across the room and stood opposite her at the table. She looked up from her phone but said nothing.

"Ames, are you okay?" he asked.

"I'm just fine, Agent Alexander, and don't call me that," Ames responded in a flat tone. She began tapping a manicured fingernail on the tabletop. "As fine as the last time we spoke. Let's see? How long has it been? Maybe fifteen years? And you? Looks like you've put on a few pounds."

Dan heaved a sigh. "Look, I was a jerk back then. And I could have treated you better."

She studied him for a moment. "Better? You left me," she said through gritted teeth. "No goodbye, no note, just gone. Disappeared."

Dan looked down, unable to meet her green eyes. He took a small step back from the table.

Her chair scraped on the hard floor as she stood. "I went to your apartment for some clue," she said. "Quite the surprise when I found that *diamond ring* just sitting on the desk. I brought in the police and filed a missing person's report. Called them every day." Ames moved around the table. "You should have heard the message the detective left on my phone two weeks later explaining how you were just *fine*, that you moved back East and joined the Navy. Implied it was somehow my fault. And me, all the while, thinking you must be kidnapped...or worse."

She stopped in front of him and raised her hand as if to strike him but hesitated. "Coward," she whispered. Her hand fell back to her side. She spun on her heel and headed for the door. "You'll have to excuse me," she called back. "I'd rather be in the care of someone a little more reliable."

His mind raced as he tried to think of some way to explain his actions from so long ago—to tell her about his mother. But no, he could never do that. Maybe something else. "Ames—" he began.

And the lights went out.

CHAPTER FOUR

Dan stood in total darkness. He reached into his pocket for his cell phone but remembered he had left it on his desk. A rectangle of dim, pale light appeared across the room as Ames opened the door.

"Dan, what's happening?" she called to him.

"Not sure," Dan said. Chairs screeched as he pushed them aside on his way across the room.

Ames stood in the dim hallway silhouetted by the emergency lights that cast enough light for Dan to see her worried expression. He stood next to her and placed a gentle hand on her shoulder. Her frown moved it away.

"It's probably nothing," he offered but looked both ways up and down the hall. He heard several indistinct voices to his right. Given the late hour, only a minimal staff would typically be in the building, the rest already home for dinner or out for drinks. But tonight, many worked late, focusing on the events at the CDC. "Let's head back to my office."

They had only gone about ten steps when he heard the first staccato echo of gunfire. He froze and swiveled his head to try to get a bearing on the sounds.

"Is that gunfire?" Ames whispered.

"Stay close," he replied.

They moved on toward his office, two floors above, where his firearm, cell phone, and keys sat securely in a desk drawer. More gunfire, a mix of automatic weapons and pistols, reverberated behind them along with a few shouts and the muffled rumble of an explosion. Dan caught Ames by the arm and broke into a trot but slowed as he approached the elevator.

"Power's out," Dan said, more to himself than to Ames, and rushed past the closed doors toward the stairwell at the end of the hall.

He hesitated outside the stairwell door, opened it two inches, and listened. More gunfire, louder than before, echoed up the stairway. Then all went quiet.

"Keep close," Dan said in a low voice. He took Ames's hand, and they moved onto the stairs. Below, beams of light from flashlights danced about, and he heard heavy boots on the stairs. Dan led Ames up two long flights of stairs and paused at the door to his floor. Unsure who approached from below, he released her hand, opened the door, and stepped into the hall, only to have the barrel of a gun jammed into his back.

"Freeze," a familiar voice said.

Dan raised his hands slowly. "It's me, Reid."

The pressure on his back relaxed, and Dan turned to see his partner and the woman agent from the ATF stood next to the wall, weapons drawn. Voices echoed from the stairwell below, and Dan reached back across the threshold to urge Ames through. Then he eased the door closed.

The twin beams from the emergency lights above the door cast shadows across the large open area of the fourth floor. A dark gloom hung over the extensive cubicle-filled area to his right, the distant lights above the north exit casting only a few shadows. To his left, the hallway to the agents' private offices remained dark.

"Are you armed?" Reid asked. His partner's eyes never left the door.

"No, my firearm is at my desk," Dan replied. "What's happening?"

Reid motioned them back from the door. "Not sure. Some kind of full-scale assault. I have no idea how they breached the external security without detection. I think this floor is still secure for now. Most of the action has been on the ground level, but I think they're moving up. Agent Torres and I took up station here." The ATF agent nodded at Dan. "Redman and Johnson are at the north stairwell. Others may be with them. There should be no other access to this floor as long as the power is off. Get the doctor to your office and wait there."

As Dan and Ames started toward his office, the stairwell door burst open behind them, and automatic weapons fire sprayed into the room.

Dan pulled Ames down behind a desk and watched as two men dressed in dark tactical gear stormed into the room. Reid and Torres put several rounds into the first, and he fell to Dan's left. The second fired two short bursts and stepped to the right toward Dan, but the gunman's attention remained on Reid and Torres.

Agent Torres leaned out and shot twice at the gunman. The man returned fire. Dan saw the ATF agent fall back, hit by multiple rounds. The gunman took a step forward and fired in Reid's direction. No one had noticed Dan hidden in the shadows.

Just like in Kabul.

Dan stepped up behind the gunman. He circled his left arm around the man's throat and leaned back while he grabbed the man's chin with his right, forced his head up, and twisted hard. He heard the distinctive crack that the C4 and C5 vertebrae make when they break and felt the abnormal, disjointed turn of the man's head to the far right. A single spasm confirmed the man's death, and the gun clattered to the floor.

Dan let the body drop to the floor and called, "All clear." He turned to Ames. She leaned forward out of the shadows—relief and revulsion warred on her face. He held out his hand, but she just stared at it.

"Need some help over here," Reid called. He knelt by Agent Torres's side.

Without taking Dan's offered hand, Ames scrambled to her feet and rushed to the ATF agent. She knelt, felt for a pulse, and began CPR. She paused after about fifteen seconds and checked again for a pulse. "Come on," she whispered as she continued the chest compressions.

Gunfire erupted from the north end of the building. Reid met Dan's gaze and gave him a nod, motioning for Dan to go assist the other agents. Still without his weapon, Dan turned back to the man he had killed, looking for the submachine gun.

As he went for the weapon, Dan saw the man's arm twitch. He picked up the submachine gun and stepped closer to lean over the body. Something about his position seemed wrong—too *normal*. Dan reached down to check the man for a pulse. When his fingers touched the man's neck, his eyes popped open, and the man smiled. He grabbed Dan's arm with his left hand, pulling him closer, and punched Dan in the face with his right.

Stunned by the blow, Dan tried to pull away, but the man still held his arm and used it as leverage to spring to his feet. A punch in the gut came next, doubling Dan over. He shoved Dan upright and kicked the gun out of his hand. The weapon clattered across the floor. Still dazed, Dan staggered back as the man drew a knife from his leg scabbard.

A gun fired twice from just to Dan's left. The man recoiled and fell back as each slug hit its mark—one to the chest, one to the head. Reid took a step past Dan, gun still aimed at the man.

"I thought you said he was neutralized," Reid snapped.

"I thought he was," Dan replied. He rubbed his ear, and the ringing began to subside. Dan approached the dead man, prodded him with his foot, but turned away as Ames stood up.

Eyes downcast, she shook her head as if it were her fault. "I'm sorry," she said. "I couldn't save her. If we had been at a trauma center, there would have been a chance, but here…" she trailed off, a doctor's frustration plain on her face.

Dan wanted to go to her, but more gunfire from the far side of the office space demanded his attention. He scooped up the submachine gun again and checked the magazine. "Meet me at my office," he said to Reid. In a crouch, Dan melted into the maze of cubicles and headed toward the gunfire.

A loud explosion rocked the north end of the room. Papers and fragments of desks and computers flew into the air. Dan crept forward, peeking around the end of a row of cubicles near the elevators. SAC Thompson and Agent Redman lay five feet away amid the debris that had been a desk. Neither seemed to be breathing, and a nasty burn disfigured the left side of the SAC's face.

Four hostiles held position near the north stairwell, and as Dan watched, two more entered from the stairs. One, probably their squad leader, gave hand motions for the rest to fan out and search the cubicles. Dan tensed as three approached his position and readied his weapon. But he knew the probable outcome, and it didn't look good.

Two rows over, Agent Johnson jumped up, fired his pistol, and took down the nearest man, only to succumb to the hail of answering bullets. Dan grimaced as he saw Johnson fall but knew he could not help the agent.

A distant rumble shook the building. The squad leader stiffened, hand going to his ear, and he began talking into his comms. Hand still at his ear, he paused for a moment, listening, before barking out commands to his men. The squad leader and two of his team charged back into the stairwell while the other two took up station by the door. Dan used the distraction to slide further into the shadows, turned, and made his way down the side corridor to his office.

He tapped lightly on the door and slipped in. Reid stood at the ready to one side, and Ames hid behind his desk.

"Situation?" Reid asked.

Dan moved to his desk and gathered his sidearm, cell phone, and keys. "We've got two hostiles guarding the north stairwell. There is a larger group on the other floors with a firefight still underway. The SAC, Johnson, and Redman are all down. We need to move now." He took Ames's hand and headed for the door.

We've got to get out of this building.

———

With his Glock in hand, Dan led the way, and they kept to the shadows as they moved down the hallway toward the south stairwell door. Ames followed close behind Dan, her hand a light touch on his back. Reid brought up the rear and covered their six. Dan felt another distant rumble confirming the fight continued on other floors, but here, silence filled the offices.

At the end of the hall, he paused. The dark interior of the cubicle area stretched out to his left. No one moved. He motioned for Reid and Ames to wait and then melted into the shadows and slipped behind a desk. All remained quiet. He had a clear view of the area around the south stairwell door, and the sight of Agent Torres's body brought a surge of anger he fought to control. The first gunman lay near her, his arm outstretched like he wanted to shake her hand. But the body of the second man, the one whose neck refused to break, was missing.

Dan drew in a quick breath and scanned the area, thinking he might get a chance for a little payback for the punch to his face. Then he remembered Reid's head shot and relaxed. No one got back up from that. They needed to move before someone came back for the other body.

He led them across the small open space to the door and reached for the knob, but the door began to swing open. Dan grabbed it and jerked hard. An off-balanced man in dark fatigues staggered across the threshold. Ames stifled a cry of surprise as Reid shoved past her to point his gun at the man's face and growled a soft, "Freeze."

The man raised both hands. A smile played at the edges of his mouth. Dan heard voices from above in the stairwell speaking in some Eastern European dialect. Boots sounded on the stairs, but Dan had no idea of their direction. With a flick of his weapon, Reid motioned for the man to move to the side. Dan eased the door back closed and then stepped forward and punched the man hard in the temple. Reid caught the man as he crumpled to the floor and dragged him away from the door.

"Go," Reid said to Dan and added a nod of his head for Ames to follow.

His weapon at the ready, Dan opened the door and moved into the stairwell with a quick glance up and down the dark enclosure. A voice called from above, again in a foreign dialect. Dan knew they only had seconds before being discovered. He pointed his gun at the stairwell above and whispered, "Reid, multiple hostiles above. Get her down."

Reid took Ames by the arm and started down. As the door settled back closed, Dan remained hidden in the pitch-black gloom. The voice called down again, followed by a few seconds of silence. More boots *clanged* on the steps, and the beam of a flashlight began bobbing back and forth as someone descended.

Dan moved down another flight of stairs and waited, gun still at the ready. He heard the door above scrape open, followed by what had to be a curse, and the man shouted back up the stairwell. Dan hurried down two more flights and almost ran into Ames as he neared the ground floor. The stairwell door sat ajar, and faint light bled through the crack. Reid held up his fist and signaled that two hostiles waited below. Dan signaled back that more were on the way down.

"Watch our backs," Dan said to Reid in a low voice. He eased the door open, slid past, and rounded the last corner. Two men in dark tactical gear stood by the exit door, conferring in low tones. With his weapon aimed at them, Dan moved into the light and called out, "Don't move."

Both men tensed and turned to face Dan but seemed to relax. "Sir," the one on the right offered in a thick accent, "this section is secure."

Confused, Dan took a step closer. He motioned with his gun. "Weapons on the ground."

The men exchanged worried looks. "Sir, we have followed the instructions," the one on the left said and gestured with a sweep of his hand. "No one has left through this exit. We have done nothing wrong."

Dan hesitated. His mind raced as he tried to make sense of the situation. A shout from up the stairwell broke the spell and forced him into action.

"I said, drop your weapons."

The two exchanged another look before the one on the left shrugged, and they placed their submachine guns on the floor.

More shouts echoed from above, and gunfire erupted in the stairwell. Ames stumbled into the light, followed by Reid, who turned and fired twice back up the stairs.

Across from Dan, the two men's eyes widened in surprise. "You are him!" one shouted and dove for his weapon.

Dan took the man down with two rapid shots. The other charged Dan, but Reid dropped him with three quick rounds. More gunfire erupted from the stairwell, and bullets ricocheted around the room. Ames ducked her head with her arms pulled tight across her chest and slid to a stop.

"Let's move," Dan called out and ran to the emergency exit door. Reid grabbed Ames, spun her toward the door, and urged her to follow Dan. Pounding footsteps reverberated from the stairwell as men raced down from the floor above.

Dan drew in a deep breath and crashed through the door. Three men held positions behind the nearest parked car with their automatic weapons at the ready. Upon seeing Dan, they all straightened and lowered their firearms. One even saluted.

What the hell?

Reid and Ames burst out behind Dan. Startled, the gunmen jumped and brought their weapons up, but they hesitated with a look back at Dan as if for direction. Reid fired once, and the man on the left toppled to the ground. The other two opened fire, forcing Dan, Reid, and Ames to dive for cover behind a large blue dumpster. While bullets clanged into the metal sides, Dan checked for an escape route. But the dumpster sat in a small alcove with high brick walls and no way out the back.

Trapped.

Dan's heart raced, and his mouth felt dry. Reid kept his gun leveled toward the door they had exited. Dan inched forward and fired around the corner of the dumpster without aiming, hoping to keep the men behind the car from rushing them.

He wiped the sweat from his brow and glanced at Ames. She crouched in the back corner, eyes wide but focused on him, lips pressed together, hands balled into fists. A burst of rounds from an automatic weapon clanged into the metal side of the dumpster like a jackhammer assaulting a granite rock.

The roar of an engine caught his attention, and he risked a quick look around the dumpster. A black four-door Jeep Rubicon raced into view from the other side of the building and slid to a stop as its large metal bumper smashed into the rear exit of the building, pinning the door closed. The window lowered, and the driver tossed something at the gunmen behind the parked car. Dan shielded his eyes, anticipating the bright flash and the loud *bang* that followed. Both gunmen dropped to the pavement, either stunned or dead.

"I told you to leave!" John shouted at them from the Jeep.

Dan heard pounding and shouts from the other side of the door to the building. Ames inched up beside him. He grabbed her hand and ran for the Jeep. The rear passenger door popped open, and both piled in. Reid rounded the back and took the front passenger seat.

With tires smoking, the Rubicon backed in a tight circle and then raced forward across the lot. Dan kept an eye out the back for pursuit. Five men burst from the building exit and began firing. A few rounds struck the Jeep but glanced away.

The building power remained off, but the streetlights revealed the remains of the front entrance—glass shattered, doors off their hinges, all signs of the explosives used to gain access to the building. Three large dark vans sat parked right in front. But Dan wondered how they had entered the lot without raising an alarm.

Dan swiveled back around as they neared the security gates. The fence could withstand an armored personnel carrier, and the large metal wedge barrier prevented any unauthorized vehicle from entering through the gate. At least two armed guards always staffed the bulletproof guard station. But someone had lowered the wedge. And the guards had exited their enclosure and now lay sprawled on the pavement. Dan shook his head as they sped through the gate.

How could this have happened?

CHAPTER FIVE

The Rubicon slid around a corner and sped down Northlake Parkway, weaving in and out of the light traffic. From the back seat, Dan craned his neck out the side window, trying to spot any pursuit. They sped through an intersection; the signal light changing from red to green reflected on the damp, empty pavement. No one followed them.

"All clear," Dan called forward.

Reid pointed to a structure in a shopping mall to their right. "Pull into that parking garage. The entrance is next to Macy's."

"We have to get out of the city," John replied in a low, dangerous voice.

Reid pulled his Glock and pressed it to John's temple. "Pull into the garage," he demanded.

With a sigh, John turned off the parkway and sped across the parking lot like an arrow fired at a distant target.

"That would make a mess in my Jeep," John said. He made eye contact with Dan. "If he accidentally shoots me, all of you are going to have to clean it up." John barked out a laugh. "And you'll get to see something you will just *not* believe."

"Like that man back in the attack?" Ames asked in a detached and clinical tone.

"Saw something, Doctor?" John said. "Something hard to explain?" She nodded with an unfocused look in her eyes. "Yeah, something like that," John continued. "Only at this close range, the smell would be awful."

The Jeep shot into the garage and raced up the first ramp. Tires squealed as they rocketed around three turns before John slowed to a stop and pulled into a slot on an empty level.

Reid lowered his hand but kept his weapon pointed at John. "First things first. I need to know who you are. Right now."

John made eye contact with Ames in the mirror. "Doctor, are you hurt?"

"I am fine," she replied in a soft voice. "And thank you for your assistance. You've saved me twice in one day."

Dan glanced at Ames, and a flash of jealousy surprised him. Feeling pain in his jaw, he relaxed his clenched teeth. "Come on, man. You obviously have some idea of what's going on. Help a friend out here."

John turned in his seat and faced Dan. "Well, first, you need to understand a little about who you've gotten involved with," he said. John glanced across at Ames. "You've already caught on to the fact that they are trying to kill you, Doctor."

"Yes, but why?" Ames asked.

Dan said, "Like I explained at the FBI. They are killing all of the experts in viruses and rapid vaccine development."

Ames heaved a sigh. "Yes, Dan, but why?"

"Let's start with the *who* first," John said. "But please get out of the Jeep. There's something I want to show you." He turned to Reid. "And put away your weapon, G-man. I'm no threat to you or Dr. Cranford."

Without waiting for Reid's consent, John opened his door and stepped out. Ames followed and rounded the Jeep to stand with John. Dan shrugged when Reid looked back.

Dan and Reid exited the vehicle and stood facing John. Reid lowered his weapon but did not holster it. With a grimace on his face, John shook his head and glanced up at the ceiling for a brief moment.

"Doctor, you should move over with the agents, or they might get agitated," John said. He fixed his gaze on Reid. "So, Mr. FBI Agent, what's your name?"

Reid's eyes narrowed, and his jaw tightened. "I'm Special Agent Zachary Reid. And who are you?"

A smile spread across John's face. "Well, Zachary, I'm going to draw a pistol from under my coat to show you something, and I'd prefer that you don't shoot me."

Reid tensed and brought his weapon to the ready. "Okay, but slowly this time."

With a chuckle, John made an exaggerated show of opening his coat with one hand and reaching in with the other. He withdrew the pistol, a long-barreled Colt Python, and kept the muzzle pointed down.

John took a moment to meet each one of their gazes. His dark eyes seem to search for something, some insight about them. "I suspect you may have seen some things today that you are having trouble explaining." He nodded at Ames. "Like the doctor did." John raised his gun to admire the weapon. "You see, there are a few of us living among you that are...*different*."

"Different?" Dan snapped. "You mean like, what, mysterious, cryptic...*strange*?"

"Give it a rest, Dan," Reid said in a low tone.

John locked eyes with Dan and held his gaze for a long moment. "Some have called me all of those things and much worse. But right now, none of that matters. You face a group that you can't stop on your own." He paused. The smile crept back onto his face. "Perhaps a demonstration will help."

His weapon held high, John turned and crossed to the concrete wall of the garage. He placed his left hand on the wall and leaned into it. John looked back, winked at Dan, and said, "You might want to cover your ears." He lowered the revolver and pressed it against the back of his hand on the wall...

"Wait!" Ames yelled.

"Stop!" Reid ordered.

...and fired.

The deafening roar echoed through the empty garage. Dan charged forward but pulled up as John bent over and placed his gun on the ground. With a grimace of pain, John straightened and raised his right hand above his head. He kept his left arm out away from his body as blood streamed from the gaping wound in the shattered remains of his hand.

"What the hell?" Dan shouted at him.

"Oh, they haven't got this in Hell, boy," John said. The pain faded from his face. "Now watch."

Reid moved closer to get a better view but kept his gun at his side.

Ames pushed past the agents. "Let me help you," she demanded.

John brought his hand close for her to see. "No need, Doctor," he said. "Just wait."

Her eyes widened in amazement. Dan gave a low whistle as the wound stopped bleeding. Dan leaned in closer and watched the tissue and muscles knit back together.

"Please...explain," Ames asked, her voice filled with awe.

The skin smoothed over, a little pink but with no scar. John held his left hand up, rotated it once, flexed his fingers, and smiled at Ames. He withdrew a large-bladed knife from his belt scabbard. Reid brought his weapon to the ready, but John just eyed him with a smirk, turned back to the wall, and ran his hand across the blood-splattered spot.

"There you are," John said and used the knife to pry out the slug. He held it up to admire before tossing it to Dan.

"A little souvenir, kid," John said. "Now, let's talk."

———

Still stunned by what they had witnessed, they followed John to the back of the Rubicon. He swung open the rear door, raised the back window, and began rummaging through his gear. Dan leaned in beside him and took a quick mental inventory of the array of weapons and equipment—three assault rifles, a sawed-off shotgun, night vision goggles, a belt with five flash-bangs and an empty clip for a sixth, three large boxes of ammo, and a wide assortment of duffel bags and other items.

"You starting a war?" Dan asked.

John picked up a revolver, flipped out the cylinder, spun it, flipped it back closed, and stowed the gun behind a box of ammo. In a tired voice, John said, "I've been fighting one for a long time." He dug through the gear for another moment and then smiled as he pulled out a small black duffel. "There you are." With a small flourish of his hand, he unzipped the bag and withdrew a large thermos and a stack of Styrofoam cups. John turned to Ames and raised his eyebrows. "Coffee?"

She stared at him for a moment, brow furrowed. "Yes, please," she replied. John passed her a steaming cup, and she held it with two trembling hands.

The fragrant aroma smelled like heaven to Dan, and he met John's questioning eyes with a quick nod. Dan relayed the first cup to Reid and waited with anticipation as John poured him another. John passed Dan the cup and filled one for himself.

Setting the thermos aside, John rested back against the rear bumper and looked up with his head cocked to the side as if listening to some faint music. Dan only heard the occasional traffic sounds from the streets below.

After a long moment, John nodded, looked down, and took a sip of the steaming coffee. "I was born this way," he began in a soft voice. "A long time ago. I'm not like any of you. Once I crossed over, I stopped aging. I don't get sick. I'm not going to die." John paused. He met each of their gazes as if he expected them to object.

Dan looked down at the man's hand. He had seen it heal, but he did not understand how. "What do you think, Ames?"

She pressed her lips into a thin line. "It must be some form of advanced cellular regeneration with a rapid muscular response. But it must be more at the cellular level. Maybe a by-product of a hormonal effect on the mitochondria in the—"

"I'll take that as a *maybe possible*?" Dan interrupted.

"I wouldn't have thought so an hour ago, but you saw the same thing I did," Ames said. She frowned, but her gaze drifted back to John's face. "Do you understand the process?"

John's smirk returned. "I've heard it's biblical." He turned his back to them and started sorting the gear.

"So, how many of you guys are there?" Dan asked. "The you-shoot-me-and-I'm-still-okay types?"

"I don't know the exact count of Discovereds, but Luke estimates we are about three hundred."

"Who's Luke?" Ames asked.

John's head snapped up to stare toward the front of the Jeep. Silence hung in the air. As the seconds ticked past, Dan considered shaking the man.

John finally answered in a soft voice. "He hasn't used that name in a long while." His voice hardened as he continued. "He went by Josef the last time I saw him, but that was several decades ago. I've heard they call him *the Professor* now." John turned to look back at Ames. "He's the one trying to kill you."

"But why does he want to kill me?" she asked, anger rising in her voice.

"Oh, it's not just you, Dr. Cranford," John said. He laughed a humorless laugh. "I think he is trying to kill all of you."

"All three of us?" Reid asked.

John exhaled hard and shook his head. He reached up and pulled down the rear window, took a step away from the Jeep, and slammed the back door. "No, he means to kill *all of you*. All seven billion of you!" John yelled with a dramatic sweep of his arms. He stomped away from the Jeep and looked up at the concrete ceiling, talking to himself in a low voice.

Dan glanced to his partner. Reid replied with a shake of his head and placed his hand on his weapon while moving to stand between Ames and John.

With his eyes locked on John, Reid said, "Dr. Cranford, you're our responsibility. Your safety is our top concern. We need to get to a secure location and contact our superiors. The FBI has several safe houses in the area. I'll direct us to the nearest one and—"

Without turning to face them, John called out, "Your superiors are all dead, or have you forgotten? And do you mean the small duplex on University?"

Stunned, Dan asked, "How do you know that location?"

John spun toward them and marched back to the Jeep. "Let's just say your safe houses aren't all that safe." John slapped his hand on the side of the Jeep. "We need to get out of Atlanta. Dr. Cranford, the only people you can trust are standing right here."

"No can do," Reid said in his I'm-in-charge voice. "Procedure dictates that we get to a secure location and contact FBI headquarters for instructions. If our locations are compromised, we will need to find an alternative."

John ran a hand through his dark hair. He asked, "Is today Wednesday?"

Ames glanced at her watch. "Yes, for the next thirteen minutes," she replied with a quizzical look.

John gave her a crisp nod and smiled. "That's great. It will be Thursday by the time we get there. Thursdays mean Maccabees. It's just the place. Not far." John motioned them all into the Jeep.

Ames asked, "What is a Maccabees?"

John winked at her. "It's my favorite home. You're going to love it."

As they settled into the Jeep, a cold lump formed in the pit of Dan's stomach.

———

With Reid again in the passenger seat and Dan and Ames secure in the back seat, John gunned the engine and headed out of the garage. The Rubicon raced down the exit ramp with the engine roar amplified by the close concrete walls. Dan ground his teeth as they bounced through the exit at just over sixty miles per hour. The Jeep glanced off a large green plastic trash can, sending a spread of garbage hurtling through the air.

"Where did you learn to drive, NASCAR?" Dan asked.

"Maybe we should assume a lower profile. We don't want to attract attention," Reid said.

John ignored them both and sped across the parking lot to the nearest street. The tires screeched as they turned and rocketed into the late-night traffic. The Jeep weaved in and out of the lanes. Horns shouted their disapproval on all sides. After three blocks, they made a hard left, skidding in front of the oncoming traffic. An oversized Dodge Ram pickup locked its brakes and swerved to avoid them. They cleared its bumper by inches and sped up the on-ramp to the I-285 loop.

Dan shot a glance at Ames. She stared straight ahead, face a little pale, and clung to the overhead grab handle with white knuckles.

"Really, man. Slow it down!" Dan shouted at John.

John shot Dan a withering look in the mirror, but he eased up on the accelerator. "We're fifteen minutes out. Keep it together back there." John reached up and rotated the mirror to look at Ames. His eyes and tone softened. "Just trying to get you somewhere safe."

"It might help if you filled us in a little more," Dan said. He leaned forward with a hand on the back of each seat. "Starting with who you are. We don't even know your last name."

"I've had many last names, but none of them were mine," John replied and paused. He continued in a softer voice as if talking to himself. "He used to call me Thunder. But that was a long time ago." After a moment, he added, "As to who I am? Right now, I'm your only friend."

Dan exhaled his frustration. "Could you *please* lose the cryptic answers, Mr. John *Thunder*?" He leaned further forward. "How about the terrorists? Who are they, and why are they trying to kill Ames?"

John met his eyes in the mirror. "As I said, their leader is like me. I've known him for a long time. And I told you, they are out to kill all of you."

John's gaze found Ames. "I think you are more than just one last target for them, Doctor. They wouldn't be this reckless if you weren't a serious threat to their plan. It will be easier to explain when we get to our destination," John said. "Sit back and relax for a few more minutes. You'll like me a lot better once we are inside."

Dan glared at the man, but John did not seem to notice. Dan sank back into his seat and said, "So, Reid, do you think we can get him to run by Starbucks on the way? I mean, if we are just out for a ride, a triple, grande, nonfat, one-sugar latte would go down great right now. What about you, Ames? Want some more coffee?"

"Cut the crap, Dan," Reid said from the front seat without looking back.

Silence settled over the Jeep. John leaned forward, hit the power button on the audio system, and selected a playlist. The iconic drumbeat and mournful guitar intro of "All Along the Watchtower" by Jimi Hendrix filled the cabin as they rode on into the night.

They exited the freeway, made three turns, and meandered down a dark tree-lined lane. The sparse streetlights revealed a large hedge that flowed down the left-hand side of the road. After about a quarter of a mile, they turned left and pulled up to a ten-foot-high, solid wood security gate.

John rolled down his window and reached out to a small box with a keypad sitting on top of a dull metal pole. He keyed in an elaborate code of at least fifteen digits. A voice barked from a hidden speaker in a language Dan did not recognize. John replied in what sounded like Klingon. The gates began to slide open like the ones to Jurassic Park, and John eased the Jeep forward. Dan looked back to see them lumbering closed behind them. John let one hand fall to his lap and relaxed back in his seat.

Dan scanned their surroundings. The well-lit, manicured grounds spread out over a three-acre yard. Green grass carpeted a lawn absent of trees. Rosebushes in full bloom lined the exterior walls. The tall shrubs by the road hid an impressive wall with security cameras placed at even intervals along the top. The wall extended around to the back of the house on both sides.

The house looked more like a small fortress than a home. The two-story stone bunker loomed over the peaceful yard. Security lights and cameras lined the front just under the eaves. Storm shutters reinforced each window. Dan rolled his shoulders and felt some of the tension drain away.

John pulled the Jeep around to the side, and light spilled out from the waiting four-car garage. As the Jeep eased in, Dan saw three identical Rubicons in the other slots. He exchanged a puzzled look with Reid. The steel garage door trundled down as soon as they parked.

John stepped out without a word. He walked around the front of the Jeep, removed his duster, hung it on a peg next to the interior door, and began pulling weapons from various holsters and scabbards. Dan saw at least three handguns, one a very old-looking Smith & Wesson like something Wyatt Earp might carry. Two long knives followed the guns, and John placed them all in a neat row on a table next to the door.

"I still don't trust him," Reid said.

"But we don't have much choice, do we? And he has great taste in cars," Dan replied. He exited the vehicle and rounded the back of the Jeep. While Reid got out and moved to the front, Dan stepped up to Ames's door and tried to open it for her but found it locked.

She looked at him through the window, her green eyes wide and a little panicked. "I just need a minute," she said, her voice muffled by the glass.

Dan put on his best smile. "Please, Ames, you need to come in with us. I won't let anything happen to you." He silently counted to five. "Please?"

The lock clicked up, and Ames shoved the door open. "*You* won't let anything happen to me?" she replied angrily. "*You've* been doing an excellent job so far. We don't know what's happening. You don't know how to keep us safe. Simple platitudes won't get us through this, *Agent Alexander.*"

He took a quick step back and held up both hands chest-high, palms turned out. Ames glared at him and stepped out. She glanced both ways like a runner looking for traffic on a busy road, stepped past him, and crossed to stand by John.

"Weapons on the table," John said. "I don't allow instruments of violence within Maccabees."

Dan looked to his partner. To his surprise, Reid straightened his tie, withdrew his Glock, and placed it on the table. But Dan met John's stare with lips pressed together and gave him a shake of his head.

No way I'm leaving my weapon again.

With two quick steps, John got right in Dan's face. They glared at each other like two prizefighters at a weigh-in. Although John was several inches shorter, Dan felt the danger in the man.

"Look," John hissed through clenched teeth. "You are welcome to camp out here in the garage. But you are *not* bringing your weapons inside."

A tense moment passed before Dan glanced at Ames and saw a look of anguish on her face. Without stepping back, Dan slowly withdrew his forty-five and let it hang by one finger on the trigger guard. "Any other obscure rules we should know about?"

John glared at him. A light seemed to burn in his dark eyes. "Jackass," John whispered. He turned on his heel and stalked to the interior door. "Just put it on the table." John slapped his hand onto a biometric scanner by the door. He looked up at the ceiling and muttered, "See what I mean." The door slid open, and he stepped in without looking back.

Dan cursed softly. Stepping to the table, he laid his sidearm down next to John's weapons. One of the knives caught his eye. The nine-inch blade gleamed in the light. The initials *JB* carved in the worn wooden handle failed to provide Dan with any concrete clue to its owner's true identity. A dull ache began to form right behind his eyes. With a nod, he motioned for Reid to follow John.

Reid gave him a shake of his head and pulled out his phone. "I'm going to contact DC first," Reid said. He typed a four-digit short code and held the phone to his ear.

Ames closed her eyes for a moment before moving to the opened door. Dan followed her and glanced past Ames into the room. Soft light filled a large area. Several couches and tables were grouped together across the room. John had disappeared to somewhere further in the house. "Wait inside, Ames. We'll be right with you," Dan said and turned to face his partner.

When his call connected, Reid provided identification and security codes in quick, staccato bursts to the station supervisor Dan knew he had on the other end.

"Yes, sir. We are at what we believe is a secure location," Reid said and paused to listen for a moment. "Yes, Dr. Cranford is with us and is unharmed," he said. "Yes, sir. He's also not injured." More listening. "That bad, sir?" Reid began to pace. "All of them?" He placed a hand on his forehead. "Yes, sir, I knew him well. Has anyone let his wife know?" Reid looked around and moved to lean on the Jeep. "I understand, sir. We are at a secure location and can await pickup until morning. Yes, we will make sure she stays safe."

Reid disconnected the call and seemed to fold in upon himself. He rubbed his eyes and heaved a sigh. After a brief moment, Reid straightened and pushed off from the Jeep. "The bastards killed everyone in the building—Thompson, the other agents, security, techs, even the cleaning crew. Only left one guard at the front gate alive, but he is still unconscious."

White-hot fury burned inside of Dan, and he wanted to punch something. Someone. "But how did they get in?" he demanded.

"They don't know. No alarms triggered. Communications from the building must have been jammed. Local PD heard about it from some passing motorist. They contacted DC, and the team has only had twenty minutes on-site. It's going to be a long night for them, but they want us to remain here till morning. You and I only have one mission, and that's the doctor."

Dan forced his hands to relax. Without another word, Dan turned and crossed the threshold to find Ames.

Only one mission.

CHAPTER SIX

Ames left the garage and stepped into a large room. Couches and tables sat across an area designed to hold about forty people. Impressionistic art hung on the cream-colored walls, and a single door faced her from across the room. She rubbed her right temple and glanced at the digital display on her watch. *12:33 a.m.* Voices drifted in from the garage as Dan and Reid debated what they should do next. She let her head hang forward.

My protectors.

Questions swirled through her mind. She meandered across the spotless room to look for John. As Ames approached the door, an older woman breezed in, carrying a silver tray. She wore a full-length dark robe, like a grandmother on a winter morning, and upon seeing Ames, she smiled a warm, inviting smile that made Ames feel she already liked the woman.

"There you are, my dear. Welcome to Maccabees. Master John said you've had a most miserable day." Her smile grew wider, and her dark eyes twinkled. "He thought you might need a little refreshment." She held the tray forward. It contained a stack of small, moist-looking towels, three crystal glasses filled with a pink liquid, and four baklavas on white medallion doilies.

The woman spoke with a slight accent that Ames could not place. She started to refuse the offer but realized she felt spent. And unclean. Ames reached for a towel, not surprised but very pleased with its warm, moist feel. She wiped the grime from her hands and face and looked down the short hallway beyond the door. It emptied into a large foyer at the front of the house, but she saw no trace of John.

"Thank you," Ames said.

"You're most welcome, Dr. Cranford. Please try a glass. You will find it a most refreshing hibiscus tea."

"Please call me Ames." She took one of the offered beverages. "It's what my friends call me." In response to a quizzical look, Ames added, "Short for Amelia. But I need to speak with John. Can you please direct me to him?"

"And you may call me Martha. Master John will be along in a moment. You may wait for him here," she replied in the same warm voice, but Ames had the impression that no other option was available. Martha nodded toward the garage. "Oh, and here comes your friend."

Ames looked back to see Dan stalk into the room like a tiger on the hunt. It had been just twelve hours since he had been waiting for her at the CDC. Why had they sent *him* of all people? She had not even known the Navy had released him.

And he had changed.

Martha engaged him halfway across the room. He smiled a distracted smile at her, ran a rough hand through his brown hair, and bobbed a polite nod to her while taking the offered towel.

He killed that man with his bare hands.

Part of her knew he had done it to protect them, but it left a feeling in her that she could not wash away with just a warm cloth. Ames felt light-headed and collapsed into a nearby chair, setting her glass on a table.

With a troubled look on his face, Dan slid past Martha and drew close. "Are you okay, Ames?" His eyes never stopped scanning their surroundings.

She put her head in her hands. "Stop asking me that." Then, with more heat in her voice, she added, "And stop calling me Ames."

"Is it Dr. Cranford then?"

She looked up at him. His face looked almost the same as the one she used to adore. But a few wrinkles and lines had found their way onto that boyish face, and not the kind that came from too many smiles. "I don't know, Dan. I don't even know who you are anymore."

Will you abandon me again?

A tightness formed around his eyes as his gaze settled on her. "I'll get you through this. You need some sleep. We all do."

"We *need* to know why this is happening. I don't like being in the dark," Ames replied. She rose and started for the door. "I'm going to find some answers."

"I can help with that," John said.

Startled, both Ames and Dan jumped and spun to see John step out of the shadows in the corner of the room. He looked freshly showered and had exchanged his fatigues and combat boots for jeans and a loose-fitting white linen shirt. With wet hair pulled back and his dark beard still unruly but now damp, he seemed relaxed.

"And rescues always make me hungry," John continued and rubbed his hands together. "I woke Petros. He's making us a late-night snack. Martha, would you please fetch Agent Reid? He's making more calls but is getting very frustrated that he can't obtain any additional information."

"But how—" Ames began.

"Please," John interrupted. "You're safe here. Come." He motioned to the door. "Join me. Be at ease." He offered Ames his arm.

She looked at John for a moment before she placed a light hand on his arm. As they headed toward the hallway, Ames sighed and shot Dan a glance. Whom could she trust—the strange man she had just met or the one she had tried so hard to forget?

———

Reid eyed the older woman as he continued to talk with Sergeant Barnes of the Atlanta PD's 103rd precinct. Sergeant Barnes—the policeman who knew nothing but took a long time letting you know. The woman stood there in her dark robe with white lace, arms folded behind her back. An obvious housekeeper, she still managed the your-call-must-be-really-important-so-I'm-okay-waiting-but-I'm-not-going-to-leave look better than any he had ever seen.

"Thank you, Sergeant. Please call me at this number if you receive any information," Reid said to the too-friendly officer and hung up.

"Special Agent Reid," the woman began the instant the call ended. "Master John wishes you to join him and the others within Maccabees right away. Please follow me."

She turned and walked into the house without waiting for his agreement. Reid rubbed the back of his neck.

I wonder what she would do if I don't follow?

But someone had tried to kill their doctor—his responsibility. They had killed all his friends at the field office, and he was going to make them pay. And he did not buy that Wolverine stunt in the parking garage. He needed one thing. Answers. If he had to humor this John guy, then humor him he would. Just so long as he cut the nonsense and gave him what he needed to know.

It took seven precise steps to reach the door and then twenty-three to cross the beige room filled with what appeared to be a random collection of couches, chairs, and tables. But to Reid's trained eye, their arrangement provided specific areas of cover and two fields for overlapping fire. He also noted the faint outline of a hidden door in the shadowy corner.

At least this John knows how to plan his security.

Miss Marple had waited for him across the room at an interior door and now provided his escort like a Praetorian Guard. The short corridor opened into a rotunda that doubled as the main entryway. The dome above the circular room had a fresco painted across it that reminded Reid of the Sistine Chapel. They marched straight across the hard, blue tile floor with the clack of his footfalls echoing through the space above.

Reid followed her down another short hallway and came to a set of double doors. The housekeeper opened them without breaking stride and smoothly moved to one side to allow his entry. She nodded with a warm smile and a hint of mischief in her eyes. "Master John is so looking forward to your company."

He managed not to frown at her and continued into a large rectangular dining room. The dark paneling provided a warm backdrop to the brightly lit room. A long table, elegant in its simplicity, dominated the area. With seats for thirty, it held only three occupants at the far end.

As Reid approached, John looked up, smiled, and rose from his seat. He swept his hand in a wide arc. "Zachary, please join us."

Confused by the gracious greeting, Reid stopped and considered the man. The white linen shirt and dark hair neatly pulled back made him look more like an imam than an antiterrorist vigilante. Reid remained standing.

"Petros," John called toward a rear door. "One more, please." John eased himself back into his chair.

A short, barrel-chested man clad in a chef's white jacket over dark trousers pushed through the door carrying a silver tray in his large hands. With the overhead light gleaming off his bald head, he paused and gave Reid a questioning look.

"Over there is fine," John said and pointed with his fork at the seat across from his. "Please, Zachary, Petros makes fabulous omelets. Just ask your partner."

Dan looked up and gave Reid a nod as he set his fork down on an emptied plate. Dr. Cranford's plate remained mostly untouched, but she did appear to be enjoying the coffee.

"I'd rather have answers instead of a midnight snack," Reid said in a flat tone.

"Why not both?" John replied with a smile. "Your life is too short for you not to enjoy it."

Reid allowed his voice to slip one step toward anger. "Answers first."

John's smile faded. His eyes hardened. He set his coffee cup down and pushed back from the table.

"Your hospitality has been very kind," Dr. Cranford said. "But please, John, you offered information about the terrorists."

John glanced at the doctor and sighed. "It's a very long story, I'm afraid. And the hour is late. Let's just say I know your adversary very well."

"Okay, you've told us that, what, three times now? But we don't," Dan said. He leaned forward with his elbows on the table, hands folded together. "So how about you get your Greek cook back in here with a big pot of coffee, and you get on with this long story."

Reid slid into a chair, ready to lead the interrogation. John looked down and paused as if considering what to tell them.

Or maybe making up some elaborate tale.

"I'll tell you this much tonight. First, I met the Professor in my home country when I was just a teenager, and we became friends," John said. He glanced at Dr. Cranford. "He was already a physician like you, Doctor. And like you, the Professor wanted to understand, to explain, *our condition*. He became obsessed with understanding it."

John stood and moved to stare at the single painting in the room—an excellent reproduction of da Vinci's *The Last Supper*. Reaching up, John let his hand glide just above the surface until it stopped over the image of Jesus. After a brief moment, he let it drift on to hover above the disciple to the left. "Over the years, he lost his way and has done terrible things in the name of his science."

John turned to face them with a sad look on his face. "But if you live forever, what is the one thing you would fear?"

Reid felt time slipping away. *No one lives forever.* They needed to be doing something. The weight of the next impending fatality rested on his shoulders. Sitting around did nothing to stop the terrorists. One thing was for sure—he did not trust John. Reid rose from his chair and buttoned his jacket. "He should fear what we will do when we catch him."

John met his gaze with cold eyes. "Exactly." He stepped back to the table and appeared to press a hidden button. "Doctor, Martha will escort you to the guest quarters."

The housekeeper appeared in the doorway with a smile for Dr. Cranford.

"There are rooms nearby for you gentlemen," John said. "I suggest getting some rest. Tomorrow will be a long day of travel." Without another word, John turned and stalked out of the room.

"Wait," Reid called after him. But the man disappeared through the rear exit. Reid turned to Dan and slapped his hand on the table. "We are taking him into custody first thing tomorrow morning. I'm tired of this cryptic crap. And we are not going on any *road trip* with him."

"Maybe we should discuss that later, partner." Dan nodded his head toward the housekeeper.

Reid shook his head, angry at his own impatience. They had to stick to the mission.

Protect the doctor.

———

Dan woke with a start. His hand reached for his gun but only found the empty holster on his belt. He glanced around the room, trying to get his bearings.

Early morning light streamed in from windows set in the opposite wall. Dan still sat in the chair he had occupied for the night outside Ames's room. His stiff neck complained, and he stood, rubbing the cramped muscles that came from sleeping in a chair. A glance at his watch confirmed his *too-early* feeling. *6:12 a.m.* A ring from Reid's cell phone echoed down the quiet hall.

Dan ran his hand through his hair and went to join his partner. Reid had just sat up on a couch and squinted at his phone. He said, "DC," to Dan and then answered the call with "Special Agent Reid."

Dan parked himself on the end of the couch to listen to Reid's half of the conversation.

Reid sat up a little taller and replied, "Yes, I'll hold for him." He stood, facing a window. After a few seconds, Dan heard a muffled voice from the phone as someone came on the line.

"Director Adams, I was not expecting your call," Reid began but fell silent. He listened intently to the caller, and he managed to straighten his tie with his free hand.

Reid spun to look at Dan. A puzzled look spread over Reid's face. "That's not possible, sir. He's right here with me," Reid said. He stared at Dan and continued to listen to the man on the other end of the call. "There must be some mistake."

Several more seconds ticked by. Dan saw a bead of sweat form on Reid's brow.

"No, sir, he was with me all day."

More unheard conversation.

"Well, I can't account for every moment. He did step away to get something to eat, but I don't see how—" Reid continued but was interrupted by the Director.

Dan strained to hear the conversation but could only pick up angry-sounding tones.

Reid began to pace. "Sir, that will not be necessary. Let us come to Quantico. We can catch an early flight and have Dr. Cranford there by noon."

More raised voices from the other side.

Reid spun around. He looked up and down the hall and then hurried to the window and pulled the drapes wide. "They are already on the way?" Reid asked the Director. "Sir, this is a mistake. Agent Alexander is no more a part of this than I am."

Dan moved to the window and looked out across the green lawn. Nothing seemed out of place.

Reid pointed up at the blue sky and mouthed *helicopter*. Seconds later, Dan heard the *thrump, thrump, thrump* of the blades from an inbound aircraft.

Reid stood straighter. With his voice filled with urgency, Reid said, "Sir, your team is arriving. It is imperative that you remind them that we are also federal agents and are just coming in for a debrief." Reid paused and listened. "Yes, sir, I will," he finished and hung up. He took a step away from Dan. Reid's gaze moved from his partner to the hallway leading to the garage.

And their weapons.

"What's going on?" Dan demanded.

"They say it was you," Reid began in a flat tone. "That the security cameras showed it was you that let them in." Reid took one step toward the hall.

"You know that can't be true," Dan shot back, but he also took a step in the same direction. "Think, Reid. Something else is going on here. We need to sort this out."

Reid heaved in a deep breath and seemed to relax a little. "I know," he said and rubbed his brow. "But they are coming to take you into custody. Got our location off the tracker in our phones."

John burst into the room and ran to the window. "You fools! What have you done?"

Through the window, Dan saw the black helicopter touch down on the lawn, fifty yards away. In an instant, the doors flew open, and a team of six armed men poured out. Dressed in FBI labeled tactical gear and armed with automatic weapons, the men sprinted toward the house.

"They cannot be allowed inside Maccabees," John spat out. He ran to a control panel on the opposite wall, slapped his hand on the biometric reader, pressed a green button, and spoke into a small microphone, again using Klingon. His voice echoed through the house.

John glanced back at Dan. A wicked grin spread across his face. "This is going to hurt." John laughed as he pressed a small red button.

CHAPTER SEVEN

Dan groaned. A thousand hammers pounded on the inside of his skull. Pain tried to keep him from opening his eyes, but he forced them to obey. Bright sunlight made him squint as he sought to recall what had happened.

His head bounced hard against the thick glass of the window. It gave him another round of searing pain at no extra charge. Black dots swam across his vision. He forced in a quick breath and pushed himself upright.

Unconscious, Ames leaned against him with a grimace on her face. He gently brushed a lock of black hair from her face and eased her onto the seat.

John drove the Jeep wearing sunglasses, a Yankees ball cap, and a bright Hawaiian shirt. "Carry On Wayward Son" by Kansas blared from the sound system while John tapped the steering wheel in time to the music. Reid sat slumped forward in the passenger seat with his head resting against the dash.

"What did you do?" Dan managed just above a whisper.

"What's that?" John asked. He looked in the mirror as he turned the volume down.

Dan rubbed his forehead with his left hand. "What did you do?"

"I just saved the doctor one more time," John replied coldly. Then he added, "Hold tight."

Dan bounced into the door as the Jeep turned hard through an intersection. He managed to get a hand on Ames's shoulder to keep her from rolling onto the floor.

Reid moaned as his head rebounded off the dash. He caught hold of the grab handle above his door and looked around. "Where are we?" he croaked.

"We are *not* in FBI custody, no thanks to you," John said. He swung the Jeep around another hard corner. "And *we* are on the move, making sure *we* stay that way. You shouldn't have called them. If the doctor didn't need you, I would have left you."

"We didn't call them," Dan said.

"Then why did they come?" John asked. He used the rearview mirror to gaze out the back for a long moment. "I liked that house. It will take time to find another location that good."

Dan looked out the back. A column of dark black smoke rose from the horizon. As a knot formed in his gut, Dan's hand went to his still-empty holster. "Did you kill them?"

"No, you fool. When you value your privacy as I do, you take the time to develop some very effective countermeasures," John replied. He steered them onto I-85 and merged the Jeep into the morning traffic. "But I don't kill people unless they give me no other choice."

———

A light-gray, fixed-wing drone circled high above the Atlanta freeway. Its long-range camera whirred as it zoomed in on the Jeep below. A blinking green light changed to red, and the drone banked hard to the left to pursue its target.

———

Dan fell silent and gazed out the side window of the Jeep.

"Oh, God," Ames said in a pained voice and sat up, rubbing her temples. She glanced left and right, frowned, and glared at Dan. "What did you do?" she demanded.

"Me? Blame your Israeli friend," Dan retorted. "Seems he had the phasers set to stun."

"Israeli?" Reid asked. He stared intently at John.

John favored Reid with a nod and said, "It's been a long time since I've been home." His face hardened. "But why did they send a tactical team?"

Reid shot Dan a glance. "They made a mistake. They think Dan is involved with the terrorists. That he aided them in the attack at the field office."

Dan's breath caught, and he looked at Ames. Her deep green eyes studied him. Lips drawn into a thin line, she sat a little straighter and asked, "Why?" Dan wondered whom she was questioning, him or his accusers.

Reid came to his rescue without even realizing it. "Something they saw on the security footage, but I'm not sure. It must be a mistake. We will clear it up when we head in."

Ames's gaze did not soften, and her posture remained tense. "Are you sure that would be wise?"

"She's right, Zachary," John said. "You can no longer trust the FBI." He cut in front of a brown UPS truck to make a last-second exit from the freeway and looked back and forth between his mirrors as he watched the traffic behind them. "They won't believe your story and will separate you from the doctor. They'll make the same mistakes that led to the attack on your FBI offices. And that will end with her being dead."

Dan also checked out the rear window for a tail. No vehicles exited from the freeway, and the access road remained clear. Satisfied, Dan settled back and waited for his partner to start the argument that had to follow. Right on cue, Reid swiveled his body in the seat to face John.

Reid's face reddened. "Look here, we have procedures for handling terrorists. We are the FBI." He reached inside his coat. "I'm going to call for instructions..." but trailed off as he felt his various pockets and then glared at John. "Where is my phone?"

"You mean that little homing beacon that you said led them straight to Maccabees? Gone with everything else. I think you *agents* will need to plan on being my guests for a little while longer. What the doctor does past that is up to her, but I strongly advise her to remain with me."

They turned into a quiet neighborhood and wound down a tree-lined avenue across from a golf course. Dan watched Reid fume in the front seat and considered how to head off a physical altercation with John—if he even wanted to. Dan glanced at the rearview mirror and saw John staring at him.

"Wondering if you can take me at the next stop?" John asked.

You think you could stop me?

Dan fought down his anger and rubbed his jaw. "No," he said, drawing the word out. "Just wondering how long it will take to get anything close to a straight answer out of you."

John heaved a loud sigh. "Okay, let's get two things settled. First, you've already seen that your adversaries are well equipped and trained. So, you need to be off-the-grid long enough not to get killed. I can help you with that. Second, you need a chance to think through your next steps carefully. These are not ordinary terrorists. Standard FBI procedures won't cut it. Their leader is a genius scientist who has no scruples about taking human lives. You have to be very smart, or you are going to be very *dead*."

Heading out of the neighborhood, John turned onto a boulevard with a strip mall on one side and a Target down the block. "You'll need a change of clothes and personal items for a couple of days. After that, you can decide what to do," John said. They pulled into the strip mall parking lot and rolled to a stop in front of a small restaurant called the Rise-and-Dine. "Zachary, why don't you come with me to Target? Dan, wait in the diner with Dr. Cranford and get something to eat."

"We should all stay together," Reid countered.

John sighed and leaned back in his seat. "Too many security cameras. A group is much easier to spot. Trust me. I've been evading your types for a long time."

Ames sat back and folded her arms. "You guys are great at making plans for me. Thanks for the careful consideration of my input," she said. "But I'd prefer Agent Reid to stay with me." She kept her eyes fixed forward.

Surprised, Dan stared at her and swallowed hard. He opened his mouth to reply. To say they had it wrong, to remind her that she could trust him.

But why would she?

A fifteen-year-old memory played through his mind—the one of the voice mail she had left after the police told her he had joined the Navy. The hope that he was okay. The plea for him to contact her, to help her understand. He leaned back and managed, "That's probably a great idea."

John made eye contact with Dan in the mirror and added a soft, "We all have secrets, don't we?" He opened the middle console, withdrew Reid's pistol, and offered it grip-first to the agent. "You take care of the doctor."

Reid took the weapon and lingered for a moment with the muzzle pointed at John. Then he nodded and slipped it into his shoulder holster. "Doctor, you're with me," he said and opened his door.

Ames did not move. "Let me just ask you one more thing, John," she demanded. "If we're up against some super-genius and we can't trust the FBI, then just how are we going to stop them?"

"Well, Doctor," John said. He leaned into the gap between the front seats to face her. "I've seen your file. I think you're actually smarter than he is." He reached up and took off his sunglasses. A smile spread across his face for the second time that day. "And you have me."

Dan felt his heart sink as he looked from Ames to John and back.

———

Three men sat in a dimly lit room. Large monitors glowed in front of each. One moved a joystick that controlled the drone now circling above a dark-gray Jeep Rubicon. He zoomed in on the driver and captured a still-shot that the software immediately began processing through facial recognition. The match took only three seconds.

"Tell Cain we've found them," he said into the microphone of his headset.

CHAPTER EIGHT

Cain walked through the automatic door without slowing. "We've found your old friend. I'm getting the team together."

The man sitting behind the mahogany desk did not acknowledge him. As always, he wore a loose-fitting, white lab coat that made him look even shorter than his mere five foot seven. The desktop held two curved wide-screen monitors, some kind of VR device, and stacks of files. The man had an iPad in one hand and tapped on a keyboard with the other. His eyes never left the screens. Cain marched up to the front of the desk and waited.

Cain scanned the very familiar room with boredom. Spotless as always, the laboratory equipment that occupied the right half of the large room held little interest for him. The examination chair in the middle of the room sometimes provided entertainment, but today, it sat empty. The two chairs to the far left had a tray of tea sitting on the small, elegant table between them. Steam rose from the pot.

The enormous tapestry on the wall behind the desk caught his attention. He had seen the pattern too many times—hundreds of small circles with names in each, all connected by thin lines. It spanned from one wall to the next. He once marveled at the details—how the many names on the right stretched back to just a few on the far left. But that had all become mundane years ago. Today, however, a new blank circle sat to the far right.

"Professor, are you examining someone today?" Cain asked the man behind the desk.

"Yes, but a low-probability candidate," the Professor replied without looking up.

Cain waited. After a few more moments of scrutiny for the iPad and the monitors, the Professor looked up and ran his hand through his thick black hair.

"So, you have found him? And she is with him?"

"Yes, sir. As you predicted," Cain said.

"And the FBI agents?"

Cain frowned at the mention of the agents. "Yes," he replied. "The drone images clearly showed them in the Rubicon. But how did you know *he* would be one of the agents assigned?"

The Professor rose and strolled around the desk like a teacher at some university. "It was all about the timing. It's why I saved her for last," the Professor said. "I calculated the probability as high that he would be selected, and you have to admit it has worked to our advantage." He stopped in front of Cain and stared up into his eyes. "But you have not succeeded in your assignment, and that is disappointing to me."

Cain let his gaze fall to the floor.

As the Professor continued, he tapped on Cain's chest with his index finger in time with each of his words. "I want you to eliminate her today, Cain. But something quieter. Something they will blame on *him*."

"I can do it within the hour. I will find a way," Cain replied.

The Professor walked over to the examination chair and let his hand slide across the back. "Make sure that is the case. I don't want your lack of execution to impact the project schedule. The first test is in eight days. I don't want any lingering distractions."

Cain felt his anger rising. "You should have eliminated John a long time ago."

The Professor's head snapped up, and his dark-brown eyes locked onto Cain's. "I have told you before. There is an 87 percent likelihood that he will still join our cause once we have begun. Once *they* are no longer here, he will have nowhere else to turn. I will not waste such a valuable resource just because you are incapable of eliminating the woman."

Cain squeezed his hands into tight fists. But any further argument faded from his thoughts as the door swished open. Two muscular guards entered. They dragged a third man between them. A dark hood covered their prisoner's head. A fourth man in a white lab coat followed behind the trio. They forced the hooded man into the chair. He struggled and thrashed about as they attached the restraints to his arms and legs.

With a smile, Cain stepped forward to jerk the cover from the man's head. He blinked under the onslaught of the bright, clinical lights. As the man's eyes adjusted, he stared up at Cain in fear.

"Where am I? Why am I here?" the man sputtered.

"We all asked that at first," Cain answered. He wandered back to the side of the room. Cain knew the Professor's opening question. It was always the same.

The Professor studied the man. "Tell me, Robert, do you know your Bible?"

Confusion clouded the man's face. He expressed his ignorance with a small shake of his head.

The Professor said, "What a pity. So much history. So much knowledge."

Cain watched the Professor move, like he did every time, to gaze up at the mural hanging behind his desk.

"Why, the Bible even spells out the origin of our little community— for any that are intelligent enough to look," the Professor continued. He raised a delicate hand to the weave. Not quite touching it, his hand glided along and traced a path from right to left.

"Genesis 6 tells an interesting tale. When the Immortals of heaven had offspring with humans." The Professor glanced back at the man in the chair. "Can you imagine the outcome of shared DNA from an immortal being?" His gaze returned to the wall and lingered over one section, his fingers near a particular circle. His voice became almost a whisper. "Their descendants were called mighty men. Men of renown." He paused and then stalked back to the far right of the tapestry and tapped a small empty circle near the bottom. "Now, as for you, Robert, we shall see if your name should be added."

The Professor reached across the desk to pick up a small recording device and moved to stand by the man strapped in the chair. As he placed a hand on Robert's shoulder, the man looked up into the Professor's eyes.

Hope joined the fear on Robert's face. The Professor leaned a little closer. "Tell me, Robert, if someone dies, can they live again?"

Sweat appeared on the man's brow, and he looked right and left, searching for some help with the question. "I don't understand," Robert whispered.

"It is a simple question, my boy," the Professor said.

"No, of course not," Robert answered. "Dead is dead."

The Professor eased to the other side of the chair. "But what if it was possible for some to live again? Would you desire it? Eternal life?"

The man stared up at the Professor. His hands tensed into fists of fear and confusion. After a long moment, he added a single nod of agreement.

The Professor straightened and folded his arms behind his back. "Now, Robert, an acquaintance of mine once said that no one can have eternal life unless they are born again. But so many have misunderstood what he meant." He leaned down beside Robert's ear and whispered, "Would you like to understand, Robert? Do you want to be born again?"

Cain took a step closer. He always enjoyed this part. The man looked at him for understanding. Cain smiled and gave him a small nod of encouragement.

"Yes," Robert stammered. "Yes, I would like that…to be born again."

"That is good news, Robert," the Professor said. He reached out and took the man's hand. "But I am afraid you will not *like* it. Unfortunately, I will have to eat your flesh and drink your blood, in a manner of speaking of course. But it will be worth it if you have been chosen by your genetics to be blessed with eternal life."

The Professor spoke into the recording device. "Commencing examination of test subject 20143. We will start with the standard benchmark to ensure that the subject has not already crossed over. Let's begin with the removal of the fifth digit on his left hand at the proximal phalanx. Anton, the number-four shears, please."

The man in the white lab coat picked up a pair of medical cutting shears and slapped them firmly into the Professor's outstretched hand. "Number-four, sir."

Cain's pulse quickened. He always enjoyed the examinations. The bright-red blood and Robert's initial screams brought a smile to Cain's face. But he sighed. Today, he had more pressing matters. His promise to the Professor outweighed the possibility of entertainment. He needed to see the woman dead within the hour and by his own hand this time.

He turned on his heel and moved with purpose out of the room. The screams cut off abruptly as the soundproof doors slid closed behind him. While Cain waited for the elevator, he wondered with another smile if Robert had what it took to be born again.

He paused as he exited the elevator to peer through the heavy glass into the nursery. Medical equipment surrounded the nine small cribs in the center of the room, holding nine small, wailing infants—each one labeled with consecutive numbers from CA-8 through CA-16. He tapped on the glass, but the babies ignored him.

Give them a few years, and that will change.

As Cain marched down the hall to the garage and his waiting car, a plan took shape in his mind. With a single loud clap of his hands and a nod, he smiled again. "I'll do it with my knife," he whispered to himself.

He always liked using his knife the best.

CHAPTER NINE

Ames paused just inside the door to the Rise-and-Dine. The inviting smell of bacon and coffee greeted her. She was surprised that only two of the twenty-odd tables had patrons.

Reid followed her through the double glass front door and stepped to the right, just in front of Ames. He surveyed the room before folding his arms behind his back, apparently satisfied that no one posed a threat.

The one waitress, a fiftyish plump woman in a bright yellow uniform with a red apron, looked up as she refilled the coffee cup of a grandfather-looking customer. With a wave, she motioned to the empty tables and called out, "Anywhere y'all like."

Reid nodded to himself, adjusted the half-Windsor knot on his tie, and marched into the room without waiting for Ames. She frowned but followed him to the table he had selected. With red seats, the booth was on the far wall near the door to the kitchen. Reid took the side facing the front door, and Ames slid in across from him.

The waitress breezed over and laid down two white paper napkins, plopped a fork and knife on each, and asked Reid, "Will this be one check or two, honey?" She beamed a smile at the agent.

"One," Ames replied. "And, *honey*, why don't you order first?"

Reid shot Ames a look. "Oatmeal, skim milk, an English muffin, and coffee."

"Skim milk?" the waitress asked with a wink. "Why, I'd never take you for the skim milk type. And you can call me Karen," she added. She placed a hand on his shoulder. "And how about your sister here?" She turned to Ames with a raised eyebrow.

"Coffee and wheat toast, please. And I'm not his sister."

"Hmmm," was Waitress-Karen's only reply. She turned and walked away, yelling their order to the cook through a small open window to the kitchen. The cook's muffled reply echoed back.

Ames smiled. "I think she likes you, Agent Reid."

Reid's brow tightened, but he offered no reply as he kept his eyes locked on the front door.

Waitress-Karen swung back by with two white mugs of coffee and slid them onto the table. Her smile faded when Reid failed to acknowledge her, and she shuffled past to stand near the kitchen window.

They sat in silence. Ames stirred her coffee and glanced back at the entrance. Two of the other customers left, leaving only them and the grandfather in Waitress-Karen's care.

The strong coffee spurred her thinking, but the questions outnumbered the few answers. "Agent Reid, what are we going to do?"

Reid straightened his utensils in a neat row on top of the paper napkin and then met her eyes. "I'm not sure yet. Things got out of control," he said. "There has never been a successful attack of this size directed at an FBI field office. The pieces don't add up. And then there's John and all his talk."

Ames stirred her coffee again and sat watching the dark swirl. "And what about that terrorist? The one that got back up after Dan…you know…broke his neck," she added in a soft voice, not wanting anyone else to hear.

Reid straightened his silverware a little more. "I've lived through some major shifts in thinking. The end of the Cold War, 9/11, Trump, the Taliban. But nothing like this."

The kitchen door swung open behind Reid's seat. Ames looked up in surprise as Dan strolled into the room. He now wore a long black coat over a white shirt and jeans and sported dark, stylish Ray-Bans. Upon seeing her, he pulled off the glasses, smiled a winsome smile, and said, "Just like I hoped."

———

Reid heard the swoosh of the door as it opened behind him. He saw Dr. Cranford's eyes widen in surprise but not fear and heard his partner's familiar voice say, "Just like I hoped."

He wanted to talk with Dan in private. "Doctor, please excuse me for a moment, I need to speak with Agent Alexander," Reid said. Dr. Cranford frowned and started to object, but he rose and turned to face his partner. He only saw Dan's heel a moment before it connected with his temple.

Pain exploded in his head, and he staggered to his right. His vision swam. He tripped over a chair and fell onto his back. Only instinct saved his life. He rolled to his right as Dan slammed down on top of him and a six-inch blade buried itself in the linoleum just to his left—where his heart had been.

Reid struggled against the weight on top of him. He tried to slip his right hand inside his jacket to draw his weapon, but a powerful hand pinned it to the floor.

Dr. Cranford jumped up. Reid saw her swing her coffee cup at his partner's head.

But so did Dan.

He ducked his head and rolled his body down on Reid's right arm. The doctor's cup only swooshed through the air, and Dan kicked her hard with his right foot and sent her stumbling out of Reid's field of vision.

With his right arm still pinned, Reid punched Dan in the face with his left. His partner rolled away and sprang to his feet. Still on his back, Reid drew his weapon, but Dan kicked it from his hand the next second. Reid rose to his knees and anticipated the follow-up roundhouse kick in time to deflect it with his left arm. He countered with a punch to Dan's stomach. The man's *Oof* confirmed he had connected, and his partner staggered back.

Reid managed to get to his feet before the attack resumed. Dan moved in, throwing two quick jabs, which Reid blocked, and one body blow that he did not. The air shot from his lungs in a whoosh, and he staggered back.

A plate bounced off Dan's back and shattered when it hit the floor. A glass followed. It sailed past his partner's head and exploded against the mirror on the back wall. Both men looked to the center of the room. Dr. Cranford stood ready to launch another cup.

"Run!" Reid yelled.

Dan spun toward her and took a quick step in her direction. Seeing the opening, Reid lunged at his partner's back.

But it had been a feint.

He ran straight into Dan's sidekick. Reid rocketed into the wall and crumpled to the ground. The big man moved in and delivered a quick kick to Reid's midsection. Reid tried to rise, only to receive a powerful punch to the side of his head that drove him back to the hard floor.

Dan turned toward the doctor. She took a step back toward the exit but kept her gaze locked on Dan.

Reid scanned the floor for his weapon, but it lay across the room. He forced himself up on his hands and knees. His head swam, and black dots flooded his vision.

The cook burst through the kitchen door with a "What the hell?" only to turn and run when he saw Dan pull the knife free from the floor.

Reid struggled to his feet and stood with his hands on his knees. "Why?" he shouted at his partner's back.

"Why?" Dr. Cranford asked softly.

"You know, I used to ask myself that all the time," Dan replied.

Reid heard the waitress talking to 911 from behind the counter. He knew they would be too late.

Dan began flipping the knife from handle to blade to handle as he stalked closer to the doctor.

"Run!" Reid called out again. He stumbled forward two steps. The pain in his side flared with each breath.

The bell above the entry door jingled. A six-foot-two man with a rumpled suit jacket and a crooked tie walked in with a plastic Target bag in each hand.

The man with the knife paused in the middle of the room. He said, "Well now. This just got interesting."

Still by the door, Dan swayed a little. His mouth hung open. The Target bags slipped to the floor, but his hand still hung in the air. He uttered a strained, one-word question.

"Cain?"

The man glanced back at Reid and smiled. He whispered, "Bet you didn't see that coming, did you?" The man turned back to Dan, squared himself up, and asked, "Well, Brother, have you missed me?" Then he hurled the knife at Dan.

———

Dan stepped out of the Jeep in front of the diner, and John pulled the vehicle around the corner of the building to park it out of sight. Dan carried a change of clothes for himself, Reid, and Ames in two large Target bags. The tempting smell of bacon reached him even through the closed restaurant doors, and his stomach grumbled its agreement with the idea of breakfast. He proceeded into the Rise-and-Dine without waiting for John.

Hands loaded, Dan pushed the restaurant door open with his backside. The bell jingling overhead brought back a childhood memory—one of meeting his grandfather at a small restaurant in Gainesville that also had a bell above the door. He smiled at the thought of that happier time when both his brother and mom had still been with him. Now, both were gone.

The door swung wide, and Dan froze as he turned into the restaurant. His tactical training made him record the details: Chairs scattered. A few smashed dishes on the floor. A crack in the mirror on the back wall. Two overturned tables. Reid staggering out from the far wall. Ames standing with her back to him, hand raised, poised to throw a coffee mug, and the man with the knife.

But all of it faded when he looked at the man. He spoke the name without thinking.

"Cain?"

Cain said something to Reid that Dan did not catch. Then he turned back with a smile, squared himself up, and asked, "Well, Brother, have you missed me?"

Without waiting for a reply, Cain hurled his knife at Dan. Sunlight glinted off the six inches of steel as it flew through the air. Dan dodged to his right and the blade embedded itself in the wall an inch from his head.

"Cain, it's me," Dan blurted out.

Standing in the center of the room with his hands balled into fists, Cain spat back, "I know it's you, Brother." Then he laughed. "Just how many identical twins do you think we have?"

The sound of approaching sirens drifted in from the street. Ames looked at Dan, swiveled back to Cain, and turned to Dan again. Shock and fear filled her eyes.

"Ames, you need to move to the door and wait for John," Dan said. He took a step forward and kicked aside the bags of clothing. Ames backed toward the front window, away from both of them.

With a smile, Cain faced him, loosened his shoulders, and rolled his neck. "I've dreamed of this for a long time."

Dan watched as Reid eased toward the counter, and he saw his partner's gun by the far wall. Sirens wailed out front as a squad car slid into the parking lot. Two officers sprang from the vehicle and drew their weapons. They took up defensive positions behind the car doors.

Cain looked out the window at the policemen and sighed. "Do you remember, Brother? How mom always hated it when we fought?" He turned to Ames. "And, Doctor, you're last on my list. I always say, *save the best for last*. I am so looking forward to the next time we meet. Maybe somewhere a little more private."

Reid made a rush for his gun. Cain pivoted and launched a chair at him. It struck Reid high on the shoulder and knocked the injured agent off his feet.

"I'll see you soon, Brother," Cain called back as he walked casually toward the kitchen door.

"But, Cain," Dan said. "Where have you been?"

Cain shook his head. "Where indeed?" He pushed through the kitchen door and was gone.

"Who was that?" Ames demanded.

Another squad car pulled up out front. "No time now," Dan said. "We need to move. Reid, can you walk?"

Reid managed to get to his feet and nodded his head. Hand pressed to his side, he made his way to his weapon and picked it up with a grimace of pain.

Ames looked out the front at the police. "Maybe we should just surrender to them?"

"That would be a serious mistake, Doctor," John said. "One that will surely get you killed."

With no surprise on her face, Ames turned to look at John and sighed. "Are you sure?"

"Do you want to bet your life on me being wrong?" John replied.

Reid straightened with a grimace and walked to the entrance. He smoothed out his jacket and tried to look normal. "I'll flash my badge and tell the local PD we broke up a fight. I'll give them some bogus descriptions and send them on their way. John, where is your Jeep?"

"Parked on the east side of the building. You handle the cops. We'll leave out the back," John replied.

Reid nodded and headed out the front. John turned to Dan. "And I can't wait to hear about the look-alike that just left. I thought it was you, Dan, but he seemed to think that was hilarious."

"Well, John, how did you put it? That's a long story, and we don't have time for it now. Maybe when we are safe," Dan said with a bit of sarcasm. "But, Ames, we need to go." He moved to stand next to her.

She tilted her face up at him. Her eyes searched the lines on his face. "I thought it was you. That you were trying to kill me."

"It's okay. But we have to go," Dan said. He took her arm and urged her toward the back door.

She stood firm for a moment and stared into his eyes. "Dan, what is happening?" she whispered.

I only wish I knew.

CHAPTER TEN

Dan stepped into the alley behind the diner. He glanced both ways, saw no one, and motioned for Ames to follow.

John slid past. "Wait here," he said.

The Rubicon sat in the side lot to their right. John sauntered toward the Jeep like a kid walking to the park on a Sunday afternoon. Arms swinging. Hawaiian shirt bright in the morning sun. He began whistling as he crossed the side lot and glanced toward the front of the building. With a smile, he waved at the unseen officers before he entered his Jeep.

John's smile faded as he eased the Jeep to a stop next to Ames and Dan. Ames grimaced as she pulled herself up into the back seat.

Dan stepped to her side. "Are you hurt?"

"Just a bruise. It's been a few years since I was in a fight." She pushed her hair back from her face. "I'll be fine. But what in God's name is going on?"

"We've got to move," John called from the front.

Ames grabbed his arm. "Dan, I have to know." Her piercing green eyes demanded an answer.

He looked down. "I don't know."

"Talk later. Cops coming. Partner's hurt. Move it!" John yelled.

Ames released Dan, and he hurried to the other door.

Reid waited at the corner of the building, and John approached with the Jeep at a slow roll. Reid managed to hoist himself into the passenger seat. He slumped back with a ragged breath.

As they rounded the corner, the group of about ten police eyed them with suspicion. Reid waved to the officers. He said, "I'm not sure they bought my story. Let's not give them any more reasons to doubt us, John."

"You don't like my driving, do you, Zachary?" John said. "I can be a good boy when I have to." He merged the Jeep into traffic and headed back toward I-85.

Dan looked out the side window. His heart raced, and his thoughts swirled in confusion. It had been Cain. He was sure of that.

But how was he there?

Where had he been all these years?

And why did he try to kill Ames?

Dan had trouble catching his breath. A warm hand touched his arm. "Dan, talk to me," Ames said. "Who was that?"

Dan swiveled his head to look in her direction. He saw John watching him in the mirror.

Reid looked back and winced. "Dan," he said. "That guy kicked the crap out of me. I want to know who he is."

Dan leaned his head into his hand and rubbed his temple. "I had..." he began but trailed off with a sigh. "I have a twin brother. He was kidnapped when we were seventeen. We...I thought he was dead."

"You had no idea he might be alive?" Ames asked.

Dan hesitated. He felt a gentle squeeze of encouragement from her hand that still rested on his forearm. He looked out the side window and hoped they did not see the guilt on his face. "None," he replied flatly.

"Think, Dan. Any family ties to these terrorists? Any clue as to how they recruited him?" Reid asked.

"They didn't recruit him," Dan shot back. "They *took* him!"

"You're right. We don't know that this is the same group that kidnapped him," Reid conceded. But he shifted back into interrogation mode. "John, what do you know of how this group operates? Is this their MO?"

John eased the vehicle into the flow of traffic and headed south on I-85. His frown seemed to indicate a struggle within as if he was trying to decide what to tell them.

Reid pressed for more. "You've shown up at each of their attacks. You must have some idea of how they operate."

John sighed and glanced at Reid. "I just haven't been sure you are going to believe me." He paused and looked at Ames in the mirror. "But

I guess we are way past that now. As I told you, their leader calls himself the Professor. And like I said, I've known him for a very long time. For most of that time, he's focused on understanding how we, the *Discovered* as he calls us, are made. During the last one hundred years, it has become an extreme obsession." John lapsed into silence.

Ames leaned forward and asked softly, "Just how old is he?"

"I don't know for sure. When I first met him, he called himself Luke. But he changes his name about every seventy years to help remain hidden."

Ames frowned. "Hidden?"

John gave her a wry smile. "I asked you once before, if you live forever and can recover from any injury, what is the one thing you are afraid of?"

"What people would do to you if they found out," Reid said in a low voice.

"Of course," Ames said. She leaned back as she considered the implications.

John said, "After 2020, with the racial unrest, protests, election controversy, Capitol riot, and COVID, the government stepped up surveillance of the general public. And with all of the talk of domestic terrorism and pandemic worries, everyone accepted increased government oversight as the new norm. I think the Professor is afraid that we can no longer stay hidden," John checked the traffic in his mirror and changed lanes. "And he is the premier geneticist in the world. He discovered the characteristics of DNA before Watson and Crick were even born. And who do you think mastered the use of mRNA that led to the advances in vaccine production?" John slowed as a police car sped past, lights flashing. "But I'm betting he's got something other than vaccines in mind."

Dan squinted out the side window. They continued south, passing the I-285 loop and heading into the heart of Atlanta. "But that still doesn't explain anything about my brother."

Ames leaned forward again and rapid-fired her questions. "But how have you known about each attack? Do you have a way of monitoring them? Or a spy in their organization?"

"No. Nothing that sophisticated, I'm afraid. I haven't been able to track their specific movements for the last seven years."

Ames frowned and seemed unsatisfied. "But how were you able—"

"You, Doctor," John interrupted, "have been quite the opposite. I've had you under surveillance since my AI flagged you for observation."

"Your AI?" Dan and Ames both said. Ames sounded surprised, but Dan felt his anger rise.

"Yes, once it became clear that you would be a primary target. My AI detected the pattern after they assassinated your colleague in England last week." John signaled and moved into the right lane. "When they killed Dr. Restor two days ago, it flagged you as the next high-value target. Their move at the CDC was unexpected. It was fortunate I was nearby. The attack showed a change in their tactics. I think they must be preparing for something big."

"You could have clued us in," Dan said. "We might have been able to prevent this."

John shot him a hard look. "Would anyone at the FBI have believed me, Dan?" John's answer to his own question echoed what Dan thought. "Not a chance in hell."

They exited the freeway on Tenth Street and headed west. A university campus soon surrounded them as they wound down the tree-lined lane. Dan saw the large letters of TECH emblazoned on the top of a steeple in the center of the campus.

Dan asked, "Why are we at Georgia Tech?"

John pulled the Jeep into a garage next to a building with an impressive sign that announced it as the Klaus Advanced Computer Center. He used an ID card to gain access to the faculty parking area. "In exchange for some rather large donations, I have access to the research facilities here. Over the years, I've built a base of operations under the campus." He parked the Rubicon next to a set of elevators in the back corner of the garage. "And I'm one of the tenured professors in their advanced computing department." With a smile, he stepped out of the Jeep. "And, Dan, you'll never guess what my specialty is." He glanced back, met Dan's glare with a twinkle in his eye, and mouthed *artificial intelligence*.

They followed John to the elevator. He placed his hand on a biometric reader next to the elevator door. The door slid open, and John motioned for them to enter. "This is my most secure location. We will be safe here while we plan our next steps."

Dan clenched his fists to keep from shouting. As he stepped into the elevator, he saw the same frustration on Reid's face. One thought shouted in Dan's mind: *What is going on?*

———

The three drone pilots sat in a dimly lit room. Large monitors glowed in front of each. One reached forward, pressed a button on the console, and spoke into the microphone of his headset.

"Cain, sir, you asked to be updated regarding the location of the target."

He waited for some confirmation, but the silence in his headphones drilled a hole in his confidence. "We tracked them south from your location. They exited the freeway in midtown."

More seconds of continued silence slipped by. He held his breath. He concentrated, trying to eliminate a slight tremor in his hand on the joystick controlling the drone.

"And?"

He flinched at the single word. A wave of dizziness washed across him.

"We lost them on the campus of Georgia Tech, sir. The buildings are—"

"*We* lost them?"

He glanced around the room, looking for a place to hide. "I...I lost them, sir."

The expected tirade did not come. The flat, emotionless reply he received sent a chill down his spine.

"Forward their last known coordinates to me. Place your drone in auto-return and report to Angela for reassignment."

"Please, sir," he pleaded. "I can do better. I can find them. I'm sure Ms. Angela is very busy."

"No need to worry. I'll speak to her myself. She will help you see your future duties, if any, more clearly."

"But, sir, I can—"

His comms went dead.

———

John rarely brought people to this location. He eyed his three wards as the elevator descended into his complex. Dr. Cranford leaned against the back wall and rubbed her temples. The two agents glared at him. Reid gripped his hands tightly behind his back. Dan balanced his weight on the balls of his feet.

He knew how to deal with their anger. But the appearance of Dan's brother presented an unexpected complication.

The elevator doors slid open. John took a deep breath and stepped into the dark room beyond. In the high ceiling, automatic lights clicked on. He moved to the center of the large circular room and turned back to face his companions. The three hesitated in the elevator.

He gave them a slight bow and, with a sweep of his right hand, said, "Welcome to Crac des Chevaliers."

Dan shook his head and stepped out first. "What now? Is this your Fortress of Solitude?"

John smirked at him. "You think I'm Superman?"

"I wish," Dan muttered under his breath. John still heard and gave him a small shrug.

John turned his attention to Ames with a smile. "Dr. Cranford, you look like you could use some refreshment. Martha and Petros will arrive soon, but I'm sure we can find you some tea."

She took one step into the room. Her face remained blank, but her eyes flashed anger. "Let's see... How many times has someone tried to kill us in the last twenty-four hours, and you're offering us tea?"

John maintained his smile. "Please, what you need is a moment to rest. A little time to let your heads clear of the adrenaline of combat."

Dan marched across the room and stopped inches from John. He poked John's chest hard with his index finger. "How about I use some of that adrenaline to whip your ass?"

"I am *not* the one who took your brother," John replied in a low voice just for Dan's ears.

Dan glared at him a second longer, but the rage on his face began to melt into something else, perhaps sorrow. Dan wheeled about and stalked to the far side of the room.

Reid leaned against the wall nearest the elevator. He held his side with labored breathing. John knew Reid needed some attention, but the man's pride prevented him from asking for help.

"You're all safe here. And I will answer all of your questions without delay. Please come with me, and I will tend to your needs," John said. He held out his arm to Dr. Cranford like a nobleman offering to escort a princess.

She looked at his outstretched offer of protection, slowly stepped forward, and took it. Her eyes held his for a moment before she glanced around the room at the art on the walls—four of his earlier works spaced evenly around the circular walls.

"They're beautiful," Ames said. "Da Vinci reproductions?"

As John guided her toward the interior hallway, a smile played at the corners of his mouth. "You might say."

———

Dan watched as John guided Ames toward a dark hall. Chaos ruled his mind. Memories of Cain sat in every corner of his thoughts. He shook his head. He needed to concentrate, but he only saw Cain's seventeen-year-old face as his brother stood in the mall parking lot. His first words at the Rise-and-Dine echoed in his thoughts.

Well, Brother, have you missed me?

Lights flickered on in the hallway. Dan followed, not wanting to let Ames out of his sight. Reid grimaced as he pushed away from the wall and trailed behind Dan. Soft light filled the fifty-foot corridor from the sconces spaced down the walls. Like a museum, the left side held a series of ten glass display cases. The right held a variety of more paintings. A few seemed familiar to Dan. Halfway down the hallway, a small writing desk sat to one side with several thick tomes scattered across its top.

"What is this place?" Ames asked.

John paused at the first display. "These are items of importance to me that I've collected over the years," he said. John waved a hand toward the desk. "And where I like to do my research."

Dan looked over Ames's shoulder at the first display. It contained a series of black-and-white photographs of scenes from the 1940s, most from the war. Many showed the gaunt, malnourished victims of the Holocaust. Others showcased generals and overweight politicians. A collection of documents and letters rested on several small stands. Dan leaned forward to get a better look at the photos. One eight-by-ten sat in the middle and pictured just three men with arms around each other's shoulders. Two Dan recognized. Albert Einstein stood to the right.

Ames pointed at the same picture. She asked, "Is that Robert Oppenheimer on the left?"

Dan leaned near the glass. His mouth went dry. The man standing in the middle was John.

Dan straightened and looked at John more closely. He seemed to have not aged a day since the photo. He glanced back at the display. A handwritten note sat under the picture. The few words scrawled on the faded paper spoke of the writer's remorse.

John, you were correct. We should never have done it. May God have mercy on our souls. Albert.

With a sigh, John let his chin drop a little. He moved on down the hallway with Ames close at his side. Dan tried but failed to ignore the tightness in his chest.

The following display contained an odd collection of replicas of US historical items. A few caught Dan's eye—a picture of Lincoln with a pistol lying next to it, a copy of the Declaration of Independence with a note from Thomas Jefferson sitting to its right, two western-style revolvers with a gun belt and a card with *For Doc* written in a flowing script. John only paused briefly before he led Ames further along the hallway.

As they proceeded down the hall, Dan took a moment to glance in each case. They all contained historical items, each more ancient than the previous. One held things a Samurai might carry or wear. Another had a suit of armor with a two-handed sword. An even older one displayed a Roman-looking shield and short sword.

John did not stop until they neared the end and then only for a moment to gaze at the display second from the last. It held a simple gold ring, a woman's dark-blue scarf, and a single red rose—wilted with age.

John started forward again, but Ames pulled him to a stop, looking back at the prior presentation. It held a thick old book opened to the last few pages.

"Is that a Gutenberg Bible?" Ames asked with awe in her voice.

John glanced into the display with the book. "Yes, it was a private printing for me in English. A gift for my help in creating his press."

"You're telling me you knew *the* Gutenberg?" Reid asked with obvious sarcasm.

"Yes," John replied.

Reid looked away with a shake of his head. He walked on down the line of displays.

John sighed. "And you wonder why I've been reluctant to tell you my story."

Dan stepped forward for a closer look. The Bible sat open near the end of the book of Revelation. *Chapter Twenty-Four* stood out at the top of the page, noting the exact location in the text. Something from Dan's Catholic school training struggled through his memory. "This isn't right," he exclaimed. "Revelation only has twenty-two chapters."

John just smiled at him. "Well, I remembered a few more things and added them in for this printing."

Dan stared at him in disbelief. "You remembered a few more things?"

Reid stepped up to the last display and tapped on the glass. "And what is this? More fakes?"

A dark cloud spread across John's face. He drifted away from the displays and into a shadow.

Dan moved around Ames to look into the final collection. Three items sat behind the glass under twin spotlights. The first was a circlet about six to eight inches across formed out of petrified wood with spiked thorns. The second, lying near the back, was a cloth of fine linen displaying the imprinted outline of a man's face. The third item sat a little more forward of the rest—a metal blade about eighteen inches long. Not a knife, more like the long tip of a stabbing weapon or spear but without the haft. He looked at John, wanting some explanation. He saw sadness in the man's eyes as John stared at the relics.

John shouldered past Reid to stand closer to the glass. "These I collected when they murdered a friend of mine. Some might even think of them as sacred. To me, they're only reminders of how long I've had to wait." He rubbed a rough hand across his face and then tapped the glass to point at the blade. "And that one," he said, "is the only thing I have ever seen that can kill an Immortal."

CHAPTER ELEVEN

Cain sped down Piedmont in his Maserati and rocketed around a corner. An old man and woman in the crosswalk had to jump out of the way. He thought about running one down, but the Professor had rules.

Always stay incognito. Never draw attention.

And a splattered pedestrian might draw some attention. Cain pulled the car into the garage of his Buckhead condo and hit the button to close the door. He remained in his seat and struggled to slow his breathing.

Dan.

He had surveilled his brother many times over the years, but speaking with Dan had unsettled him. And the woman had gotten away *again*. The bitch had even thrown coffee on his shirt. He liked this shirt.

His grip tightened on the steering wheel. The Professor would be disappointed.

He hit the steering wheel several times before he realized what he was doing. He rocked back in the seat and stared out the windshield.

Dan!

Cain wished he had put the knife right through Dan's neck. Or had the time to break his neck. But the stupid cops had ruined his fun. Maybe it was for the best. After all these years, he needed something special to settle the score with his brother. He rolled his neck.

Something memorable.

His breathing slowed.

Something extraordinary.

An idea began to take shape, and a smile crept at the edges of his mouth. His cell phone buzzed in his coat pocket. Cain sighed, glanced at the caller-ID, and then answered without hesitation. "Professor, how can I assist you?"

Cain heard a few muffled words on the other end of the call as the Professor finished another conversation. He waited.

After a long moment, the Professor cleared his voice and addressed him. "Cain, this is not like you."

"Sir, they are proving more difficult than expected. But we are tracking their location."

"I have been told that you have lost them."

Anger crept into his voice. "That is inaccurate."

"Angela is evaluating your tech as we speak. But he is one of us."

A bead of sweat ran down his temple. Only the Professor passed judgment on his Discovereds, but Cain did not care about the tech. Someone else dominated his thoughts. His heart beat a little faster. "I saw *him* today. Can I kill him?"

"Soon, perhaps. We shall see," the Professor said in a soothing tone. When he continued, his voice hardened into ice. "We are too close to executing our next phase, and I will not tolerate delays caused by your failures."

Cain squeezed his eyes shut and held his breath.

"I want you to come and see me. I think you need an examination," the Professor said. "Come see me within the hour."

Eyes still closed, Cain let his breath escape in a soundless whistle. He replied with a simple, "As you wish," and disconnected the call.

Cain reached into the console and withdrew one of his knives. He opened the door, swung his legs out, and sat, leaning forward with his elbows on his knees. With delicate precision, Cain ran his thumb down the blade. It sliced deep into the flesh. Blood ran down his wrist as he held his hand out away from the car. Large red drops began decorating the pavement. He inhaled a sharp breath and cut a second deep groove into his thumb.

His calm began to return with each slow exhale of his breath. He closed his eyes and let his thoughts drift back to Dan.

Something extraordinary.

CHAPTER TWELVE

D an stood next to Ames in front of the last display, the one with the circle of thorns, the cloth, and the spear. His mind reeled with the implications of what John had just told them.

As they both stared at the artifacts, Ames broke the silence. "Are these the originals?"

Reid sagged against the wall. "Originals of what?" he said. "You expect us to know what any of this means?"

Dan frowned and tried to put the pieces together. "Okay, a crown of thorns is supposed to remind us of Jesus. But what are the other two?"

John shook his head and turned away, but Dan grabbed him by the arm and spun him back around. "Look, John, we've had a couple of tough days. And I'm apparently not as bright as I thought I was. No more mysterious mumbo jumbo." Dan thrust a finger at the display. "If they're important, then tell us what they are!"

John stared back with cold, hard eyes. He shook Dan's hand from his arm and gritted his teeth. After a long moment, John turned to look at the items again and seemed to relax.

"Yes, Doctor, they are originals. They were the last three things I could get," John said. He stepped up to the display and touched the glass with a soft hand. He fell silent, lost in some memory.

"You were there?" Ames asked softly.

"Where?" Reid demanded. He gestured with his hands above his head, only to grimace in pain and drop them to his sides.

"In Jerusalem, the day they killed him," John said in a somber tone. "I haven't shown these to anyone in over five hundred years."

"Five hundred years!" Dan exclaimed. "Jesus, man, how could you be five hundred—"

John spun around on him. "Aren't you listening to anything I'm saying? I'm not Jesus! He's the one they killed."

Ames put a gentle hand on John's forearm. "He meant no disrespect. Tell us about the items, and we will understand better."

John's face flushed, and his lips pressed into a thin line. He exhaled hard. "You're right, Doctor. I have forgotten my manners. A good host must be more forthcoming."

John took a step back and motioned to the glass with a sweep of his hand. His next words sounded like those of a hawker at a sideshow. "Behold, three artifacts from ancient times. Three relics, often discussed, rumored to be in many places, but only found here." He took another step back to make sure they had an unobstructed view. "I present to you first, the Crown of Thorns. Woven by a Roman soldier and placed on the head of Jesus the night of his trial in mocking tribute to his claims. Step closer, step closer." He beckoned them forward. "Note the dark stains of the blood where they pierced his brow."

Dan let his hands tighten into fists. "What the hell?"

John fixed him with a stare and offered a fake smile. "Next, we have the famous Shroud. The cloth that covered the face of Jesus as he lay in the tomb. But being the only perfect Immortal ever, he had other plans and had no need for burial clothing."

Reid shook his head and grumbled, "This is a load of crap."

John shifted his cold eyes to Reid. "And finally, the most sought after of all. Fabled to possess supernatural powers. Often copied, but only this one is the true original. I give you the Spear of Longinus, known to many as the Spear of Destiny." John finished with a deep bow.

No one spoke.

John looked up and met each of their gazes one by one. "The Spear of Destiny?" He stretched his open hand toward the display. "Anyone? Anyone?"

Ames's face darkened. "John, you mock us. We only want to understand."

"And you have no appreciation of my circumstance," John shot back. His hand began to tremble, and he forced it behind his back. "I was there, just a teenager. I had no idea what he meant when he said that I wouldn't die before he returned. I believed him…I still do. I just didn't realize that he wanted me to wait this long."

Dan felt a tightening in his chest. Doubt raged through his thoughts. *Could he be that old?*

Reid stepped up and tapped on the glass. "But what is this Spear of Destiny?"

John looked down. "It was on that hopeless day. I went with his mother to the hill where they nailed him to a cross. He hung there for hours. The sky grew dark when he died. A soldier wanted to be sure, so he stabbed him with his spear. His name was Longinus. There was an earthquake, and Longinus dropped the spear and ran. I've had it ever since."

John pressed a hidden button, and the glass in front of the display slid into the wall. He reached in and took the long blade by its base. John held it closer to the light. His eyes ran down the length of the weapon. He rotated it for them to obtain a closer look. Dark stains remained on its metal surface.

Lost in some thought, John continued to study its length. A frown furrowed his brow. "Many think it has the power to control the destiny of the world. That's just a myth." His voice fell into a whisper. "But it can do something special."

Dan eased himself between John and Ames. The blade looked old but still razor-sharp.

John fixed him with another cold stare but placed the spear back in the display. The glass front slid back into place with a *click*.

Dan shot Reid a weary glance.

This just keeps getting better and better.

———

Ames pushed past Dan to get a better look at the spear. A dull ache simmered in her head, and she struggled to clear her thoughts. Ames did not need Dan to protect her from John. No, she needed him to help them find a way out of this. But he still seemed to either be in the way or not there when it mattered.

And his brother, that no one knew he had, just tried to kill me.

John took her arm gently, and she met his gaze. His dark eyes filled with concern. He said, "I let my frustrations get the better of me a moment ago. I ask your forgiveness for my poor manners. We are all weary, and I still owe you breakfast. Please come."

Ames let him lead her past the final display. The hallway ended in a T-intersection just beyond the display. Though a closed door blocked any view to the right, the left revealed a large room that beckoned with warm lights and an array of comfortable-looking furniture. John led them into the room and motioned toward a set of couches across the room.

"Please sit," John said. "Let me see if Martha has arrived." He headed to a desk and picked up the telephone.

Ames paused in the doorway. The contemporary decor felt inviting. Several pieces of art hung on the opposite wall, each an impressionistic view of a major world city. The center of the room held a conference table with maps and schematics of some device spread across its surface.

John spoke into the telephone and motioned again for them to enter. Standing behind her, Dan cleared his throat. Ames took the hint and went three steps into the room. Dan shot her a questioning look as he passed but proceeded to the table to scrutinize the maps. Reid shuffled in and took up station near the door. The grimace on his face reminded her he was injured.

"Let me take a look at those ribs," she said.

"I'm fine," he replied through gritted teeth.

She called out to John, "Do you have a first-aid kit? Agent Reid needs some attention."

Reid straightened. "I said I'm fine."

She shook her head. "And I hope to be home this evening. But just saying it doesn't make it true. Now sit down before you fall."

Reid frowned but moved to the conference table and eased himself into a chair.

She took his face in her hands and prodded the various contusions on his cheeks and brow left by the beating. He scowled, but he did not complain.

"No apparent facial fractures," she observed. "Any dizziness?"

He shook his head in reply.

"Take your jacket off. Let's have a look at those ribs."

"Whatever you say, Doctor."

His solo attempt failed, and she had to assist him. With his jacket removed, Ames ran her hand across the left side of his shirt. A small groan got past his best efforts to hide the pain.

"Can you take a deep breath?" she asked.

"Only if I want to black out."

John approached with a small duffel bag with a red medical cross stenciled on the side. She opened it and began rummaging through the contents. Ames withdrew a stethoscope and pressed the chest-piece to his back.

"Breath in," she ordered.

Reid sucked in a slow breath.

"Out."

He flinched as he exhaled.

"Your lungs sound okay, but the ribs feel broken. You're lucky not to have a punctured lung." She dug through the bag again and pulled out a roll of wide medical tape and a bottle of ibuprofen. She popped the lid off the plastic bottle and handed him four tablets.

Reid downed the pills without water and began unbuttoning his shirt. A dark, mottled bruise covered his left side. With a nod of satisfaction, Ames knelt beside him and started applying strips of tape to the area. He sucked in a sharp breath and held it while she worked.

Two layers of tape later, she stood and placed a hand on his shoulder. "I wish I could do more, but that should hold you over until you can get some real care."

Reid looked up with strained eyes and breathed a simple, "Thanks." He gingerly began buttoning his shirt.

A door at the back of the room swung open, and Martha and Petros marched in carrying trays of food and a silver pot. They began arranging a table near the back wall. The pleasant smell of coffee drew Ames toward the table. Dan rushed to arrive first and slid a chair back, offering it to Ames.

She had let her guard down with him after the attack by his brother. He had looked so vulnerable. The dull ache behind her eyes matured into a pounding headache. Without meeting Dan's gaze, she moved to the far side of the round table and slid into another chair. She let her forehead rest on her hands. The others took their seats, and silence fell across the table.

Martha slid a china plate in front of her. The decorative display of fruit and the mouthwatering smell of cinnamon toast reminded her of home. Ice clinked in water glasses, and Petros placed steaming mugs of coffee at each setting. Eyes still focused on her plate, Ames took a sip of the delicious coffee and selected a small fork to skewer a defenseless strawberry. The grapefruit slices went next, and without thinking, she cleared her plate.

Her headache subsided, and she began reviewing what she knew. After fifteen years, Dan Alexander had just shown up in a parking lot, claiming to be there to protect her. Someone named the Professor wanted her dead. They had tried twice with bombs and guns. Dan, his partner, and the rest of the FBI had failed to keep her safe both times. But John, the handsome mystery man, had shown up to save her each time.

Until the diner.

The fight replayed itself in her mind. She'd been terrified when she thought it was Dan, only to find out it was his identical twin—the brother Dan had presumed dead but who was alive and well and working with the terrorists.

Images of her friends at the CDC and the people at the FBI office floated through her thoughts.

A lot of people have died because of me.

A wave of nausea swept over her. She pushed her plate away and gave Martha a pleading look. The woman favored her with a gentle smile and motioned toward the rear door with her head. Ames bolted through the door and found the bathroom a few steps down the well-lit corridor. Her breakfast waited just long enough for her to reach the toilet.

After the heaving subsided, she turned to the sink and splashed cold water on her face. With hands on the basin to support her weight, Ames stared at her pale reflection in the elegant mirror. The wall behind her held an impressionistic painting of a lovely young woman in a white dress with a parasol and wearing a blue scarf. The woman stood in a field of flowers with a young boy. The painter's signature caught her eye. *Claude Monet.*

She spun to examine it more closely. Not a simple reproduction. It looked like an original work.

What kind of man has a Monet in a bathroom?

John's fanciful tales seemed to close in around her. She sucked in a quick breath.

Could his claims really be true?

———

Dan watched Ames push away from her breakfast and hurry from the room. He rose to follow, but Martha stopped him in his tracks with a smile and a firm, "If she needs your help, I'm sure she will ask." With his attention still focused on the door, Dan slumped back into his chair.

He rubbed the back of his neck. Dan thought Ames had begun to trust him again. But now, she did not even look at him. His mind raced between worry for Ames and trying to understand what to do. And above all else, one face dominated his thoughts.

Cain.

They needed a plan. No more waiting and hiding.

"Look, John," Dan said. "I'm at my wits' end. Either tell us what you know, or I'm taking Ames and hitting the road. We can be in California in two days."

John set his coffee mug on the table and met Dan's glare. "Do you think you are ready for what I have to tell you? Are you ready to believe?"

Dan shook his head and stood up. "That's it. I can't take any more of your cryptic BS. We're leaving as soon as Ames gets back."

"Don't you think she might have an opinion on that?" John asked in a low, dangerous tone.

Dan balled his hands into fists. "Right now, I think I can convince her that we need to get out of Atlanta."

"Funny, that was the first thing I told you. Right after the CDC. Right before you got everyone at the FBI killed."

Reid slapped his hand down on the table and yelled back, "Those were our friends. They died doing their jobs. Too bad they were in the dark because you won't tell us anything but a bunch of mystic *we are a group of immortals* baloney that none of us believes."

"I believe him," Ames said from the doorway.

Dan whirled around to look at her. "What did you say?"

Ames stepped back to the table and took a drink of water. She looked across the table at John but addressed the agents. "I said I believe him."

She eased back into a chair. "But you must tell us more, John. No more holding back. Don't worry if we will believe you. And it has to be now, or I will leave with Dan."

John accepted her statement with a small incline of his head. He rubbed his chin and leaned back, thinking.

Dan took a chair next to Ames. She favored him with a quick smile that bolstered his confidence. He folded his hands in front of him on the table. "Just tell us, John."

A smile spread across John's face, and he motioned to Martha. "I think we will be here a while. Please bring more coffee and let Petros know we will be having lunch and dinner here today." Martha dipped her head in agreement and glided from the room.

John sat up straight, rubbed his hands together, and asked, "Let me see. Where should I start?"

Dan opened his mouth to deliver his frustration, but John silenced him with an outstretched hand. "I know, Dan, at the beginning. Please relax. I'll fulfill the doctor's request." John studied Ames for a moment. "And while I appreciate your vote of confidence, Doctor, I think even you'll still find some of this hard to believe." He leaned forward and met each of their gazes. "But I promise you—every word of this is true."

CHAPTER THIRTEEN

They all sat in silence, waiting for John to begin his story. As the moments ticked by, Dan wondered if John had reconsidered. Martha breezed in with a silver pot of coffee and filled their mugs. Petros followed on her heels with a tray of pastries. With a slight bow, he slid it onto the table. Dan offered him a smile of thanks and reached for a cinnamon-raisin muffin. The warm pastry melted in his mouth.

The staff left, and John leaned forward, took a sip of his coffee, and sat gazing into his cup for another long moment. With a nod to himself, he looked up.

"I was born in the year 3,774 on the Jewish calendar in the month of Sivan," John began in a soft voice. "That would be in June of AD 14 in a small—"

"Really?" Reid interrupted. "You're really going there?"

Dan placed a hand on Reid's arm. "Let's hear him out."

Reid shook Dan's hand off and grimaced at the pain the sudden movement caused. His hands balled into fists.

John stared at Reid with unreadable eyes and continued, "In a small fishing village on the Sea of Galilee in northern Palestine. My older brother had some friends over in Nazareth. When we were teenagers, we used to sneak out after the day's fishing and walk over to the town." A rueful smile edged onto his face. "There were more girls in Nazareth." He paused as he considered some memory. Then his face took on a darker expression. "That's when I first met him."

"Who?" Ames asked. "The Professor?"

When John remained silent, Dan answered for him. "No, Ames. That's when he first met Jesus." John met his gaze with sad eyes.

John's eyes lost their focus as he drifted into the memory. "We had no idea who he was…what he was. But he knew everything about me. Even my *condition* before I ever did."

Reid shifted in his seat, grimaced again, and shook his head. "You're telling us that you, this Professor, and the rest of you with this live-forever *condition* are like Jesus?"

"We're nothing like him," John growled back. "He was a true Immortal with pure DNA. We're just the leftovers from someone's mistake a very long time ago."

Ames frowned. "But you have similar DNA traits, correct? Something that allows for rapid cellular regeneration and the regrowth of tissue?" She paused and nodded to herself. "It would explain the Resurrection myth."

"I was there. It's no myth. But yes, I think the process is similar," John replied quickly.

Reid continued to fume. "So, you're saying this all started with Jesus? Like you were what, all related?" He turned to Dan. "This sounds like that cult in Idaho last year. Only they're all still dead."

John sighed and rose from his chair as if to leave.

Dan shot Reid an angry frown. "Just ignore him, John."

"You're buying this crap?" Reid fired back.

Not waiting for Dan, Ames replied, "We want to hear him out, Agent Reid. Please remain quiet."

Reid's face darkened. "I'll—"

Dan interrupted him with a sweep of his hand. "Look around, Reid. All of this didn't just drop out of the sky. And what about his little *demonstration* in the garage?"

Reid stiffened but held his tongue.

John looked up at the ceiling. "See, I told you they wouldn't believe me."

Dan looked at Ames for guidance. She shrugged with her hands raised a little, palms turned up, and gestured with her head toward John. Dan frowned at her, and she motioned again at John.

Dan rose and eased to John's side. "John, help a brother out here. It is just a lot to take in at one time."

John continued to peer up. He cocked his head to one side as if listening and then nodded. Dan followed his gaze. He wondered if there was some surveillance device monitoring them.

"Okay, Dan, let's get to the good part," John said and eased back into his chair.

Dan remained standing and looked from John to the ceiling and back. A knot formed in his stomach.

Is he insane?

"You must be wondering if I've lost my mind along the way," John said. He ran his hand through his thick dark hair. "Oh, sit down, Dan," John added. "I know he's not listening anymore. It's just an old habit from when I thought he did." He shot Dan a look. "And be careful. Faith is easy to find when you don't need it."

Ames reached out and took John's hand like a doctor trying to encourage a terminally ill patient. "It must have been hard for you, losing him as you did?"

John leaned back. He let his hand slip out of hers and coughed out a small laugh. "Hard for me?" he countered. "The hard part was being left behind and getting to watch the *greatness of man* unfold all around me. For a long time, I believed I was part of his plan. The fool that I was." John let his head sink into his hands.

The concern on Ames's face echoed the feelings in Dan's gut.

———

Ames heard a soft noise from the corridor, and Martha swept back in from the other room with the coffeepot in hand. The housekeeper paused in the door, taking in the scene. She focused on John for a moment before her gaze slid to Ames. Eyes filled with compassion, Martha seemed to try to convey an unspoken message to her.

He needs me?

Martha made a graceful turn and left without leaving the coffee. Ames decided on a new tack. "What about the Professor? Where did he come from?"

After a moment, John glanced up with a faraway look in his eyes. When he spoke, his voice remained flat with no emotion. "He told me once that he had a five-hundred-year head start on me." The edges of his mouth bent toward a smile. "He'd always been a physician. Might say he was the original one."

A twinkle returned to his eyes, and his smile broadened. "He always wanted to understand things. He journaled everything. He just showed up one day in Jerusalem the year after Jesus left us." John gave Dan an amused look. "He went by Luke back then. We became friends and moved to Ephesus in the first wave of persecution." His smile faded. His face darkened. "That was before I knew."

"Knew what?" Ames prodded.

"Before I knew what he was or what I would become," John replied.

"It was around AD 65. Nero had been emperor in Rome for about fifteen years, and he'd blamed that damned fire on Paul and the Christians. Luke and I went to Rome to see Paul one last time."

Ames felt her patience running thin. "But that was long ago," Ames pleaded. "Why is he trying to kill me now?"

John seemed not to hear her. Lost in his remembrance, he continued, "My real story started there in Rome. In the Colosseum. When I learned the truth."

CHAPTER FOURTEEN

Rome, AD 65

Rome had changed. John and Luke arrived six months after the fire ripped through the city, but the rains had failed to wash the stench from the air. They came seeking Paul, only to find the man already dead—executed in the Colosseum two months before they arrived.

The surprise raid had caught John as they packed to leave for Ephesus. And now, he sat in a holding cell in the bowels of the Colosseum, waiting his turn. The warm-up spectacle had started about five minutes earlier. They usually did not last long. The guards told him he had the honor of being the main attraction. Nero himself was in attendance. And they had something special planned just for him.

He sat in the dim cell and stared at the chain linking the manacles on his wrists. He whispered a word of thanks that Luke had avoided capture. Even this far underground, the roar of the crowd made it hard to think. But one haunting thought refused to remain silent.

This was not the way it was supposed to end.

John had been doing his part. About thirty years had passed since Jesus left them, but he had promised to return. John kept the faith, even as they took the others. His brother James, Peter, and now Paul—all murdered. And none of them had been reborn.

Is this what he had planned?

The crowd above hushed as some announcement began. Two guards rounded the corner and marched up to his cell. One unlocked the cell door while the other drew his sword and stepped back.

The guard at the door clicked the keys back on his belt. "Okay, swine. It's your turn now. Will you walk like a man, or do we need to bind you like the pig that you are?"

John pushed himself to his feet and tried not to let his fear show. "I'll walk," he replied, surprised at how calm his voice sounded.

"What, no begging?" the guard asked and glanced back at his partner. "It's always more fun when they beg. Well, let's move then. We don't want to keep our good emperor waiting."

John's heart pounded. A wave of dizziness made him stagger into the wall. They marched him up a steep ramp.

He tried to slow his breathing...but failed.

He wanted to pray...but the words did not come.

After a turn, the ramp continued up, and he saw daylight. The muffled words of the master of ceremonies ended, and the roar of the crowd made John stumble.

"Keep moving, pig," the guard said. He shoved John in the back.

The three emerged from the tunnel into the bright morning light. Sand crunched under John's feet. Squinting, he saw thousands filled the stadium. The frenzied mass crammed together reminded him of the fish piled in the bottom of their boat so long ago. Only a few clouds dotted the blue sky, giving heaven an unobstructed view.

John looked across the arena. His breath caught. Each moment seemed to stretch out toward eternity.

In the center of the arena, a massive fire raged under a large metal cauldron. Shimmers of heat rose above it. A raised platform supported by six massive, knot-filled wooden posts sat next to the blazing fire. Ten steps led up to the rectangular platform. Two men waited at the top. Behind them, a fifteen-foot-high scaffold arm rose from the decking and cast a shadow toward the cauldron. A chain swung from the end of the wooden arm.

The crowd began to chant the emperor's name. One of the guards shoved him again, and he shuffled forward.

John gazed at the sea of faces in the crowd as he climbed the steps. An old woman in expensive clothing stood, hands clapping in excitement.

A small boy next to his father, tugging on his sleeve. A pretty young girl holding hands with a tall boy, a broad smile on her face. All there to see him die. And in the middle of the third row, one face stood out from the rest.

Luke.

John stumbled as their eyes met, and Luke frowned. He raised his ever-present notebook and began to write. Luke kept glancing from the page to John and back.

"Keep moving," the guard barked from behind him.

John's hands began to tremble, and his field of vision narrowed into a dark, long tunnel. He tripped on the last step, and the men at the top each grabbed an arm and hurried him into the center of the platform. One looped his wrist shackles over a large hook at the end of the dangling chain.

John stared at the hook. He did not understand what it meant until the guards pulled down on a counterweight, and he lifted from the platform. Suspended with his arms over his head, he cried out as the wrist manacles dug into his flesh. He kicked about but found no purchase or relief.

But he did not have to wait long.

The wooden arm started to swing. John looked down at the cauldron and screamed. Heat rolled over him as the wooden arm stopped above the center of the eight-foot-wide maw. A dark, bubbling liquid filled the metal container.

A voice sounded from across the arena. All eyes turned to the emperor's box as Nero shouted to the crowd, "Hanging before you is the last of those responsible for the great tragedy you have suffered. The fire they brought upon us has been repaid with their deaths. Today will be the final day that any choose to follow their cult of the dead Jew. Witness the punishment of the gods!"

John sought his friend's face one last time. Luke stood with the rest, and he leaned forward to get a better view. In that final moment, John wondered how Luke had evaded capture.

Then he fell.

The boiling oil splashed as he struck the surface. John emptied his lungs of air in one long scream as he sank into the blinding pain. His arms snapped tight as the chain stopped his immersion with his head and shoulders still above the scalding liquid.

He thrashed about. The pain became his existence. He inhaled only to power the next scream. The pain had to stop. But it still had plans for him. Seconds became years. Images flashed in his vision. His heart wanted to explode in his chest. He tried and failed to draw another breath.

Darkness closed in. The pain faded, and he slipped away into the welcoming arms of death.

———

John heard the roar of the crowd. He felt hard wood under his back. A strange thought flitted through his mind. Something he needed to remember. Something he needed to do.

A rough foot poked him in his side. He considered opening his eyes but could not recall why he wanted to. He needed to remember the other thing first.

Another poke followed by a man's voice. "What is happening?" the voice asked.

"Never seen anything like it," another voice answered.

He remembered.

Breathe.

He drew in a sharp breath and opened his eyes. Three faces stared down at him, and they all jumped back.

"Jupiter's breath!" one cried out.

Am I alive?

He rolled to his side. Wrists still chained, he managed to push himself up into a sitting position. His clothing had burned away, but his smooth skin showed no burns or trauma. He ran his hands over his chest, remembering the suffocating pain.

He glanced about the arena. A hush fell over the thousands in the Colosseum—every eye locked on him.

The guards backed away toward the edges of the platform. They exchanged hurried glances. One turned and looked at the emperor's box for instructions. He frowned and looked back at John.

"They want him to stand up," he said to his fellow guards. No one moved toward him.

"You," one yelled at him. "Can you stand?"

After a moment's consideration, John scrambled to his feet, hands held in front of him for modesty. The guards stumbled back another step. The crowd hummed with a collective intake of breath and then fell silent again.

John watched as the emperor rose. The man squinted like someone trying to decide if the fruit on the plate had spoiled.

"Again," came the royal command.

The three guards eyed John. No one spoke. One glanced toward the emperor's box, exhaled, and drew his sword. He motioned with his head toward the counterweight. When the other two guards hesitated, he turned the tip of his blade toward the nearest.

"But it is a miracle," the hesitant guard whispered.

John looked skyward and smiled.

———

John sat on the floor of his cell. The hard stones of the wall behind him dug into his back, but he no longer cared. He tossed his collected pebbles one at a time toward the far wall.

Three weeks of throwing pebbles.

He thought back to those final moments in the arena. The second trip into the cauldron proved shorter than the first but was still excruciating. That time, John felt the healing begin even while in the oil. He did not know how to explain it other than to give thanks for the miracle. The crowd had gone wild seeing it twice. They needed an entire squad of guards to get him back inside the cells. Even the guards had argued, some wanting to free him.

But cold steel has a way of making a point.

They had dumped him in this cell and given him some old rags for clothes. Other than when the slop came twice a day, he had seen no one.

John tossed his last pebble, sighed, and rose to his feet. With a stretch to limber his stiff back, he moved across the room and retrieved his collection. With his twenty-one small stones in hand, he sagged back to the floor and began tossing them one by one at the far wall.

The scrape of the outside door startled John. With the morning bowl of slop still resting on the floor by his cell door, he glanced nervously down the corridor. Voices drifted to him from the guard station. Footfalls announced someone's approach. John grabbed the bars and pulled himself to his feet.

To his surprise, Luke rounded the corner. John craned his neck to see if the guards followed his friend. None appeared.

"Luke, what are you doing here?" John whispered. His eyes darted from Luke to the hall and back.

Luke strolled up to the bars of the cell. He wore a quality robe, and he carried his journal in one hand. "I've come to see my friend," Luke said. He gave John a warm smile.

"But if they discover who you are, they'll lock you up like me, or worse."

Luke chuckled a deep, humor-filled laugh. "Oh, my boy. You don't need to worry about me. I've spent years in Rome and have many friends."

John's stomach fluttered, and he looked down the hall again.

Luke reached through the bars and took his hand. "It's okay, John. They all saw. It caused quite a stir in the city. Many have joined the Way."

John shuddered as the memory coursed through him. "It was a miracle."

Luke's smile faded. "Yes, it is. But not the kind you think."

John leaned in closer to his friend. He smelled the clean floral scent of a recent trip to the baths. His mind raced as he tried to fit the puzzle pieces together. "What do you mean?"

Luke's eyes searched John's face. "I didn't know for certain. But I've heard Jesus hinted about it. I think he knew."

Luke released John's hand and began pacing. "There is not much time. They didn't know what to do with you. The idiot emperor wanted them to try again, maybe with lions." Luke pointed up with one finger, like a professor lecturing his students. "I convinced them that another attempt would fail and likely cause a citywide riot."

He stopped pacing and turned back to John. "But we can't let you just leave. We must get you out of the public view, or they will make you into another god. Oh no, we can't have that."

"But the miracle can't be hidden. God has a plan," John said.

Luke chuckled. "Well, he didn't mention any plan to me. So, I've made other arrangements for you. It's a nice little Greek island. They call it Patmos."

"I don't understand what you mean?"

Luke stepped back to the bars. With his left hand, Luke withdrew a set of keys from the folds of his robes. A knife slid out from his right sleeve, and he held it up, examining the blade. A dark look spread across his face.

"Then let me show you."

CHAPTER FIFTEEN

As John told his tale, Dan leaned back to study Ames. She stared at John and alternated between nodding her agreement and shaking her head in disbelief. Dan rubbed the back of his neck.

How could any of this be real?

"What did he do with the knife?" Dan asked.

John's brows furrowed. He held his hand up in front of his face and rotated it for examination. "His demonstration was even more dramatic than mine in the parking garage. We had only a few days before they sent me away, but Luke taught me what I need to know to survive with our *condition*. How to stay hidden."

Ames pressed for more. "Did you know you had this *gift* before they tried to kill you?"

John shook his head. "No," he said. "It's called *crossing-over.*"

"Remarkable," Ames whispered.

Reid folded his arms across his chest. "You can't be believing this."

Dan felt like they were falling down the rabbit hole. He did not want to be at odds with his partner, but this mess fell outside of standard procedures.

Way outside.

Dan exhaled slowly. "I don't know, Reid. Everything we've seen supports what he's told us."

Reid gave him a cold stare. "Everything we've seen? But we still don't know squat. Next, I suppose John's going to offer us a red or blue pill."

Dan frowned at his partner. But he agreed they needed to know more. He leaned forward and said, "John, this doesn't explain what the Professor and his group are doing."

John rose and walked toward the door. He placed an unexpected hand on Dan's shoulder as he passed and then opened the door. Martha waited on the other side.

John said, "Martha, we'll be staying for a few days. Please arrange for a change of clothes and other personal items for our guests." He glanced back at Dan. "We had some but somehow misplaced them along the way."

Dan thought back to the dropped bags of clothes at the diner. The knot reformed in his gut.

Cain.

John moved along the wall looking at the artwork. "I spent forty years exiled on that island. That's when I took up painting. I got pretty good at it. I saw Luke again after I left my little Greek resort. We worked together for the first few centuries. Me trying to make things better for the early Christians, him wanting to understand what we were," John said.

He stepped to the large desk at the side of the room and picked up an iPad. He tapped the screen on the way back to their table.

"After that, we went our separate ways. Luke pursued science and medicine. Me, my art. But we got together in Rome every twenty-five years." John set the iPad on the table and slid it toward Dan. "Things changed in the fifteenth century."

Dan picked up the tablet. "What is this?"

John wandered back to look up at his paintings. "Let's just say it's a journal of sorts."

The screen showed an image of a page from some timeworn book, written in a language that Dan did not know. A Roman number IX monopolized the top of the page. Colorful drawings, one with a lion that looked like a coat of arms, accompanied the text.

Ames slid her chair closer and peered over his shoulder. "It's in Latin," she said.

Reid circled behind them to get a look for himself. He asked, "Can you read it?"

"Some of it. It's recounting the saving of Emperor Constantine's life by a physician and a prophet. It attributes his conversion to Christianity to their efforts."

To the right of the text, a pencil drawing depicted two men in remarkable detail. One was a royal of some kind. Maybe the emperor. Next to him stood a short, broad-shouldered man with a thick head of hair.

Dan advanced the app to the next page. It held a colored drawing of a circular stained-glass window centered within various blocks of text with lines pointing to different parts. The date of AD 535 sat in the bottom right corner of the image.

Ames passed her finger along a line of the text. "It's a recipe," she said with a smile. "For stained-glass windows."

"Yes," John offered from across the room. "I thought that up one summer. Used it in the Saint Sophie Cathedral. It took forever for the concept to catch on."

"So, you have a scrapbook," Reid said. He approached John in three quick steps. "How in God's green earth does this help us with the terrorists?"

John met Reid's glare. "We all come to fear something, Zachary," he said. John's shoulders drooped, and he let his gaze fall to the floor. "And many of us find hate inside our fears." John rubbed the knuckles of his left hand with his right. "In some ways, this may all be my fault. Perhaps if I had acted sooner."

Ames heaved a sigh and began drumming her fingers on the table. "John, we still don't understand."

John strode back to the table and leaned onto his hands. "Dan, turn to image one seventy-eight. Let's see if this clears it up."

Dan began paging forward. Various images flashed by. A few he recognized—a pencil sketch of the Mona Lisa, a map of what looked like Turkey with dotted lines denoting military maneuvers, and many others that held no meaning to Dan. Several had dates, and he noted the progression through time.

He slowed around image one twenty-five when about thirty images all seemed to be in the same few years. He saw AD 1460 and AD 1461 on several pages. Each contained drawings of the same man with long black hair, wearing a royal robe and a crown. Amid the series about the man, one page portrayed a long metal blade. Dan recognized it as John's

Spear of Destiny. The next image, number one fifty-nine, dated AD 1462, contained a sketch of the man on the ground, with another man standing above him.

Dan paused and looked closer at the image. The man on the ground had John's spear protruding from his chest. And the man standing above the corpse was John.

Dan turned the pad for John to see. "What's this?"

John sank into a chair and lowered his head into his hands. "The Professor and I often wondered if we were the only two like us. We searched everywhere we went for some hint of others, but in over a thousand years, we had never found anyone. The Professor's obsession with understanding what made us this way had surfaced, and it consumed most of his time. We still met up every twenty-five years in Rome and sometimes worked on projects together. Around AD 1450, I stumbled on a recurring story of a man in Eastern Europe. One that claimed he couldn't be killed."

Martha pushed through the door carrying a long sketch pad and lightly touched John on his shoulder. He looked up, and his sad expression brightened a little. She handed him the pad and produced a set of charcoals from her pocket. Dan felt a twinge of anger when Martha made eye contact with Ames and made a slight dip of her head toward John before she retreated through the same door.

Ames took the iPad from Dan and flipped back a few images. "Who was he?" she asked.

"I traveled to what is now Romania in search of that answer and found him to be the prince of Wallachia. I hid among the nobles of his court for about three years. Followed him into battle and saw him take many wounds, but he never stopped."

John opened the sketch pad and began drawing with the charcoals. His speech quickened with his rapid hand movements. "His troops followed him fanatically, spurred on by his invincibility. They took many prisoners. His opponents in battle often surrendered when they saw what might be a miracle." He drew men on a desolate field under a dark sky. "And he slaughtered them all."

He drew faster, adding details across the page. "His name was Vlad III," he said. John spun his finished drawing for them to see. Men on wooden stakes dotted the landscape. "But they called him Vlad the Impaler."

Dan's eyes widened as he took in the surprising details on the simple drawing. The man standing in the field of carnage was the same as the one in the images. "You mean Dracula?"

"A vampire?" Reid barked out.

John took back the pad and turned to a fresh page. "No," he replied and began another sketch. "But that is a great example about how legends spring up regarding my kind."

"Legends?" Ames asked.

"Of course," Dan added. "Like the legend of the *Wandering Jew.* I bet that one is about you!"

"Yes," John conceded. "But I find that one offensive."

Dan felt his cheeks flush, and he averted his eyes. "So, what happened to Vlad?"

John continued his drawing with a series of broad strokes. "I convinced the Professor to join me, and we tried a few things to eliminate him."

"You mean *assassinate him*, don't you?" Reid asked like he was grilling some perp.

"Yes," John replied. But his focus never left his sketch.

Reid leaned in from John's side and continued his interrogation. "What did you do?"

John's hand stopped moving. His fingers quivered, the charcoal millimeters above the page.

"I killed him," he said just above a whisper.

"But how?" Ames asked.

John's hand moved again, finishing some small part of the picture, before he turned it around for them to see. It contained a familiar depiction of the crucifixion of Jesus, three tall wooden crosses with men nailed to each. The man on the center cross hung with his head down. Dark, ominous clouds filled the sky. A few onlookers huddled in the background. A soldier stood near the cross in the middle and had thrust his spear up into the man's side.

John spoke in a soft voice, "Jesus was a true Immortal. But the spear pierced his side while he was dead. Before he crossed over—was resurrected. The wound never healed."

He dropped the charcoal onto the table, and it broke into several small pieces. He stared at the blackness on his fingers. "It was the Professor's idea. He guessed the spear might have retained something from that moment." He reached across to the iPad and turned it to stare at the image of him standing over the body.

"We overpowered the guards, and I entered his bedchamber. He drew his saber but just taunted me. He thought he was invincible." John drew in a slow breath. His eyes lost focus as the memory consumed his thoughts. "I stepped up and drove the spear into his chest. The look on his face was so surprised. Then afraid."

"So you're judge and executioner?" Reid challenged.

John pointed at the iPad. "I drew that from memory." He turned his sad eyes to the ceiling. "I keep it as a reminder of how events can drive any of us to desperate actions." John reached over and tapped the screen. "Whether they are good or evil is for God to judge." He tapped the display again, causing it to zoom in on his own face. "But that deed, I believe, he will call evil."

They all sat looking at the image until John broke the silence. "But you still haven't seen image one seventy-eight."

———

Ames sipped some water. She felt light-headed. Picking up the iPad, she began flipping the numbered images forward. Various scenes of beauty and tragedy sped past, along with samples from historical accounts—something about the black plague, copies of some of da Vinci's work, nautical charts of the tip of South America with the date November 28 scrawled across the top, and much more.

She slowed as she approached number one seventy-eight. Newspaper articles appeared, some in English, French, and perhaps German. Stories about their colonies and talk of war between London and Paris.

She paused on a letter, image one seventy-six, written in a precise script. The date, June 12, 1664, stood out at the top of the page as well as the salutation, addressing it to John. Written in English, the dialect still proved cumbersome. The letter offered thanks regarding some introduction. A pronouncement that meeting Galileo had been most fortunate and led to his breakthrough understanding. A precise signature revealed the author. *Isaac.*

Ames looked up at John, and her heart seemed to skip a beat. She felt drawn to him by the pages of history that he claimed to have helped write. From the corner of her eye, Ames noticed Dan staring at her, and she glanced down to hide her embarrassment. With the iPad gripped in her left hand, she advanced the image to one seventy-eight.

Reid sat in the chair next to John and waited. Dan moved to look over her shoulder. His closeness reminded her of another day, long ago. With a sigh, she leaned a little forward over the table.

Image one seventy-eight showed two documents side by side. Ames zoomed in on the first, a handbill to a sideshow. Large letters, printed at an angle across the top, declared the show offered the *Most Astonishing Feats Ever.* The pencil drawing next to the headline depicted a man standing with chains binding him to the floor. Around him, a circle of men with swords and spears pointed their weapons at the man. The captive strained against his bonds. Violence filled his face. The bottom of the handbill held the promise of *Be Amazed! Come See the Man Who Cannot Die.*

The second image held the front page of the *London Daily Courant* newspaper and set the date as June 23, 1706. It contained several stories from the day. One described the Battle of Ramillies, a major action in the war with France. Another noted that Sir Robert Walpole assumed leadership with the cabinet of ministers in King George's absence. All seemed unrelated to their dilemma.

Dan reached past her arm and pointed at a small article in the bottom right. "There," he said.

The block letters of the headline announced "Doctors Baffled." The three-paragraph article described a horrific sideshow on the outskirts of London where they dismembered a man every night. The police had been called the first night, only to be baffled as the man seemed to regrow limbs and not die. The doctors in attendance failed to describe how the act was perpetrated on the unsuspecting public.

Ames rotated the tablet toward John. "Was this you?"

"I only wish it was," John said. He began trying to wipe the black charcoal from his hands on a napkin. "That was my friend Luke...the Professor."

"Was he a captive?" Dan asked.

Reid took the iPad and scrutinized the images. His cold, steel-colored eyes kept jumping from the tablet to John and back.

"Yes. Luke had stayed in France for several years to chronicle the wars. Perhaps he stayed too long," John replied. "After my time in Florence, I traveled to Japan following a legend of an Immortal." John picked up a piece of the shattered charcoal and stared at its jagged edge. "I stayed in the Far East for about seventy years. I missed two of our reunions in Rome but felt sure he'd forgive me."

John picked up another piece of charcoal and began trying to fit them back together. "Luke missed the next one." He fidgeted with the broken black bar. His voice increased in tempo as he proceeded. "No one had seen him for some time. I launched a search for him. It took me ten years to find him." He dropped the pieces back onto the table.

"What had happened?" Ames asked.

"A traveling circus found out about his...*condition*. Later, Luke told me he attended one of their shows out of boredom. There was an accident, some lion got free, mauled him and a few others. They killed the lion. The other spectators died. But when they saw him heal, they took him captive."

"No one objected?" Reid asked, sliding the tablet back onto the table.

"No one," John replied with a sigh. "And I wasn't there to help him."

Ames stood and began pacing. She thought of the fear and misery an abduction would bring. Her skin tingled as sweat formed on her brow. "But why did they take him? Why didn't anyone help him?"

"They claimed it was black magic," John said.

Ames stopped at his side and placed a hand on his shoulder.

John did not meet her gaze but sank into the memory. "And they enjoyed the spectacle."

CHAPTER SIXTEEN

London, July AD 1706

John moved down the narrow, crowded street on the east side of the city. He had not been in London for almost five hundred years, and nothing remained familiar. The dirty, crowded neighborhood surrounded the center of the city. Dirty, angry people filled the houses. Angry, degrading words dominated the talk on the street.

He looked over his shoulder for the twentieth time since leaving the hovel that some called an inn. No one ran after him. No one pointed and shouted, "Dark magic." He shook his head.

I have to find him.

He carried the crumpled handbill in his left hand. It described the Jonas's Freak Show, the one claiming wonders and horrors never before seen. A man from Germany with two heads. A painter with no hands.

And the man who would not die.

A small boy stood on the next corner shouting, "*Daily Currant*, one pence." He waved a newspaper in his hand.

John stopped, and the boy shoved a newspaper at him with a grimy frown. John held up a shilling, and the boy's face brightened. John showed the handbill to the boy. "Can you lead me to this place?"

"Right away, Guv'nor. It's not far," the boy replied. He tried to snatch the coin, but it disappeared from John's hand. The boy looked about, hoping John had dropped the coin.

John reached behind the boy's ear and let the coin drop back into his hand from his sleeve. With a flourish, he presented it in front of the boy, holding the coin just out of the boy's reach. "What can you tell me of the men who run the show?"

"I don't know, Guv'nor," the boy replied. He looked down at his tattered shoes. "I've heard they're mean ones."

"How many work there?"

The boy kicked at the dirt in the street. "Five or six. And that Jonas, he's a big one."

"Have you seen the man? The one they say won't die?"

The boy looked up—smile wide, eyes glittering. He said, "Most amazing thing I've ever seen. Billy said it has to be a trick, but I don't know. It looked so real. And the blood…" His smile faded. "He screamed at them. Said horrible things about what he would do to them." His gaze returned to his feet. "And us. I'm glad he was chained."

John pressed the coin into the boy's hand. "Take me."

———

The sun dipped low in the west, lost behind the tenement buildings that surrounded the city park. John approached the brightly lit tent with the throng of people. They milled about the entrance as any semblance of a queue disintegrated into chaos. Hawkers swam through the crowd calling out outrageous claims of awaiting marvels. Arguments sprang up—shouts heard over the buzz of the crowd told John some thought it was all a hoax. Others called it black magic. A few claimed a miracle.

Only John knew the truth.

He paid the admission price, an exorbitant two shillings, and stepped into the tent. The tiered seats formed a circle around an open area in the middle of the tent. Wooden planks covered the ground, providing a hard surface for the performances. A large orange circle painted on the boards outlined the center of the stage. Two gaps in the seating allowed people to move in and out of the arena and provided an entrance for the acts once the show began. Huge shadows danced across the canvas, cast from the oil lamps that hung around the center.

People jostled for the best seats down front. John hung back and remained standing near the entry. A man strode in from the opposite side and stopped in the center of the orange circle. Tall with broad shoulders, he wore a bright-red jacket and raised his hands above his head. The crowd roared with applause.

Excitement filled most faces, but some held frowns. John spotted a group of about ten men sitting in the center of one of the sections. They all wore black coats, and most stared straight ahead with a hard, determined look. But a few glanced about while fingering something under their jackets.

The man in the center of the stage called out, "Welcome to my humble house of the strange and extraordinary. I am Jonas, collector of the unimaginable. Tonight, we only have one performance. The one you all have come to see."

The crowd cheered again. A few stood to shout their approval.

Jonas motioned to the side. The tent flaps drew back, and the crowd fell silent. The creak of metal sent a murmur of anticipation through the audience. People leaned forward to get their first glimpse. Out of the shadows, three men entered the tent. Lamplight glistened off their faces as they strained against a load. They pulled ropes attached to an upright cage about six-foot square with no top. It rolled on squeaking wheels as they hauled it to the center.

The cage held a short man. Iron bands pinned him to a vertical wooden wall, like the kind John had seen in knife-throwing acts at the circus in Paris. Multiple restraints bound each arm and leg, causing him to hang with his hands and feet spread wide. An iron collar encircled his neck, anchoring his head to the wall. Long, tangled black hair and a tattered beard surrounded a face filled with rage.

Luke!

"Behold," Jonas bellowed with a sweep of his hand. "I give you Prometheus of legend."

The crowd roared again. The sides of the cage fell outward with a loud *bang* and left the chained man hanging in the open.

Jonas drew a rapier from his side and approached Luke. "Punished by the gods for giving us fire. Cursed to be dismembered each night but never granted death."

Luke looked about with wild eyes at the crowd. "Why have you come?" Luke screamed at them. Jonas stepped closer. Luke sneered and spat at him.

The ringmaster turned to the audience. "He may look like you and me, but this is no mere man. No, my friends, he is something else." Jonas slashed his blade through the air a couple of times and then whirled back to Luke.

And stabbed him through the heart.

Luke screamed in pain. A flower of blood blossomed across his dirty shirt. His head slumped forward, and he stopped breathing.

The crowd gasped at the vicious act. But they had come for this—and much more.

John took three steps forward before he managed to control himself. He gripped a tent pole with both hands until his hands throbbed. He tried to swallow but failed. Nausea flared in his stomach.

Luke stirred. His head rose back up. Madness filled his eyes. "I will kill you," he shouted. "I will kill you all!"

A woman on the front row swooned. Others jumped to their feet and yelled insults at Luke.

Jonas held the rapier high. The bloody tip glistened in the lamplight. He turned and threw it to a waiting attendant. The man caught the weapon by its handle, spun with a dramatic flair, and tossed a hand ax back in return.

John watched the ax spiral through the air, and dread filled his gut. Jonas caught it by the haft and spun to face the crowd. With a flourish, he held it high above his head.

"Witness Prometheus! Ever tormented. Never granted peace," Jonas said.

Two of his attendants rushed forward, spun Luke's platform around, and lowered it to one side. Still bound to the wall, Luke now lay on his back. He struggled against his bonds and ranted words in a language John did not understand.

Jonas stalked across the stage to stand over Luke and hefted the ax from one hand to the other. He cried out, "Behold the punishment of the gods!" The ax swung down in a powerful arc and severed Luke's left hand. The hand plopped onto the wood. Blood gushed from the wound for a moment before the red fountain slowed to a trickle and stopped.

Luke screamed and struggled against the iron bands that held him. Cords stood out on his neck and shoulders, but the bonds held. He fell back and whimpered. Then he shook his head and yelled, "You are dead! I will tear you apart. I will rip your heart out while it still beats."

Some in the crowd roared their approval of the act. Some shook their heads in disgust. A young boy vomited off the side of the bleacher.

But no one looked away. They had heard the stories. They wanted to see it.

John rubbed his shoulder, remembering another day and a Viking's long sword. He knew what to expect.

The stump at the end of Luke's arm began to pulsate, and the mangled flesh smoothed over. More than a few mouths fell open as a new hand started to form. Silence fell across the tent. White bones protruded, followed by muscle and flesh knitting around them.

Movement in the crowd caught John's eye. The block of men with black coats all stood. As one, they all reached inside their jackets and withdrew weapons, several long knives, short swords, and a few pistols.

"Spawn of Satan!" one in the center of the group yelled. "We will send you back to hell."

Jonas motioned at Luke and called to his attendants, "Get him out of here." He rounded on the group, ax in hand. "This is my establishment. You will not threaten me and mine!"

Two of Jonas's men began rolling Luke away. Two more rushed to stand with Jonas, sabers in hand.

With a yell, the dark-coated men rushed forward, and Jonas hurtled his ax at the closest. Shots rang out. A lantern fell to the ground and exploded in flames. Tongues of fire reached the canvas. Pandemonium broke out across the tent. People rushed for the exits. Some fell to the ground. More shots echoed over the mass of people. A woman screamed.

Surrounded by chaos, John shoved his way through the crowd. He caught sight of the two men struggling with Luke's platform. John ducked under the side of the tent and ran toward the rear exit. As the two men emerged from the tent, he came up behind them. John slid his katana from its sheath. The twenty-inches of folded Japanese steel glimmered in the moonlight. He gripped the handle tight in his right hand and used the butt to strike one of the men hard on the back of the head. The man crumpled to the ground. His partner spun around only to find the tip of John's blade an inch from his throat.

"Release him," John growled.

The man's eyes flitted from the blade to the burning tent. He raised his hands and offered a friendly, "Anything you say, mate. Just take it easy."

John let a smile spread across his lips. In a cold voice, he said, "Help will not arrive before I slit your throat."

The man's eyes flared wide in fear. He began to tremble.

"Now move," John barked. The man fell to the ground and began unfastening the restraints that held Luke.

When the man removed the last one on his right arm, Luke's hand shot up and grabbed him by the throat. The man clawed at Luke's arm and beat on his face, but Luke snarled and squeezed harder.

"Luke! It's me. John. Release him. I need him."

The man's face turned purple, and John heard the sickening crack of his windpipe. Luke tossed the man to the side and began struggling to remove the remaining bonds.

John placed a hand on Luke's shoulder. "Lie back. Let me help you."

Luke grabbed his hand and yanked him close. "I'll kill you!"

"It's me, Luke. It's John."

Recognition crept into wild eyes, and the vice grip relaxed on John's arm. John worked to remove the remaining bonds and helped Luke to his feet.

CHAPTER EIGHTEEN

Poland, September AD 1943

John lay on the bunk. Faint light edged its way into the room through the single dirty window as dawn approached. The bell began sounding from the tower in the center of the complex, calling the weary workers out of their beds. He rolled up into a sitting position and scanned the long row of bunks. The one hundred and twenty discouraged souls that shared the M142 dormitory began milling about the room. They clung to the hope that they would return at the end of the day. They knew some would not.

He rubbed his forearm. Even after six days, the tattoo still itched. He glanced at the dark numbers.

875267

His new identity. His new existence.

He shook his head. Anger burned at his own stupidity. Trusting the woman, Stella Kubler, had been his first mistake. Thinking he could make a difference—perhaps his last. He looked down at the ragged shoes they forced him to wear and wondered how many others had worn them before they became his. "Stupid, stupid, stupid," he whispered.

The call to assembly blared over the camp PA. He forced himself to stand and headed out the door with the others. They merged into the flow of gaunt bodies shuffling to the open area near the munitions factory. Next to John, an elderly man stumbled and fell to his knees in the mud. John scooped his hand under the man's arm, pulled him to his feet, and set him staggering forward.

But not before a guard had noticed.

"Those too sick to walk must report to the infirmary for processing," the guard shouted. With his hand on his submachine gun, the guard took a step toward them.

A younger man broke ranks and stepped into the guard's path. "He's fine," the young man said.

The soldier struck him in the face with the butt of his weapon. The blow knocked the young man from his feet, and he tumbled to the ground.

The guard towered over the young man. "Get up, swine. It's good you are young and still have work left in you, or you would join him. You! Old man. I said report to the infirmary."

A whimper escaped from the old man. He looked up at John with a nod of thanks before he straightened, turned, and started a slow march toward a gray canvas structure across the yard. John ground his teeth as he watched him go. He had heard that none returned from that place.

A familiar voice spoke from behind John. "I'll take this one." He whirled about to see a man in a white lab coat standing next to the guard and pointing at the young man on the ground. John's movement caught the man's attention, and their gaze met. John saw the surprise he felt reflected in the other's eyes.

Luke.

The surprised look faded in an instant, and Luke stared at him with two pools of dark madness. As a smile crept onto Luke's lips, he raised a hand and pointed at John. "And that one, too," Luke said. "This is most fortunate." Two more guards rushed forward and pulled John out of the line.

"What is your designation?" one barked at him.

"I'm called John."

The backhand caught him by surprise. "Your designation," the guard demanded.

John wiped the blood from his lip and met the man's gaze. "Eight-seven-five-two-six-seven."

The guard shouted across the milling group of men, "Remove eight-seven-five-two-six-seven and…" He paused to grab the young man's wrist. "Eight-seven-two-three-nine-five from the roster. The rest of you, get in line!"

Rough hands propelled John and the young man across the yard toward a building. Painted white, it stood out from the other structures and had a raised porch. Two guards flanked the set of double doors. They wore the SS insignia. The other guards saluted from the bottom of the steps but went no closer.

Luke pushed past them. "Bring them to examination room three," he said to the SS guards.

The one on the left swung his weapon to point at the young man, and the other guards backed away. "Approach and remove your filthy shoes," the SS guard ordered.

John glanced at his companion. A bruise had blossomed on the young man's cheek, and his hands trembled. John reached out and put a hand on his shoulder. John said, "It's going to be okay."

But they both knew it was a lie.

—

John opened his eyes. He blinked at the bright overhead light. His head pounded. John tried to raise his hand to shield his eyes, only to find his arms bound by restraints. He attempted to look about the room, but a strap across his neck and some other restraint across his forehead held his head in place. He lay on a long table. Cold metal pressed against his naked back.

They forced him to drink something when they entered the facility. Dizziness had washed through him, and he remembered seeing the young man collapse. No one bothered to catch him. But John's mind had cleared a few seconds later. He remembered Luke's smile as he encouraged the guards to use other measures. The struggle had been short, ending with them clubbing John unconscious. And again, each time his eyes had fluttered open—except for this time.

Soft voices murmured somewhere. John heard a groan to his right and strained to turn and look, but he only succeeded at making his headache worse. With his head locked in position, his peripheral vision revealed little of the room.

"Where am I?" a voice to his right asked.

"You are at the beginning of a great journey," Luke's familiar voice replied. "One that may reveal the most phenomenal treasures."

"I don't understand," the voice said.

"Of course not," Luke replied. "But you will soon. What is your name?" Silence filled the room. "Come now. Don't be shy."

"Abram," the young man replied.

John's heart raced, and he struggled to slow his breathing. He tried to make sense of his surroundings. But he failed. The throbbing in his head increased, and his field of vision narrowed.

"Luke," he managed to force from his dry throat. "What are you doing?"

A woman's face appeared inches above John's and peered down at him. "He's conscious again, Professor."

"Please record his blood pressure and then assist me. My old friend will wait his turn. Now, Abram, do you know the Torah?"

After a silent beat, Abram offered a timid reply. "Yes, my parents trained me, and I attend the rabbi's classes."

"That is good. Very good," Luke replied. "I'm sure you remember the First Book of Moses. Its stories shed light on many things—the tales of creation, of original sin, and a fascinating tale of the sons of God having children with the daughters of men."

"The mighty men of old," Abram whispered.

Luke chuckled. "Yes! You remember. And now let us see if we can learn how to create one."

The screams began a moment later.

"Stop!" John shouted.

In a clinical, almost bored voice, Luke said, "Clamp the veins here and here. Control the bleeding, or he will not last long enough. Hand me the rib-spreader."

A wail of terror followed.

John endured another ten minutes of screams from the unseen table to his right. They ended in an abrupt gurgling sound. A cold silence followed, interrupted only by the metallic *cling* of metal instruments and the soft *swish* of surgical fabric.

"Your technique is improving," Luke said. "But let's see if you can speed up the severing of the vocal cords the next time."

"Yes, Professor," his female assistant replied in a submissive tone.

Luke continued his dry observations. "He appears stable for the moment. The major organs are visible and appear ordinary. Very unremarkable."

John heard the shuffling of metal trays. With more enthusiasm, Luke said, "But let us begin the comparative examination."

Luke appeared next to John on his right side. A surgical mask covered the lower portion of his face. A white cap hid his dark hair. The woman assistant popped into view on John's left.

John's pulse raced. He struggled against his restraints, but they held him like shackles of iron. "Luke," John managed. "It's me."

"Yes, old friend. It surprised me to see you. But you have come at the most opportune time," Luke replied. He held out his hand to his assistant and said, "Scalpel."

The pain of the first incision shot through John like a surprising mixture of fire and ice. He bit into his lower lip to keep from crying out, but a small moan still escaped his throat.

Luke continued in an almost casual conversation, "Helga, this reminds me a little of the years I spent in London." He held his hand up for a moment. The scalpel shimmered in the bright overhead lights, and Luke used it to point at John. "My friend here took his own sweet time finding me." A small drop of blood pooled at the tip of the blade and then leaped toward John's chest. "But that is all in the past. But, Helga." Luke leaned in a bit closer. John thought he heard a hint of amusement in Luke's voice. "You are about to see something most remarkable."

Helga's eyes widened in surprise. The cut on his chest must have healed.

Luke patted John on the shoulder. "It is a remarkable trait. I have only found two others like this man in all of my studies. We have a rare opportunity to include him in our research. Such a gift." Luke paused for a moment of consideration. "It will require some special procedures to allow us to make our comparative observations. Something to keep the incisions from closing too rapidly."

"Would some form of splint work?" Helga asked, awe in her voice.

"Perhaps." Luke peered down into John's eyes. "But first, let me show you something you will find amazing. Pass me the bone saw and observe while I remove his right hand."

———

Dan watched as John continued to craft his drawing with many rapid, small strokes of the charcoal. A bead of sweat had formed on John's brow.

"He kept me for months. Performed many experiments, each one more gruesome than before. He became fixated on the recovery process and the magnitude of injury that still allowed recovery. I only escaped when the Russians liberated the camp." John paused and drew in a sharp breath of remembrance. "He learned many things."

Ames reached out and placed a hand on John's arm. "But why?" she asked. "Why did he do it?"

Reid slapped his hand onto the table. "To punish you," he said.

"No, Reid," John corrected him. "He was looking for a way to create others like us. He wanted to grow a copy."

Dan glanced at Ames. The puzzled look on her face matched the questions circling in his mind. John spun the drawing around for them to see and slid it across the table. It showed a desolate landscape. A solitary man stood on a small hill surrounded by bodies everywhere. In the far distance, a single man stood on a similar rise.

John stood and gazed down at his drawing. "When he found a way to kill all of you, who was he going to spend eternity with? Just me?" He turned and left the room without another word.

CHAPTER NINETEEN

Ames glanced at her watch for the third time. *11:32 a.m.* Twenty-four hours ago, she had just stepped off the plane from California. The warm Atlanta sun had greeted her, and she had looked forward to seeing her friends and colleagues at the CDC.

But are any of them still alive?

She roamed around the room, studying the paintings, looking at the items on the desk. All the while wishing she was somewhere else. She rubbed her hands together and rechecked her watch. *11:33.* It had been forty-five minutes since John disappeared.

At least no one has tried to kill me in the last three hours.

Martha strode into the room from the rear door. Her warm smile greeted them as she proceeded across the room to the far wall and pressed a hidden button. A panel slid back, revealing a sizable television. Martha turned to look at Dan. "Master John said you might be interested in the news." She picked up a black rectangular remote from an end table and pressed one of its many buttons. The television sprang to life. She left the remote and headed for the door. As she exited the room, she called back, "Petros will serve lunch soon."

Dan and Reid crossed to stand by the couches, and Ames joined them. The screen showed a local anchorwoman in front of a news desk. The video image from a helicopter displayed to her left with a red block-letter headline declaring "*Suspects Still at Large.*" Ames recognized the scene as the Rise-and-Dine. Police cruisers and black SUVs crowded the parking lot, and yellow crime-scene tape barred the door. Dan grabbed the remote and turned up the volume.

The news anchor stared into the camera with bright-blue eyes. "The authorities are still sorting through the details, but it appears this incident is related to the attack at the Atlanta FBI offices and the tragic bombing at the CDC. The FBI has launched an investigation into this man." She paused as the image cut to a close-up of a hard-faced Dan.

"Not my most flattering photo," Dan said with a frown.

The anchorwoman continued her monologue. "Daniel Alexander is a person of interest in the FBI incident, the CDC bombing, and the abduction of this woman, Dr. Amelia Cranford." The image changed to a stock photo of Ames. "Dr. Cranford is a leading virologist in the United States and works with Stanford University and the CDC. Anyone with information regarding either of these people should contact the FBI at this number." An 800 number began scrolling across the bottom of the screen.

The camera cut back to a close-up of the newscaster. "And whatever you do, do not approach them. Daniel Alexander is considered to be armed and very dangerous."

Ames sat down on one of the couches. She took a moment to study Dan. He and Reid stood huddled off to the side, talking in low tones with an occasional hand-wave from Dan or a tie-straightening from Reid.

What am I doing here?

She let her mind wander down the clinical explanations for John's condition. She itched to do some blood work and get someone started on mapping out a DNA profile. But all of that had to wait.

She stood and began pacing. Ideas raced through her mind. She tapped her finger to her lips and smiled as a hypothesis formed in her thoughts. Ames stopped in the center of the room and turned to the agents. "I have a theory on how it works."

They both looked in her direction. Her breath caught for a moment. Dan's face held the same excited, curious look she remembered from their days together in college. The one she always loved.

She gave her head a quick shake and frowned. "John demonstrated the ability to regrow and repair injured bone and tissue in a remarkable way. It must be an advanced form of stem cells coupled with an extremely high metabolic rate. Based on his descriptions and stories, I think it must lie dormant until triggered by some enzyme or hormone released at the last moments of life. What John calls *crossing over*."

Dan wrinkled his brow. "I'm not sure I follow. Is there any way for us to use this?"

Ames paused and thought for a moment. "Well, it's just a hypothesis. Without the proper equipment, I can't even begin to—"

"What would you need?" John interrupted from across the room.

Ames jumped with a start but refused to whirl around to look at John. Instead, she met Dan's gaze. "I'd need a full lab, John. I can give you a list, but it will be difficult to assemble on short notice."

John chuckled. "You might be surprised."

She glanced back. John leaned casually against the wall just inside the room.

With an overhead sweep of his hand, John said, "I have access to all of the computing and medical research facilities at this university. And an army of grad students to do my bidding. I'm not just an artist," he said. He smiled and pushed off from the wall to stroll toward them. "I was never as good as Luke at science, but I do like collecting gadgets." John paused and looked at Dan. "I even have an Illumina 2000 DNA sequencer. Want to see it?"

Dan frowned at the man. "I have no idea what that is."

John gave Dan a wink and nodded toward Ames. "Oh, but she does."

Reid folded his arms across his chest. "But how will all of these *gadgets* help us stay alive and stop them?"

Ames's mind raced. The lab gave her an opportunity, but how could she use it? Then one idea silenced her other thoughts. "John," she began. "Why is the spear different? Why does it create a wound that does not heal?"

John's eyes narrowed. "I always assumed it was just some divine curse, given how it was used on Jesus."

Reid shook his head and turned away. Ames heard him mumble something about *religious nonsense*.

She took a step closer to John and spoke in a soft voice. "But what if it is *more*? What if he left something behind when it pierced him? Something we can use—maybe reproduce?"

John took a step back. "But that could mean…" A mixture of emotions played across his face. Ames thought she saw hope.

And fear.

She reached out and took John's hand. "Can I see it?"

———

Dan sat at the table, picking at the lunch Petros had provided. Some concoction of fish and greens over something he called quinoa.

I wonder where a guy can get a burger and a beer down here.

At Ames's urging, John had retrieved the spear, and the two disappeared down the hall to the lab and his fancy Hal 9000 or whatever. Dan looked across the table at his partner and smiled. Reid had organized his plate into three separate piles of fish, vegetables, and the rice-looking stuff. The man sure had his quirks, but he always had his back.

Reid noticed his attention and pushed his plate away. His frown confirmed he doubted if Dan had his.

But Dan needed him. "It sounds like Ames might be on to something," Dan said.

"And we're just going to sit here?"

Dan considered their predicament. "Yeah, I hear ya. We don't even know where the terrorists are or what they have planned. And then there's…" He paused and held a deep breath.

"Your brother," Reid finished the thought.

Dan let his breath escape. "I just don't know what to think, Reid."

"He would have killed her, Dan. Probably me too."

Dan looked down at his hands. "I had no idea he was alive. I'd given up so long ago."

"You have to put all of that behind you now. It may come down to some tough choices if we see him again."

"Maybe," Dan replied.

Maybe I can save him.

Reid left the table and paced with his hands behind his back. "Let's say the doctor works some magic and comes up with something. We still need to find these guys."

Dan leaned back. "And find a way to stop them without getting caught by the FBI. I wonder who they have leading the task force."

"Probably Jameson. He's predictable. They'll be pushing their CIs, expecting you'll need guns and supplies to keep this up."

"Well, we will need guns and supplies to do anything."

"I can help with that," John said.

Reid glared at the man. Dan spun around and said, "What is it with you? Did you graduate from some ninja school?"

"Well, I did train under Master Hattori Hanzo, but that's for another time. Dr. Cranford thinks she is on to something and thought you might want to join us in my lab," John said. He headed back out of the room without waiting for a reply.

Finally.

———

Dan stopped a few steps inside the lab. John stood just to his right. Three steel lab tables stretched the length of the forty-foot room. Each held an array of microscopes, computers, test tubes, and other equipment. The bright overhead lights and white walls reminded Dan of the research facilities he had seen in sci-fi movies. The kind that always created a monster.

Only they already had one trying to kill them.

Reid eased into the room to Dan's left. The slight grimace on his face reminded Dan that his partner was still injured.

Ames sat on a lab stool and peered into the eyepiece of a massive microscope. She paused every few seconds to make notes on a nearby pad.

"Fascinating," Ames whispered. She followed with a few "*Remarkables*" and at least one "*Impossible.*"

After two minutes of waiting, Reid cleared his throat.

Ames failed to notice. She spun around to a computer screen and began typing on a keyboard.

Dan started to move further into the lab, but John stopped him with an arm across his chest and a shake of his head.

Dan frowned at him and then said, "Ames?"

Her head popped up. "Oh, Dan, there you are. I've made some significant discoveries. There is so much more, but I have some idea how we can use the spear."

"That's great," Dan said. He started forward. John's firm arm stopped him again. Dan sighed and waited for Ames to continue.

"It has to be a new type of stem cells. Once they're activated, they can replace or repair anything at a cellular level. They permeate John's blood and tissues. But they only replicate things when connected to some vital source within the body. It will take weeks to unravel the process any further, but this…" She paused and raised the spear. "…is another matter." Ames beamed a smile at them and waited for them to reply.

Dan exchanged a look with Reid. His partner only shrugged.

"And?" Dan asked.

Ames clasped her hands. "Oh yes. You see, there is a remnant of a substance on the blade. It may be some of the triggering enzymes at the moment of death. An Immortal pierced by it after they had died but *before* the activation of the stem cells could have left some of the triggering material."

Dan waited for more.

A small chime caused Ames to glance back at the computer screen. She studied the screen for a moment and then shouted, "Yes!" Ames bent a little forward and began typing like a hacker with only seconds to crack a code.

"Ames?" Dan tried again. "What does it mean?"

She finished a long string on the keyboard and then whirled around in a flourish. "It means I may have a way to neutralize the effect. To stop the stem cells from working."

Dan frowned in his confusion. But his pulse quickened as her excitement bled over to him.

Ames beamed him another smile. "Don't you see? It could make them mortal again. At least for a short time."

Now we're talking.

"But there are a few problems," she continued.

"Problems?" Reid asked.

"Well, the first is we don't have much of the material. We can only use the spear a few more times before it is all gone."

Dan glanced at John. "So we stop stabbing people with it."

"What else?" Reid prompted.

"Well, as John found out, the spear has the advantage of being able to deliver a fatal wound and the enzyme simultaneously at the same site. I may be able to duplicate more of the enzyme by studying the material on the spear, but I don't know how we will be able to use it."

"And we need to find a way to stop them without murdering them all," John added in a low, flat voice.

They all fell silent.

"What about injecting them with it somehow? Would that make them mortal without having to kill them?" Dan asked.

Ames ran her hand through her hair. "Hmmm. That could work, but I'm not sure the enzyme would spread through the body. Perhaps if I bound it to an infectious agent."

"You can do that?" Dan wondered out loud.

Ames gave him a surprised, questioning look.

"Manipulating cells with mRNA is what I think she does, Dan," John said with a smile.

"But where are we going to get a virus to work with?" Reid asked.

John glanced up at the ceiling and then nodded. He said softly, "The CDC."

Reid slid into one of the chairs. "There's no way. It will be under heavy security following the blast. And Dan is still public enemy number one," Reid said. "We'll never get within a mile of the place."

"I may be able to help with that," Ames said. "I've done a lot of work with the CDC, and I'm part of a small team of doctors around the country that they keep apprised of any news concerning the pathogens they store. Think of it as an email alert whenever there is a change."

Ames walked back to the computer and logged into a website. "I received a flash alert about an hour ago. Due to the bombing, they're relocating all of the contagious threats stored in Atlanta." She pointed to an email she had pulled up to the screen. "And they are moving them tonight."

"You've got to be kidding?" Dan asked. He felt a little light-headed. "You're saying," he began slowly, "that all we need to do is intercept the transport, overpower the guards, and steal what, some smallpox?"

Ames laughed. "No, no, that won't work. It spreads much too slowly. No, we need something that kills quicker. Maybe Ebola." She paused and tapped her finger to her lips. "Or even better…Let's take the bubonic plague. I can alter it to a nonlethal form, attach our enzyme to it, and voila! They become mortal again, and then *no more killing all of us* because they'll be *us* again." Ames beamed at Dan. But her smile evaporated. "At least I think it will work."

Dan exchanged a long look with Reid. His partner surprised him with a nod of agreement.

Reid said, "If this levels the playing field, then I think we have to give it a try. But no casualties."

"Agreed," Dan said. "Now, John, how about showing us those weapons and supplies you promised?"

———

The pilot tried to stay focused on the screen in front of him, but his eyes kept darting to the empty seat to his left. He adjusted the path of his predator drone to maintain a tight focus on the recon team's vehicle as it approached the parking garage.

He wiped the sweat from his hand on his pant leg and tried to slow his breathing as he zoomed the camera back to its widest angle. The early afternoon sun brought many of the students out on the lawn surrounding the nearby campus buildings. Two females walked on the sidewalk next to the parking structure. The team parked their SUV in a surface lot and approached the garage on foot. They passed the two women with a wave.

His left foot bounced up and down like a fast-moving oil well. "Keep a low profile. Keep a low profile. Keep a low profile," he muttered to himself. The team of three spread out and approached the structure. They disappeared into the shadow of the building. He zoomed in with the drone's camera to watch their cautious entry through the side door.

He held his breath and waited. His hand moved to his earpiece, willing them to check-in.

A heavily accented voice spoke in his ear. "We've entered the structure. All clear." The pilot exhaled the breath he had held. "There is no sign of the Jeep. We are proceeding down one level."

Seconds passed. The static in his headset seemed to grow louder. He glanced at his watch. Cain expected to hear from him in eight minutes.

The pilot reached out and focused the already focused camera. He breathed a soft, "Come on…"

More seconds rushed by. He checked the time. Only six minutes left. He leaned in a little closer to his screen. His comms clicked, and he jumped.

"We located the vehicle on level three. We'll hold our position awaiting instructions."

He pumped his fist and then fumbled with the switch before he managed his reply. "Roger, er, roger that. Hold position."

The pilot wiped a quick hand across his brow and selected Cain's frequency. After a deep breath, he spoke into his mic, "Cain, sir." He exhaled slowly.

"You're early," came the reply.

"Yes, sir. Sorry, sir. But…we've found them."

Silence.

His left foot pumped harder as the silence stretched out. "Should I order the assault team to the location?"

"No," Cain replied softly. "Have your men withdraw but maintain the drone surveillance. I have something else planned. Something *extraordinary*."

CHAPTER TWENTY

Dan and Reid followed John down a long hall. In contrast to the other areas within John's complex, the walls in this section were a drab gray with no art or other decorations. The corridor ended at a set of double steel doors. John placed his hand on a scanner to the right of the door and then keyed a long series of digits into a keypad under the scanner.

"Dan, please place your hand on the scanner," John said.

Dan placed his right hand on the reader and felt a tingling sensation.

John keyed some more numbers into the keypad. "You're next, Zachary," he said with a wave of his hand.

Reid pressed his hand onto the device. He stepped back, rubbing his palm, and gave John a questioning look.

"It recorded your palm print and twenty-seven biometric readings," John replied to the unspoken question. "You now have access to all of the complex, save my private quarters. Take anything you need." He pulled the doors open, revealing a rectangular room with shelves stretching out in both directions.

John stepped into the room. "Flash-bangs and smoke grenades to the far left next to the assault rifles," he said. John proceeded along the wall and pointed out various rows. "Automatics and handguns over there."

Reid scanned the rows of weapons. "How large of a team do you have?"

"I like to work alone," John replied.

"Lots of hardware for one man," Dan said. He picked up a Walther PPK, checked the chamber, and placed it back on the shelf.

John stepped back and stretched. "I employ a few covert and surveillance teams," he said. "But good, *discreet* people are hard to find. They're all deployed on an operation in Europe and are unavailable to assist us."

John strolled toward the other side of the room. "Narcotics and gases down this row. Check the labels to prevent a lethal dose." He rounded the end of an aisle and pointed toward a well-lit area. "Fake IDs and document prep down there. And over here..."

As they neared the back, Dan pulled up in surprise. The shelves along the rear wall held stacks of currency. More than Dan had ever seen in a bank vault.

"...is a supply of cash. US dollars to the left but also some Canadian dollars, euros, and yuan down to the right if we need them."

John wandered back toward the doors. "Just take whatever you need." With another wave of his hand, he left the room.

Reid reached out and grabbed Dan's arm. "Look at all of this, Dan. Do you buy the *I like to work alone* bull? Looks more like a base of operations for a terrorist cell to me."

Dan scanned the arsenal, and doubt began to work its way into his gut. Questions paraded through his thoughts. He shook his head and turned to Reid. "What choice do we have? We've got to hit the transport tonight and get the stuff that Ames needs."

"But how are we supposed to do that without killing anyone?" Reid asked. He began pacing. "They'll have an escort for sure."

But none of that mattered. They had to protect Ames, and that meant stopping the Professor.

And finding Cain.

Dan leaned against a wall and ran through possible scenarios, all of them ending in violence. He relaxed and let his thoughts drift. After a moment, a memory made its way past the mental wreckage of his bad ideas.

"Hey, Reid. I wonder if John has a helicopter."

"Probably," Reid replied, still pacing. "Why?"

"Did I ever tell you about that covert op outside of Kabul?"

Reid stopped pacing to look at Dan. "Which one? You've told me about a lot of them."

"I was sent there about three weeks before the capital fell. The Taliban controlled much of the northern part of the country. We had about eight hours' notice that they were moving a large cache of money, and we wanted to *liberate* it from them to help fund the emerging underground militia. And all we had was a Black Hawk, a Humvee, and this goat..."

———

Dan glanced at his watch. *4:35 p.m.*

Reid stood next to a table in a small conference room wearing the dark clothing John had provided. Each man focused on packing tactical gear they might need. As Dan had hoped, John had a helicopter with a pilot, and it would arrive within thirty minutes. That should give them about an hour to get in place to stake out the transport.

Dan placed two flash-bangs in his pack. "Which CDC location do you think they will head for?"

"DC is my guess. It's the most secure and closest," Reid replied.

"But we're still short one man for this op," Dan said. "I hope John comes through with someone qualified."

Ames exploded through the door like a clap of thunder. She flew into the small meeting room with her white lab coat billowing out behind her. Red-faced, Ames glared from Dan to Reid and back. "You have to take me with you," she demanded.

"We don't *have* to do anything, Dr. Cranford," Reid replied. "It won't be safe. You can't come with us."

She leaned forward with her hands on the table. "But we are going after lethal contagions."

"*We'll* be careful then," Dan replied. He chambered a round in his pistol and slid the gun into its holster.

Ames did not give up. "You won't know what to take."

"Write it down," Reid directed. He gave his gear a once-over and set his pack on the floor.

She slammed her hand onto the table and shouted, "Look at me, you fools!"

Dan stopped his preparations and let his gaze rise along with his anger. He opened his mouth to reply, but Ames cut him off with a violent wave of her hand.

"Just listen," she said. "I'm betting you've never dealt with infectious diseases." She paused with raised eyebrows to see if either dared to dispute her. "It's all I do! We're talking about some very nasty stuff. You make one mistake, and it won't be just you that dies."

Dan glanced at his partner. Reid gave him a slight shake of his head.

"But, Ames, you've never done this kind of fieldwork. Something always goes wrong." He paused and looked to the floor. "Sometimes people get hurt." His eyes came up to meet hers. "Our number one priority is still keeping you safe."

She straightened. "That's all well and good, *Dan*, but without me along, you have no chance of finding the correct sample without exposing yourself." She turned on her heel and headed for the door. Ames called back as she left the room. "I'll be changed in five. You can brief me about the plan on the way."

"This just keeps getting better and better," Reid said through gritted teeth.

Dan looked up at the ceiling, squinted, and rubbed the back of his neck.

—

Dan sat with Ames and Reid in the dark-gray Rubicon. They had been in the side lot of a truck stop on I-85 for three hours. *The goat*, John's red Shelby Mustang, occupied the space next to them. John sat in the driver's seat, drumming on the steering wheel in time with the throbbing beat of some song.

Dan knew the helicopter circled near the CDC, waiting to report on the transport's departure. Reid adjusted the earpiece on his communications gear and tapped his fingers on the steering wheel.

In the front passenger seat, Dan leaned on his door, giving him an easy view of Ames in the back seat. She picked at a piece of lint on the black jacket she wore. Her hand trembled. She folded it into her other hand and squeezed them together.

"You're sure you're up for this?" Dan asked.

She looked up with a start. "Yes, just like the last five times you asked me."

"I just—" he began but was interrupted by a squawk on their comms.

"Target on the move," a crisp, masculine voice announced through his earpiece. "Rolling north as expected. One escort vehicle out front. No one following. Estimate five minutes to your location."

Dan glanced through the window at John. He finished his drumming on the steering wheel with a series of rapid strokes and a pretend cymbal crash, before giving Dan a smile with a thumbs-up. Dan smiled back.

He's a strange one.

But maybe strange was just what they needed.

Dan looked up through the Jeep's open roof panel at the bright stars overhead. "Once I'm across and deal with the door, I'll toss you the tether. Jump quickly, or you may be pulled off."

"I've got it," she confirmed.

"Keep it close," Dan said to Reid.

"I'll do my part," Reid said. "You make sure you do yours."

Static flared in Dan's earpiece followed by a staccato, "Two minutes."

Reid touched his mic control. "Let's roll."

Dan heard a loud *whoop* from the Mustang and turned in time to see John nodding his head to another song as he floored his accelerator. He spun the Shelby into a tight doughnut and rocketed across the parking lot.

"Great," Reid muttered. "This is going to be just great."

Dan felt the corners of his mouth edge up in admiration. "Stick to the plan, and we'll be fine."

———

The plan remained simple. Simple always worked best. In and out with no one the wiser. All while traveling at seventy miles per hour. Dan ran through his gear again as they sped onto I-85.

Bolt cutters? Check.

Headlamp? Check.

Small bag with ice pack? Check.

Replacement vial? Check.

Tether for Ames? Check.

Replacement lock—drilled out to fit any key? Check.

Luck? He would have to wait and see.

He glanced back at Ames. Her face was a little pale, but her determined look gave him confidence. "You'll do great," he said. "Follow my lead, and just wait for my signal."

She reached out and grabbed his hand. "I'm scared."

"Good," he replied with a smile. "That means you know the plan." He looked out the rear window at John's red Mustang following them.

I hope he does too.

"Target one hundred meters ahead of you in the right lane," the voice from the helicopter reported.

"There it is," Reid said. He pointed at a semi and keyed his mic. "Okay, Goat, whenever you are ready."

John's only reply was a *howl* over the comms as the Mustang shot past them.

Reid eased the Jeep into the lane behind the semi, and they waited for John's signal.

———

John howled again as he shot past the Jeep in his Shelby Mustang. "Welcome to the Jungle" by Guns N' Roses blared from the two-hundred-watt speakers. Their target, a gray eighteen-wheeler, bore no identifying marks and followed the predictable black suburban at a standard four car lengths.

John smiled as he passed the truck and swerved hard into the gap between it and the SUV. He put on his right blinker as if he wanted to exit the freeway and began a gradual reduction in his speed. He could see the three heads of the security team in the SUV. Two whipped around to stare at him. He smiled, waved, and flashed his lights at them.

When they drove past the exit, the driver of the big truck grew impatient and gave him a long blast from his air horn.

John had them right where he wanted them. With a laugh, he keyed his mic. "The Goat is in place. You may proceed."

———

Dan's earpiece sounded with the words he wanted to hear. "The Goat is in place. You may proceed."

Reid glanced his way, and Dan nodded. The Jeep accelerated and closed the gap with the back of the truck.

Dan released his seat belt and turned to Ames one last time. "Showtime, Ames. Follow me."

He climbed through the open roof and slid onto the hood of the Jeep. He felt every inconsistency in the road as he stood and struggled for balance. The semi loomed just ahead. In a crouch, he made his way to the front of the Jeep and studied the back of the truck—two large steel doors, hinged on either side, with a bar-type handle in the center, secured with a padlock. He took a deep breath and glanced back. Ames pushed herself up out of the top of the jeep and slid down the windshield. Hair lashing about, she looked up at him with wild eyes. Dan gave her a thumbs-up, lost his balance, and almost fell. Laughing, he turned and leaped at the back of the truck.

Dan crashed into the steel door, feet making it onto the bumper, arms sliding down the door face. He had aimed for the door handle secured with a padlock and managed to catch it with two fingers of his right hand. Off-balance, Dan tilted back, left arm pinwheeling, until he managed to haul himself back to the door. He leaned against the cold steel to catch his breath, and his earpiece crackled.

"Goat here. These guys are getting angry. You'd better hurry."

Another blast of the truck's air horn sounded its agreement.

Dan slid to the center of the door for a better grip and withdrew the bolt cutters. He positioned the jaws over the lock, pinned one handle against the door for leverage, and pushed hard on the other. The lock gave way with a satisfying snap. He dropped the cutters back into his pack and glanced back at Ames with an okay sign. Still in a crouch, she had made her way down to the front of the Jeep, both hands pressed against the hood for balance.

Dan lifted the handle and was surprised when the door swung open. It pulled him from the bumper as it rotated out to the left. Ames grabbed his shirt as he went by and jerked him back around but lost her footing and stumbled forward.

Ames screamed as she teetered on the front of the Jeep. As she fell, Dan's door swung back, and he grabbed her by the forearm. He held her, suspended in the narrow space between the Jeep and the truck. The toes of her boots dragged on the pavement below them. With a yell, Dan hefted her up and onto the bumper, where she planted her feet. Ames grabbed the other door and heaved Dan back to the truck. He reached above her and secured a hold. She squirmed past him, climbed into the trailer, and collapsed onto the floor. Dan followed her into the truck and then secured the door with the tether he had intended for Ames.

Dan caught his breath and spoke into his comms. "Goat, we are on board. Take up station two." He offered Ames his hand. "That wasn't too bad."

She glared at him as she took his hand and pulled herself to her feet. "Let's just get this done."

Dan turned on his headlamp and surveyed the interior of the trailer. Six sizable gray plastic crates sat near the front of the trailer, strapped in with ratcheted tie-downs. He unbuckled the first container and slid them one by one back toward Ames. Each container had a manifest taped to the top and biological hazard stickers plastered on every side.

Ames flicked on her light and pulled the manifest from the first. "No, no, no," she muttered as she ran her finger down the manifest and moved on to the next crate. On the third one, she rewarded Dan with a "Gotcha!"

He shoved the other two aside and examined the container. Two large metal clamps secured the front. A rubber seal ran around the lip of the lid. He popped the two clamps up and strained to pull the top open by the handle—and failed. He tried again with an equal lack of success.

Ames placed a hand on his arm and pushed him to the side. She grabbed a black knob on top of the container and rotated it counterclockwise. Dan heard a soft hiss as the crate sucked in air.

Ames said, "The containers are depressurized to prevent any accidental airborne leaks." She gave him a mischievous grin and lifted the lid with one hand. "Guess it's a good thing I came along, huh?"

Inside, two racks held about fifty vials above a layer of frozen gel packs. Ames ran her hand down the row as she read the label on each. "This is the one." She held up the vial for Dan to see. A clear liquid filled half of the tube. "One batch of bubonic plague ready for transport."

Dan secured it in his pouch and pulled out their replacement. But before he could pass it to Ames, the truck began a rapid deceleration, and they stumbled forward. With a loud scrape on the metal floor, the two open containers slid forward. They struck Dan from behind and propelled him into the front wall of the trailer. His head slammed against the hard, unforgiving steel. Stars exploded in his field of vision. The last thing he heard before he slipped into unconsciousness was John's frantic call over the comms, "Houston, we have a problem!"

—

When John received the signal that they had gained entry, he changed lanes and passed the SUV. With everything proceeding as they had planned, he maintained his position about ten yards ahead. Give them three minutes to find the correct contagion, and it would be his turn again as the attention-grabbing decoy.

I wonder what happened to the goat in the Kabul story.

Maybe he did not want to know. He scrolled through his playlist, picked "Danger Zone" by Kenny Loggins, and began singing along. He glanced in the mirror and saw that Zachary had dropped the Jeep back about one hundred yards. He still needed to win Agent Reid over, but some things just took time.

As he belted out the song, John rechecked the mirror. What he saw made him forget the next line. The security SUV pulled hard into the left lane and slowed. The semi slammed on its brakes and swerved onto the right shoulder. John keyed his mic and yelled, "Houston, we have a problem."

He maneuvered across the traffic and into the right lane. The truck continued its rapid deceleration. John watched as Reid sped up and positioned the Jeep between the SUV and the semi, all still rolling forward but slowing rapidly.

"Reid!" John shouted into his comms. "I'll handle them. You get Dan and the doctor. Jeremy, you get ready to set that copter down."

"Set it down where, boss?" the helicopter pilot replied.

"In the middle of the freeway just beyond the truck. The freeway is about to be blocked."

Reid slammed on his brakes, and the Jeep slid to a stop. A Lexus rear-ended it, spun to the side, and crashed into a Ford pickup. Tires smoking, Reid maneuvered the Rubicon off the road behind the semi.

John put the Mustang into a spin, turning a one-eighty back toward the SUV, and shot forward. With the accelerator pressed to the floor, he lowered his window and fired a burst from his submachine gun into the air. The security SUV braked hard and swerved to the right.

"Something went wrong," Ames said over the comms. "I think we triggered an alarm when we opened the container. Dan is hurt and unconscious."

The helicopter roared by low overhead, did a flair turn to center on the freeway, and began setting down.

Still accelerating, John pulled hard on the wheel and caused the Mustang to slide sideways into the SUV. His car glanced off the vehicle and plowed into the semi. He locked his arms on impact, and the steering wheel broke off in his hands but shattered his wrists. The engine wall collapsed back, and he felt his right leg snap.

"That hurts!" he yelled. Pain radiated through him even as he felt the bones knitting back together. John pried his leg free and tried his door, but the bent frame jammed it. He tossed the steering wheel out the window and then followed it, dropping to the ground. "I'm too old for this," he muttered to himself.

He had to buy Reid some time. Pulling his Colt Python from its shoulder holster, he came up on his knees and began firing into the air above the SUV. Two doors flew open, and the security team took up defensive positions. Shots rang out, and three slugs punched into John's chest. As he spun to the ground, John saw Reid struggling down the side of the road, carrying Dan over his shoulder. Ames sprinted ahead of them toward the helicopter.

The men at the SUV shouted as they also spotted his team. Ignoring the pain, John sat back up and fired two more times into the grill of the SUV. The men ducked and returned fire. He took another round to the chest and one in his neck. He sank back to the pavement and saw Reid and Ames heave Dan into the helicopter.

John smiled. As he let himself sink into the cold darkness of death, he wondered if the other goat had made it out alive.

CHAPTER TWENTY-ONE

Cain had reported in as ordered. And man, the Professor had been angry. "You need to be reminded of our procedures and protocols," Cain said out loud in a singsong voice, mimicking the Professor's rebuke.

What did the Old Man do? He sent Cain to do filing! And three hours later, another stack of folders had just arrived. Cain shoved the stack of folders off the desk. Papers swirled through the air like a flock of angry crows. He hated this, and the Old Man knew it. He knew the Professor believed in punishment. But paperwork?

Screw this.

His phone buzzed. He looked at the screen and smiled at the one-word ID.

Surveillance.

Cain glanced down at his watch. *8:37 p.m.* He pressed the answer icon and said, "You're late."

He heard a sharp intake of breath. "Sorry, sir."

Silence.

Cain imagined burying the man alive in file folders. "Well?"

"Something is up, sir. They are involved in some operation on I-85."

Cain leaped to his feet. He wanted to choke the man. "And you're just now contacting me?"

"Well, sir, you see, sir, they were parked at a truck stop for hours and—" the man replied.

Cain spun the phone to look at the screen and put the call on speaker. He shouted, "Patch me into your video feed, and don't lose them."

His phone's screen came alive with a freeway scene of vehicles speeding in both directions. A light-gray targeting circle highlighted a Jeep in the left lane with a Shelby Mustang close behind. An eighteen-wheeler occupied the right lane about twenty yards ahead of the Jeep.

"Zoom in on the truck," Cain said. The image zoomed in and focused on the semi. No identifying marks. "Let me see the Jeep." The camera zoomed out, panned, and zoomed in until the front of the Jeep filled the screen. "Tighter," Cain demanded.

The image shifted to the close-up of the driver. Cain smiled as he recognized the driver as the agent from the restaurant. The one he had taken by surprise. The kick to his head had been the best.

Cain's smile faded when the camera shifted to the passenger. He slapped his hand down hard on the desk.

Dan.

"Where are they?" Cain asked.

"Heading north out of the city on I-85."

The image panned out to show both the truck and the other vehicles. The Mustang shot past the Jeep and the semi, only to swerve in front of the big rig.

"Stay with the Jeep," Cain said.

Cain laughed when Dan climbed out onto the hood followed by the woman. If she fell, all his problems would vanish. He yelled, "Yes!" when she slipped, only to watch Dan catch her and haul her to safety. They disappeared into the rear of the truck.

"What are you up to, Brother?" Cain whispered.

Moments later, all hell broke loose. The semi skidded to a stop. Cars crashed. Gunfire erupted.

A helicopter flew by, almost hitting the drone. The helicopter dove for the freeway, swooped past the truck, circled, and put down in the middle of the lanes.

The firefight intensified, and Cain watched the escape play out. Two figures, one with Dan over his shoulder, emerged from the back of the truck. The man labored under Dan's weight as they headed for the helicopter.

Cain's pulse quickened, and he let a "Come on" escape before he thought about it. The woman reached the craft first and helped the FBI agent dump Dan into the cabin. Cain grinned as their man by the car went down in a hail of bullets.

The helicopter lifted off, eased forward toward the man lying on the pavement, and hovered until it began drawing fire from the security team. It spun and leaped into the darkness.

"Follow them!" Cain yelled at his phone.

"No can do, sir," the voice replied. "The drone was damaged by the near-miss. I've got to bring it back, or we'll lose it."

Cain pounded both fists into the desk. He severed the call without another word.

———

Ames stood in the middle of the freeway next to the black helicopter. She ducked as a bullet ricocheted off its metal side. Her hair whipped about her face in the vortex caused by the spinning rotors. Ames glanced in the cargo compartment of the helicopter. Both doors sat open. With no seats, the space could hold maybe half a dozen people. Another round deflected off the fuselage.

"You guys need to hurry!" the pilot yelled.

She turned back to see Reid laboring up the side of the road with Dan in a fireman's carry. She hurried to him, and together they hoisted Dan into the cabin. She hopped up into the helicopter and offered Reid her hand.

"Thanks," Reid managed. He took her outstretched hand, and she pulled him into the cargo hold. Reid let out a soft groan and rolled onto his back.

Ames bent over to check Dan and stumbled forward onto one knee, hands pressed on Dan's chest as the helicopter lifted from the ground. It tilted forward to drift down the freeway toward John's position.

"Ow," Dan muttered. His hand went to his head.

Ames rocked back onto her heels at his side. "Lie still. You have a head injury." She began going through his vest pockets, searching for the vial.

Several bullets struck the helicopter. Ames ducked and looked out the side door. John lay sprawled on the pavement in a pool of blood.

"He's hurt!" she yelled at the pilot. She willed John to do the impossible again. She whispered, "Come on."

But John did not move. Ames slid to the doorway, ready to jump out. "Set down as close as you can," she shouted above the din of the rotors.

More rounds ricocheted off the fuselage. From the cockpit, a klaxon began blaring out some warning.

"Hold on," the pilot called out. Instead of landing, the helicopter banked hard to the right and shot upward at a steep angle.

Caught off balance, Ames rolled backward across Dan toward the other door. She screamed as she slid through the opening and grabbed the door frame with both hands. Ames hung for a split-second looking down at the twinkling lights of the freeway below. The helicopter leveled off, and she swung back to plant her feet on the landing skid. With a heave, she pulled herself back into the cabin and rolled onto the floor.

Pushing herself up onto one arm, Ames yelled, "We can't leave him! We have to go back."

"No can do, ma'am," the pilot called back. "The site's too hot." The pilot turned to look back at her. "And you saw the same thing I did. He's gone! Dead!"

She pounded her fist on the floor as they flew into the darkness.

———

One minute later, Cain approached the automatic door to the Professor's lab at a jog. He had to hesitate at the door for it to open. "Hurry up, hurry up." The door slid open, and he burst through the gap.

As he entered, Cain said, "They're up to something." He pulled up as he saw Angela next to the desk. She leaned toward the Professor in a subtle but provocative stance. The Professor stared at the computer monitors, oblivious.

Angela looked up and smiled at Cain like a cat caught with a toy it was not supposed to have but did not really care. She straightened and smoothed her short skirt back in place but remained close to the Professor's shoulder.

Cain frowned. He liked being with her. Most of the time. And she was hot. But he never trusted her. For now, he chose to ignore her.

Without acknowledging Cain, the Professor continued his conversation. "Angela, please forward me the new analysis numbers from all three of our online DNA genealogy services. I want to get as many potential profiles identified before we move to phase two. We must find them before the chaos spreads."

"As you wish," Angela said. She placed a casual hand on the Professor's shoulder and gave Cain a wink.

The Professor let his gaze drift to her hand. A frown flickered across his face; then his attention returned to the screens.

Oblivious of the Professor's notice, Angela smirked at Cain. She shifted her weight to stand even closer.

"What did you say, Cain?" the Professor asked.

"Sir, they've made a move. They hit a transport on I-85."

The Professor replied without looking up, "Interesting. What did they take?"

"I'm not sure, sir. They targeted an unmarked semitruck."

The Professor brushed Angela's hand from his shoulder. "Leave us," he said. Her cheeks flushed, and she stalked past Cain without meeting his gaze.

"An unmarked truck, you say?" the Professor asked. "Even more interesting. Was the doctor with them?"

"Yes, and they pulled a ridiculous stunt to gain access to the truck."

"That should tell you everything you need to know," the Professor said. He pushed back from his desk. "Get your men together. We will move our first test up to tomorrow morning. We will use the G-6.4C version of the formula." The Professor went to the closest lab table and began searching through a stack of folders.

Cain blinked in surprise. "Sir, that test is not scheduled for eight more days." Cain glanced at his watch. "We'll only have about six hours to get into position. And do we have enough of the formula on hand? I'm not sure why we have to rush."

The Professor let the stack of folders drop back onto the lab table, and he shot Cain a cold stare. "You're not sure? Not sure?" he said. The Professor rounded the table, stalked across the room to stand inches from Cain, and looked up at him. "Well, let me help you." He poked a hard finger into Cain's chest. "The woman doctor has been with John for approximately thirty-six hours. Since you've been unable to eliminate her, what do you think they've been discussing?"

Cain struggled to think. "Us?"

The Professor sneered up at him. "Very good, *boy*. And why do we care about the doctor?"

Cain's anger almost overwhelmed him. The need for violence ripped at his control. He let his knife slip into his hand before he thought about it and squeezed his eyes shut.

"Why do we care?" the Professor asked again, softer this time.

Cain let the breath he held ease out through his nose. He rolled his neck and then opened his eyes to meet the Professor's. Cain recited the memorized lines in a monotone voice. "She may be able to slow down our plan. With her mRNA expertise, given time, she might create a vaccine."

The Professor caught the front of Cain's shirt and pulled him close. He whispered, "They have stolen something from the CDC tonight, most likely a contagion. But why now?"

Surprised, the anger melted out of Cain. The CDC? Why? The Professor released him, and Cain stepped back. He began flipping the knife from handle to blade, trying to puzzle out what the Professor thought.

"Your old friend has some idea of what we are up to," Cain said. "But they don't know the details of what we have planned. And they can't know until we make our move." He caught the knife by the handle and held it up to look at the blade. "They've made another plan." His pulse began to pound, and a smile spread across his face. "They're going to try to kill you!" Cain thought for a moment. "But how?"

The Professor nodded his approval. "How indeed? I told you she was the smartest of them all." He began tapping his index finger to his lips. "She must think she has discovered something…"

Cain felt a chill run through him. "But there is nothing that can hurt you."

"That's where you are wrong, my son," the Professor said. He turned back to the desk. He rifled through a stack of papers to produce a photo of the woman doctor. Block letters across the top showed her name, *Amelia Cranford*. "There is one thing. And she may have discovered its secret. I would like for you to bring her to me." He ran his hand across her name. "She reminds me of someone I used to know."

Cain slid the knife back into his sleeve. An idea crept into Cain's thoughts.

The Professor continued his lecture. "We must force their hand and bring them out into the open. Therefore, we will execute our field test tomorrow without delay."

The man carried on about details that Cain already knew. Cain pretended to listen but concentrated on the more important things.

Cain snapped his fingers as the last piece of the plan for his brother clicked into place. He would use the new security guy. What was his name?

Tomlinson.

Cain smiled. Oh yes, this was exactly what he wanted.

Something extraordinary.

CHAPTER TWENTY-TWO

Dan sat on the hard metal floor and leaned against the back wall of the cargo space in the helicopter. The alarms continued to sound from the cockpit. The tail drifted to the right and left as the pilot struggled to keep the craft flying. Reid rode to Dan's left and checked his pistol for the third time. Ames sat across from them, closer to the pilot.

"How much longer?" Dan yelled over the noise.

"One minute out," the pilot shouted back. "Hang on. It's going to be rough."

Dan looked across at Ames. She had wrapped her left arm in the cargo netting and was studying the floor. With the doors locked open, the wind whipped her dark hair and prevented him from having a clear view of her face.

"At least we have the vial, Ames," Dan said. "And John will be okay. You've seen what he can do."

She looked up and brushed her hair back. Tears streaked down her cheek. "What if there's a limit to what he can take?"

Before Dan could reply, the pilot shouted, "Hold tight!"

The helicopter crashed into the ground, tossing Dan up in the air. He slammed back to the hard floor, and the pain in his head flared like a flash-bang grenade in close quarters. Reid groaned and struggled to sit back up. Ames looked dazed and shook her head.

The pilot unstrapped his helmet and tossed it into the empty copilot's seat. He looked back with a smile. "Well, that went better than I thought it would," he said. "You guys okay?"

No one replied. Hand to his brow, Dan managed to ask, "Where are we?"

The pilot continued unstrapping himself while flipping various switches and turning knobs. "We're at DeKalb Airport. I came in unannounced, so I suggest we get a move on before security shows up." He stepped out and jogged across the tarmac without waiting for them.

Ames exited first, followed by a slow-moving Reid. Dan slid to the side, hopped down, and staggered as he fought to catch his balance.

"Let me help," Ames said. She slid under his arm. "You've got a concussion."

They straggled across the pavement. The pilot rounded the corner in a four-door full-size pickup. He slowed to a stop near Dan and rolled down the window. "I fly better than I drive, but you guys look like you need a lift."

Reid and Dan struggled into the back seat. Ames took the front.

She grabbed the pilot by the arm. "We have to go back for him."

"No way. You saw the same thing I did. He's dead," the pilot protested.

"We don't know that," Ames shot back.

"I liked working for him and all," the pilot said. "But I'm not going back there."

Ames looked back for support, and Dan gave her a small shake of his head. Silence enveloped the cab.

The pilot left the airport and headed east on the boulevard. "Where can I drop you guys?"

Dan leaned forward and pointed at a convenience store on the left side of the road. "Just pull over there."

Reid gave Dan a hard, knowing look.

The pilot maneuvered his truck across the street and let the vehicle roll into the parking lot. A police car sped by with lights flashing. "You sure, man?"

"What's your name?" Dan asked. He withdrew his Glock and held it low.

The pilot eased the truck into a parking space and glanced into the mirror. "Jeremy."

Dan said, "Well, Jeremy." He pointed his weapon at Jeremy's head. "I'm *sure* we need your truck. Our mutual friend is still out there. And I'm *sure* he will make this up to you. Now get out."

Jeremy glared at him in the mirror. "I saved your sorry asses, and this is how you repay me?"

Ames touched Jeremy's arm, and he jumped with a start. "Thank you," she said in a low voice. "I am grateful. We don't want to hurt you, and I will take care of your truck. So, would you please get out?"

Jeremy studied her for a beat and then smiled. "You guys are crazy. Just like John." He grabbed his cell phone and eased out of the truck.

"Ames, you drive," Dan said. He slumped back into his seat and looked at his partner. Reid's icy stare seemed to lower the temperature in the cab a few degrees.

"What? We couldn't just take an Uber," Dan protested. Reid held his gaze for a long moment before he turned and looked out his window. Dan shook his head and sighed.

No choice.

———

Dan let his eyes drift closed and sought to tame the throbbing in his head. Silence settled over the truck. The navigation system showed Ames the route back to I-85. With the freeway still shut down, they followed side streets toward their destination, and Ames drove without comment.

Reid shifted in the seat next to him. Dan glanced at his partner and suppressed a grin as Reid reached to straighten his tie that was not there. He wore the black combat fatigues that John provided, but he still wanted to straighten his tie.

Reid noticed the attention and frowned, "I've never stolen a vehicle before."

Dan rubbed his temples. "I've never stolen from the CDC either."

Reid exhaled hard. "What are we doing here, Dan?"

"Whatever it takes to stop them."

"But who are they? All we've got is some wild tales."

Dan looked forward and nodded toward Ames. "We have to keep her safe. That's the mission. And that means we have to stop the bad guys trying to kill her."

"We don't even know how to find them," Reid said.

Dan sighed his agreement. "Let's just get John back and see what we can find out."

Reid looked back out his window. "Not much of a plan, partner."

The road they followed reached a bridge that spanned the freeway. Ames slowed to a stop at the middle of the overpass and pointed to her right. "There it is," she said.

Police SUVs, fire trucks, and other emergency vehicles littered the stretch of highway, lights flashing like Friday night on Times Square. The CDC eighteen-wheeler sat on the side of the road. Just behind it, a very official-looking Suburban with *CDC* plastered on its fenders was parked next to a black paneled van with *FBI* emblazoned on its side. A group of men and women stood nearby, pointing and gesturing in various directions.

John's car was gone, but small yellow evidence tags showed where he had fallen. And the blood. Lots of blood.

Ames fumbled with the earpieces of her comms and managed to key the mic. She hesitated and looked at Dan. He motioned with his hand for her to continue.

"John?" she asked. "Are you there?"

No one replied.

"John, it's Ames. We are at the scene. Can you hear me?"

Another moment of silence filled their earpieces. Then a soft chuckle made Ames smile.

"I wondered how long it would take you to get through the traffic."

"Are you okay?" she asked.

"Yes. I'm fully recovered."

Dan and Reid began scanning the men below, looking for John.

"Where are you?" Dan asked into his comms.

"Well, you see…funny thing, I've got a couple of problems," John replied.

They waited for him to continue. After a few seconds, Reid keyed his mic. "And?"

John said, "Well, you see, Zachary, they took all my knives. So, I'm stuck in a body bag in the back of some vehicle," A long silence followed.

"And?" Dan demanded.

"Well, and this has *never* happened to me before, but…you see, when I died…I think I pooped my pants."

Ames and Dan made eye contact. Ames's grimace met Dan's laugh.

———

Dan hid in the ditch with Ames and Reid not far from the emergency vehicles. He whispered, "John has to be in the ambulance. That's the only vehicle that could hold a body."

"Only one attendant," Reid said. "Ames, you stay here. Dan and I can approach together. I'll flash my badge and tell him we want to look at the body. Dan, you take care of him once we are inside."

Ames touched Dan's shoulder. "Be careful."

The two men stood and dusted the dirt from their black fatigues. Dan withdrew a black ball cap from a pocket, planted it on his head, and pulled the brim down to obscure his face. They both straightened and walked with purpose as they approached the back of the ambulance. The attendant sat on the back bumper, looking down at his phone.

Reid led the way and flashed his badge when the man glanced up. "I need to take another look at the body."

The man did not rise. "Really, man," the attendant complained. "I'm all ready to roll. Just waiting on the paperwork. Can't it wait till the morgue?"

Reid let his steel-gray eyes bore into the man. "Open it," Reid demanded through clenched teeth.

The attendant jumped up like a squirrel that had just spotted an oncoming car. He unlatched the rear door, swung it open, and stepped back. His gaze became glued to his shoes.

Reid climbed in next to a gurney with a body bag strapped to it and glanced back. "I'll need your help."

The attendant looked up at Dan and mouthed a silent *Me?*

"Better get in there," Dan said.

The man clamored up into the back. Dan pulled the door closed as he followed him into the ambulance. The man glanced back, and Dan punched him hard in the temple. He collapsed to the floor without a sound.

Reid clicked open his knife and cut the straps while Dan found the zipper to the body bag. The teeth caught as he tried to pull it open, and he fumbled with it for a moment.

A muffled voice came from within the bag. "Do you remember the sign in front of the Springfield Hospital on the Simpsons?"

Dan paused and looked up at Reid. His partner shrugged.

Dan resumed his attack on the zipper. "No, John. What did it say?"

"It said..." John began and paused as Dan managed to get the zipper unstuck. John pushed the sides of the bag back, sat up, and delivered his line. "Quality care or your autopsy is free." John burst into laughter and slapped Reid on the shoulder.

Dan and Reid exchanged a worried look. Reid asked, "Are you okay?"

John reeled in his laughter. "Yes, Zachary. Just a little oxygen deprived is all. And then there's the..." He trailed off as the pungent odor filled the cabin.

Reid coughed. Dan waved his hand and said, "Oh God, you weren't kidding."

John looked from one agent to the other, smiled, and asked, "Shall we go?" Dan nodded with an anxious frown. John added, "You guys wait outside. I'll be right with you."

The two agents hurried out the back and stepped into the flashing lights of the crime scene. Reid moved to one corner to observe while they waited. Dan stood watch at the doors and wondered what John was doing. He heard a few crashes from inside, a muffled curse, and a "There you are." A minute later, John popped out—arms spread wide, showing off his hospital scrubs under an EMT jacket.

"Much better," Dan said. They marched across the roadway like three men on an assignment and disappeared into the shadows.

Ames rose as they approached and greeted John with an embrace. As she stared into his eyes, she said, "I thought we had lost you." But Ames seemed to feel the others looking at her and stepped back, cleared her throat, and turned to face the roadway. "But I think we have a couple of problems."

Dan followed her gaze to the semi and the CDC vehicle.

"First, I think the CDC has figured out what we did. They've been taking inventory, and they all got very excited about two minutes ago.

Reid stepped up next to her. "Okay," he said. "So, they know. That shouldn't be an issue."

"Second, it will be a problem if he also finds out." She pointed at a man hiding in the shadows to the right of the eighteen-wheeler.

Dan tugged on Ames's sleeve and eased them further back into the dark. "Did he spot you?"

"I don't think so, but you guys parading around could have given us away," she replied.

"John, do you recognize him?" Reid asked.

"Nope. But I don't keep tabs on the Professor's grunts."

Dan checked his pistol and chambered a round. "We can't just leave him."

Reid rounded on Dan. "I've gotten past the *truck acquisition*, but we're not going to kill him."

Dan looked from Reid to Ames. "We may have to. But we might have another play here." He looked past his partner at the man in the shadows. "Hey, John. I bet you've got someplace we can stash him back at your fortress, don't you?"

John nodded with a smile. "What do you have in mind?"

"Well, we need information about their plans and location. I say we take him and sweat some intel out of him, then drop him off with the local PD."

Reid turned and studied the man. "Okay, but we need him to be able to talk."

"No problem, partner. Did I ever tell you about that op in Somalia?"

"Which one?"

Dan swept his hand across the scene. "It was a snatch-and-grab of a terrorist undercover operative," Dan said. "All we had was a pickup, two bandannas, and this Afghani medic." He smiled at John.

John looked skyward. "Did the medic survive?"

Dan chuckled and laid out the plan.

Reid turned and studied the man by the truck. "Okay. Remember, we need him alive."

But would he even stay dead if I killed him?

CHAPTER TWENTY-THREE

The morning sun had yet to break the horizon. The pink glow in the eastern sky always made Cain think of his mom. Growing up, Cain often woke up early. He never knew why.

Cain recalled padding down the hall in his fuzzy slippers and always finding her sitting in the kitchen, staring out the window as if she was waiting for someone to come home. The warm pink glow reflecting on her face made her look happy. It was the only time he remembered her looking happy.

Cain shifted in the passenger seat of the large truck and checked his watch. One of the thick-necked hired men sat to his left, arms resting on the steering wheel, staring straight ahead. The man alternated flexing the muscles in his biceps.

Idiots.

Cain felt surrounded by them. He knew the Professor had promised them a place in the world to come. But he also knew that was a lie.

Cain's comms crackled. "Are you in position?" the Professor asked.

"We are. Ready to activate the video feed on your command," Cain replied.

"Very well, proceed with the initial lockdown. I want no witnesses to escape. Set up the roadblocks first. Remind the men only to use deadly force on your command."

Cain frowned. He knew the details, but the Old Man insisted on reviewing them over and over and over. "Yes, sir. Proceeding as *planned*."

"Stay focused, young man," the Professor said. Cain's comms went silent as he ended the transmission.

Cain ground his teeth and looked up at the signpost just ahead of his truck. He read it aloud to himself with his best Southern twang. "Welcome to Historic Buford, Georgia. Incorporated 1872." He switched to the tactical frequency. "We have a go. Send in the drones for the first pass. Strike teams set up on Lee, Hamilton, and Sewanee. Report any encounters with local law enforcement to me. No one in or out of town. Let's move!"

Brow furrowed, Cain's Hulk-like driver leaned forward and squinted at the sky through the windshield. Two fixed-winged drones sped by on silent engines about fifty feet above the ground. The man looked back and forth. Sweat formed on his brow. He gripped the steering wheel with white knuckles.

Cain tried to remember the man's name but decided he did not care. "Relax, *Banner*. We're outside the dispersal zone."

"My name's not Banner, sir. It's Roman. But what if it drifts on the wind?"

"Well, *Roman*, that's why we're on *this side* of town," Cain replied. The man did the sign of the cross over his chest and strained forward to stare out the window again. Cain let out a laugh. "And if I'm wrong... maybe we all die."

———

Cain glanced at the lock screen on his phone. *March 18, 6:59 a.m. A day,* he thought, *people will look back on and remember.* The day the veil of their secrecy began to tear.

Just under ninety minutes had elapsed since the drones had flown overhead and released the formula. The multiple passes had blanketed three square miles from the center of town in less than ten minutes. The lack of wind helped simplify the test.

Cain ran through the rest of the timing. The Professor had been very precise in the details. Ninety-one minutes from delivery to contagious activation. Twenty-seven minutes from infectious exposure to onset of symptoms. Then the fun part began—ending two excruciating minutes later with death.

He checked his watch. *7:00 a.m.* His heart began to beat a little faster. *Any minute now.* He keyed his mic. "Suit up."

In the seat next to Cain, Roman heaved a sigh of relief. The hulk stepped out of the truck to pull on his hazmat suit. When Cain remained seated, Roman gave him a quizzical look.

"I'll just stay in the truck," Cain said. His thoughts returned to the plan. After two and a half hours, the virus would revert to its inert state and allow them to start cataloging the results by eight thirty.

And free Cain to get an early lunch by eleven.

"But, sir," Roman protested, pulling Cain back from thoughts of barbecue. "What if there is contact with the subjects?"

Cain heaved a sigh of his own. He knew the man only worried because he was Cain's driver and feared that Cain might somehow accidentally get exposed and share it with him.

Idiots.

Cain stepped out and reached for his bag. At least his hazmat suit was custom-tailored.

———

The first car pulled up to their checkpoint twenty-five minutes later. Cain stepped out of the cab of their truck and waved as the driver pulled forward. A middle-aged man, probably on the way to some unimportant job, sat behind the wheel. Cain's hazmat suit caused a look of concern to fall across the man's face, and he did not roll his window down.

Cain smiled his best civil-servant smile. "Good morning, sir. I'm afraid there is a problem up ahead." The man leaned closer to the window, struggling to hear. Cain motioned for him to roll the window down and yelled, "It's okay." The man hesitated and glanced about. The window slid down about an inch. Cain let his face show sympathy. "A tanker truck ran off the road and released some toxic chemical. The poor driver. Such a horrible sight. The road will be closed up ahead for a while."

The man relaxed but brought his hand up to rub his brow. The hand trembled, and Cain held his breath.

The man coughed and wiped his mouth only to catch sight of his hand. He held it up and rotated it right and left, mesmerized as the skin began to wrinkle. A few dark spots appeared.

"What's happening?" the man croaked.

Cain tried the door latch and found it locked. He tapped on the window with his gloved hand. "Sir, open your door. I can help you."

The man gazed up at Cain and fumbled with the door, unable to get it unlocked. Wrinkles spread across his pleading face. Amazed, Cain watched as the white film of a cataract formed in the man's right eye. The man tried to raise his right hand but grimaced at a sudden pain and grabbed his elbow with his left hand.

The fear on the man's face melted into confusion, and he managed to ask, "Where am I?" in a dry, raspy voice before a paralyzing pain gripped him and made him press back into the seat. With a moan, he breathed out one more rattling breath and expired.

Cain jiggled the door handle again and then pounded both hands on the top of the car. He wanted a closer look. Cain stomped back to the truck and pulled himself into the cab. "Let's roll."

"But, sir, the virus is still active."

"I know. I want to watch."

CHAPTER TWENTY-FOUR

The three hours of sleep Dan had managed to snag only made his headache worse. He leaned by the door and watched as Reid took his turn with the man. His partner sat at the polished, ornate table in their makeshift interrogation room. The high-backed padded chair they had lugged into the room made Reid look more like an angry Russian czar than an FBI interrogator.

Taking the man had not been a problem. Getting him to talk was another matter. So far, all they knew was his name.

Tomlinson.

Reid paused to twist the top off a plastic water bottle. The seal broke with a loud *crack*. "We know you are a part of the terrorist cell." He took a long drink and eyed their captive. The man sat strapped to a similar chair with bright-blue plastic ties. "Look, Tomlinson," Reid said. "We can ship you off within the hour, and you'll never see the light of day again, or we can set you up in WITSEC and have you in some nice comfy hotel by tonight."

Ames burst through the door. Her white lab coat flared out as she rushed into the room. "Something's happened." She took a deep breath. "I just got another flash-alert from the CDC. There's been an attack."

Dan took two quick steps to the table and backhanded Tomlinson across the mouth. "Enough of this! What have they done?"

The man sneered and spat blood back at him.

Ames grabbed Dan's arm. "Let's check the news. They're probably all over this, whatever it is." With her footsteps echoing down the hall, she left as hurriedly as she came.

Reid rose and smoothed out his suit jacket. "Guantanamo is very hot this time of year."

Dan slammed the door as the two left the room and caught up to Ames with long strides. They entered the large conference room, and Ames began a frantic search for the remote to the television. She found the black square device and studied the fifty-odd buttons on the remote. Dan smiled and held out his hand.

"I've got this," she snapped at him without looking up. Ten seconds later, she nodded and pressed a button. Nothing happened. She frowned and pushed another.

The television sprang to life. A silent scene of a small town, shot from a news helicopter, filled the screen. A red banner scrolling across the bottom confirmed their fears.

"Breaking News. Thousands Dead in Terrorist Attack."

Ames turned up the volume. The sounds of the helicopter in flight provided the backdrop for a news announcer—a female voice caught midsentence. "...with more reports still coming in. Ted, the federal agents on the scene are all in hazmat suits. We don't have a total death count, but we've not seen anyone alive in the town."

More circling images. More helicopter noises. Numerous bodies lying in the street. The camera panned to a school bus parked at a street corner. The door sat open. A woman's body rested against a streetlight next to the bus. The camera zoomed in on the scene. The picture went from a soft, unfocused fuzz to the crystal-clear, high-definition image of three young children next to the woman on the ground. One, a little girl frozen in death, still stretched a small hand toward the woman.

But the hand was deformed. Wrinkled and twisted into a knot.

Rage boiled up inside of Dan. He wanted to look away. But his eyes remained locked on the three children, lying on the hard pavement as the camera exposed them in vivid detail, each of them wrinkled and hunched in a strange posture.

"Hold on, Ted...My pilot has just informed me that the airspace above the town has been declared a restricted zone." The image spun to the clear blue sky of a beautiful afternoon as the helicopter banked hard to the left. "I'm handing this back to you in the studio. This has been Margaret Gomez above the suspected terrorist attack in Buford, Georgia."

The television image switched to a close-up of the anchorman, his midfifties face tight with concern. "Here's a recap of what we know so far. The FBI has reported that sometime this morning, the town of Buford, Georgia, was exposed to an unknown chemical or biological weapon. Initial reports confirm that there appear to be several thousand casualties. Our sources on the ground indicate that they have not found any survivors." His hand went to his ear, and he listened intently for a few seconds before his pale-blue eyes snapped back to the camera. In a grave voice, he continued, "With a population of just over fifteen thousand, Buford has existed as a quiet Georgia community for over one hundred and fifty years. But that ended this morning. As yet, no one has claimed responsibility for the attack, but this man…" The news anchor paused as an image of Dan's face filled the screen. "Is wanted in connection with several crimes, including an attack on a CDC transport last night. He is considered armed and—"

Ames muted the television and collapsed into a chair. "This is no terrorist attack. It's them," she murmured.

Dan began pacing. "Holy crap. I thought we had more time." He ran his hand through his hair. "What are we going to do?"

From the shadows by the doorway, John said, "We will stick to the plan. The doctor needs to finish the serum for us to have a chance against them."

"Jesus, man, have you seen what they've done?" Dan said.

John's face clouded, and a rebuke formed on his lips. Dan beat him to it. "Yes, yes, I know. You're not Jesus. We've got that, okay." Dan wanted to punch the man. "Sure, you knew him but blah, blah, blah. People are dead, man. A lot of them. And you're worried about what I call you? We need to be worried about what's next and how to stop them."

"He's right," Reid said in a cold voice. "We can't just *stick to the plan* when the plan is to do nothing."

John stalked into the center of the room. "Dr. Cranford has almost perfected the serum. But without it, we are not ready to move against them. You will only get yourselves killed."

Reid turned away from John with a look of disgust on his face.

Dan pointed at the television. "So, what do you suggest, John? We wait for them to release this on a large scale and kill all of us?"

John threw up his hands and spun in a circle. "I don't know," he admitted. "But we can't go for them yet. We're not ready."

Dan hesitated, unsure how to proceed. John marched to the far side of the room and stood not looking at them but up at the ceiling—his faint whispers the only sound in the room.

Dan felt a bead of sweat form on his brow. "What do you think, Reid?"

Reid eyed John and rubbed the back of his neck. "We should contact Quantico. Turn Tomlinson over, and get Dr. Cranford into protective custody."

With his back still to them, John said, "It won't work. We have to stick to the plan."

The image of the three dead children rolled through Dan's mind. "I'm sorry, John," Dan fumed. "But we are federal agents, and we cannot just stand by and do nothing."

John turned to them and shook his head. "You cannot trust the people at Quantico. They are FBI, and you can't trust the FBI anymore."

"We *are* the FBI," Reid spat back. He folded his arms across his chest. "And we know how to handle terrorists."

"Been waiting two whole days to say that?" John asked. A smile played at the corners of his mouth. "Never have quite believed me, have you, Zachary?"

Dan felt disoriented. He took a deep, steadying breath.

"You have no idea what I—" Reid began, but Dan placed a hand on his partner's arm.

"Reid, he's right," Dan said. He waved at the muted television. "The FBI thinks I'm behind all this. It will take a long time to convince them otherwise. But, John, we have to do something. They killed thousands." He took one step toward John and added, "We could use your help."

"With what? Getting yourselves killed? No way." John edged closer to Ames. "The doctor stays with me."

"Hello," Ames said. "I'm right here, you know. I think I can speak for myself."

John wheeled on her and grabbed both of her shoulders. "You *must* keep working on the serum. We need it to have any chance against them. There is no other way to stop them. Without the serum, they can keep this up forever."

Dan started forward, but John released her and took a step back. John's gaze fell to the floor, and his hand went to his brow. The images from Buford crept back into Dan's thoughts. His mouth went dry, and he shook his head. "I'm thinking a big box of your C4 might have a good chance of slowing the bad guys down," Dan said. "But he's right, Ames. You need to stay here and finish the serum just in case we need a backup plan."

"No," she replied firmly. "I need to get a sample of whatever virus they used and get ready to work on the vaccine." She touched John's arm and brought his attention back to her. "And you, John," she continued, "are going to help me. Let's let the boys *go blow some things up* the FBI way. You and I have other priorities."

Dan nodded his agreement. "But first..." He paused and cracked his knuckles. "We've got to know how to find them. It's time to make Tomlinson talk." Dan nudged his partner with his elbow, and the two agents headed for the door.

As they passed John, he grabbed Dan's arm and gave him a hard look. John said, "If you're going after them, we don't have the time for you to beat information out of Tomlinson. And are you going to trust your lives to what he tells you through his hate?" John glanced across at Ames. "Besides, my way is much more fun. Let me grab some supplies, and I'll show you."

———

Ames stood with Dan and Reid outside the door to their makeshift interrogation room, waiting for John. Reid checked his watch for the third time and muttered something under his breath. Dan leaned against the wall and rubbed his temples with his eyes closed. She reached out her hand but stopped an inch from his arm. Her fingers trembled. She curled them into her palm and let her arm drop back to her side.

John rounded the corner and jogged down the hall with a small duffel in his right hand. "Okay, I've got it." He eyed the two agents. "Gentlemen, I'll need you just to stand at the back, look entertained, and keep your mouths shut."

Reid started to object, but Ames cut him off. "Please, Agent Reid, there's not much time." Reid frowned but kept quiet.

John nodded and reached into his bag. He handed Ames two medicine vials. "Doctor, you play along, and give it your best mean face."

Ames read the labels. Both contained a simple saline solution. She glanced up at John. "I don't understand."

"You will. Put them in your coat pocket," John said. He gave her a wink and a grin. "Remember—mean face." He opened the door and led them into the room.

Dan and Reid took up position by the door. Dan straightened and folded his arms across his chest. Unsure what to do, Ames stopped two steps into the room and watched John circle the desk. Tomlinson looked straight ahead with his eyes unfocused as he tried to stare at nothing.

John leaned in close to his ear. "I know you saw what we did to the CDC truck, but do you know why?" John said, his voice smooth and confident. Tomlinson continued his fixation on nothing. "Doctor, show him what we took."

Ames hesitated but slipped her hand into her pocket and withdrew one of the saline vials. She held it up between her index finger and thumb for the man to see.

"It's the plague, my friend. The bubonic plague. The freaking *Black Death*," John said. He leaned a little closer to the man's ear and whispered, "Only she's modified it. Trying to reproduce what your boss did to that town last night."

Tomlinson's eyes locked on the vial.

"She's ready for a human trial."

A bead of sweat began its slow advance down the man's brow.

"She promised me her enhancement is spectacular." John pulled a syringe from his pocket and held it in front of the man's nose. "Here's the thing. We're looking for a volunteer. Now that can be you, but your boss kicked the crap out of my friend over there." John nodded at Reid. "And he'd *really* like for it to be…what's your boss's name…oh yeah…*Cain.*"

At the mention of Cain's name, the man's eyes widened, and he shook his head. "He'll kill me if I take you to him."

"Oh, you don't have to take us to him. We only want to know the location of the lab. We'll take care of the rest."

"I cannot!" the man said.

John sighed, straightened, and held the syringe out toward Ames. "Very well, Doctor, you may use this one."

Ames kept a grim, clinical look on her face as she took the syringe and filled it with the saline. She held the tip up like they do in movies and flicked it a couple of times.

John leaned back down close to the man's ear and whispered, "Last chance."

Ames stepped forward and lowered the syringe to the man's arm. He struggled against the restraints but looked up at her with defiant eyes.

"Even if I told you," Tomlinson said, "you'd never get to him."

"Well, I guess you'll never know," Ames said and jabbed the needle into his arm. She turned her back to the man and winked at Dan. "Start the timer. It will be fast-acting, but I want to get the exact time of the first symptoms."

"Yes, Doctor. Anything you say, Doctor," Dan replied. He pulled out his phone and selected the timer.

Chair legs scraped on the hardwood floor as John pulled the man around to face him. John leaned forward with a wicked grin. "Here's the thing," John said. "You have maybe five minutes till there's no going back." John turned to Ames and inclined his head in her direction. "But being the good doctor that she is, my friend here also has the antidote."

"That's right," Ames said. She fumbled in her pocket for the second vial. "It's right here." She held the bottle up for the man to see.

John pulled another chair over, sat down, and slouched back. He took out one of his knives and started to clean his fingernails. "Did Cain tell you what it will feel like? How it breaks your insides down into a pile of goo." He paused and tapped the point of the blade on Tomlinson's knee. "We'd like to try this on Cain instead of you, but I can understand your loyalty to him. I mean, he's always been there for you, right?"

The man shook his head without realizing it.

"Yeah, I get it," John said. "But the antidote has to be administered in the first five minutes. If we just knew where the lab was, but..."

The man turned his head to stare at the vial in Ames's hand. Sweat poured off his face.

"The subject looks feverish already," Ames observed to Dan. "How much time so far?"

"Three minutes, forty-two seconds," Dan replied.

"Just over a minute left," Ames said. "I want to stay and watch, but you gentlemen should wait outside. It's going to be very messy once he starts hemorrhaging."

John slapped his knees, slid his chair back, and stood. "Whelp, we'll just have to find Cain another way. I'll get the cleaning crew ready." He started toward the door and handed Ames a surgical mask. She smiled and pulled it on.

Dan turned to head out the door and glanced at his phone. "Forty-five seconds."

"No, wait!" the man yelled. "I'll tell you."

"Best be quick," Ames said. She drew the supposed antidote into the syringe.

"The warehouse is on Fulton Parkway. I promise. The big white one. He showed me just last night."

Ames fought back a smile. She glanced at John for instructions.

Tomlinson jerked against his restraints. "Please, I've told you what you asked."

John nodded to Ames. "Okay," he said. She hesitated and let John deliver the expected final line. Right on cue, John added, "But remember,

Tomlinson. If the address is wrong, the doctor can always come back to play."

She smiled and gave Tomlinson the injection.

———

Dan looked down the row of explosives in John's armory. Simple grenades worked their way down to C4, Semtex, and what looked like old-fashioned sticks of dynamite. He walked down the aisle carrying a plastic basket like a shopper at Walmart while calculating how much C4 and incendiaries they needed to bring down a large warehouse. He loaded several blocks into his basket and turned to leave. With a smile, Dan tossed one more in just for good measure. He heard Reid selecting pistols and assault rifles for both of them. They met up at the door where John waited for them.

"These might come in handy," John said. He held out two tactical air rifles. "They're loaded with fast-acting midazolam darts. Should keep you from having to kill the security guards."

Reid took one and held the stock to his shoulder to sight down the rifle before checking the chamber to confirm it held a dart. Satisfied, he placed both with the other weapons.

With an outstretched hand, John offered two cell phones to Dan. "And you'll want these. Dr. Cranford and I both have one, and I asked Martha to put each of the numbers on speed dial. Just in case something comes up."

"Thanks," Dan said. He slid his into a pocket of his black vest and passed the other to Reid. "We've got everything else I think we'll need. We're going to stake out the warehouse lab and hit them tonight. What's your mission plan?"

"Ames is collecting her supplies. She says we need to arrive before they finish scrubbing the scene," John said and flashed a Homeland Security ID at Dan. "I should be able to get us in. We'll need six hours to do the site investigation and collect samples. Given the drive time to Buford, we won't be back before ten tonight."

Reid nodded and headed down the hall. Dan moved to follow, but John stepped in front of him.

"I still think this is a mistake," John said. "Your partner doesn't believe in me, but I know what I'm talking about. We should wait for the serum."

Dan looked him in the eye. "I'm sorry, John. I can't sit around while they kill people. And neither can Ames," Dan said. "We have a good plan." But as he stood there, Dan felt a touch of cold dread creep down his spine.

Have I missed something?

CHAPTER TWENTY-FIVE

Ames sat in the Jeep, waiting for John. She rummaged through her bag again to make sure she had everything they might need. Sample kits for blood and tissue. Scalpels. Swabs. DNA kits. Bottles of saline, alcohol, and bleach.

She caught sight of John entering the garage and offered him a smile as he slid into the driver's seat, but he did not notice. She sighed, settled her bag in the back seat, and fastened her seat belt. John drove the Jeep down the tree-lined campus lanes without comment. They entered the freeway and headed north toward Buford.

"How long will it take us?" Ames asked.

"About an hour and a half, depending on traffic," John said. After checking his mirror to change lanes, he selected a playlist from his phone. The melancholy notes of "Behind Blue Eyes" by The Who filled the cabin.

After a moment, Ames asked, "What's it like?"

"What?"

She looked at his face. His beard hid the lower half, but the small crow's feet at the corners of his eyes revealed tension.

"Dying. The Roman guards thought you were dead. I assume they were correct."

"Yes. Some wounds push me to the other side for a short time."

"What's the end like?"

"The end?" he said. His eyes relaxed into a smile. "Gandalf said it the best. 'The journey doesn't end here. Death is just another path. One we must all take. The gray rain-curtain of this world rolls back, and all turns to silver glass, and then you see it.'"

"See what?"

"That's just what Pippin asked," John said. "'White shores, and beyond, a far green country under a swift sunrise.'"

"You've seen it?"

"Only a glimpse."

"Did you know him?"

John looked at her and smiled. "Gandalf wasn't real."

"No, silly," she said and pushed on his shoulder. "Tolkien."

He glanced down at her hand, and his face tightened. "No, I was in Poland when he was writing. I've seen the movie."

The playlist moved on to "The Sounds of Silence" by Simon & Garfunkel. Ames settled back and closed her eyes. The music brought images of John's stories into her mind. She let her thoughts drift back down the entry hall with the glass cases, each one holding special memories for John. Her reflection paused on one display—the one with the rose and the ring.

Eyes still closed, she chanced the question. "Who was she?"

A heavy sigh followed a few beats of silence. "She's been gone a long time," John said. But Ames thought she still heard the longing in his voice.

U2's "With or Without You" began to play. John sighed again and continued in a soft voice. "I met her in Florence. I had just begun my life as da Vinci."

Ames's eyes popped open at the revelation. She studied John's face, and her breath caught.

John changed lanes and continued, lost in his memory. "She was brilliant. Beautiful. She helped me with the anatomical studies. Critiqued my paintings. Managed our money." He paused. A frown filled his face. "Luke loved her too. He was always jealous. It drove Luke away for a time. But she was mine, and for a time, we had a good life together."

The music spoke to Ames, and she knew to remain quiet.

"Her name was Amelia," John said softly.

Ames felt a tightness in her chest. She looked out her window. "What happened to her?"

His whispered reply brought an ache to her chest. "She grew old...I didn't."

———

Ames succumbed to her fatigue and dozed off. She dreamed of being stuck in a room with two doors. One she remembered walking through before, and it had not been a fun trip. But fresh paint made the door seem inviting. Mysterious, detailed images covered every inch of the other door like some fresco in an ancient chapel. She felt drawn to it, wanted to walk through it, but she knew she would find it locked.

She awoke with a start as they exited the freeway. Ames shook her head as the dream faded and checked her watch. *3:47 p.m.*

John navigated the Jeep through the series of roadblocks. He continued to flash his Homeland credentials, and no one challenged them. The tires crunched across the gravel as John maneuvered their vehicle into the makeshift parking lot at the edge of town. The final checkpoint lay just ahead.

John withdrew his phone and touched the screen. "Let me check on Dan and Zachary."

"You're tracking them?" Ames asked.

He smiled at her. "Well, of course. You don't think I'd send them out all on their own? I created a secure version of those Find My Kids apps just for this kind of work." He studied the screen for a moment. "They're in position at the warehouse. Probably going to be a long wait. I hope Dan took some snacks. I'll set it to notify us when they leave."

The two exited the Jeep and gazed across the lot. Knots of men and women from various law enforcement agencies huddled together. Muted conversation drifted across the lot. The canvas of a large field tent flapped in the breeze. Signage directed arrivals to the enclosure for check-in.

"Wait here. They might recognize you," John said.

He returned moments later with a badge and protective gear for each of them. They donned the bright-orange hazmat suits and trudged into the town.

Ames took the lead and headed down the main street. Plastic sheets covered a few of the bodies, but most still lay where they fell. Orange-clad workers filled the area and came in all shapes and sizes. Some tall, broad-shouldered ones patrolled the area brandishing automatic weapons and wearing black armbands. Others clustered around a few of the bodies. Strained conversations and shouted orders filled the air. Without slowing, Ames walked by the closest victims in search of a more private location.

Three blocks down the main avenue, John tapped on her elbow and motioned toward a house on the corner. Yellow flowers filled two planters by a blue front door. The raised blinds allowed them to see into a well-lit kitchen. "Someone was probably home," he said.

Ames headed up the sidewalk to the porch steps and took the steps two at a time. She felt compelled to knock as she pushed the front door open. "Hello, anyone here?" She stepped across the threshold and took in the small foyer. A living room sat to her right—the kitchen and a hallway were off to her left. "Hello," she called again.

John followed her in and pulled the door shut. "Better let me look around first," he said. Silence filled the inviting home, broken only by the soft swish of John's suit as he passed her, rounded a corner, and disappeared down a hallway.

Ames heard him open and close doors in other parts of the house while she waited. Signs of a happy life graced the living room through its decorations. Pictures of a family filled the mantel above the fireplace. A mom, dad, and three children had occupied this home. The kids ranged in age from a preschooler to a teenager, all boys.

Maybe they weren't home.

"All clear, but you should see this," John called from the kitchen.

Ames pushed through a swinging door, and her throat caught. Five bodies littered the room; two rested at the table, three lay face-down on the floor. She bent and gently turned one over to get a closer look. From the size, it was one of the children. But the face and hands looked like they belonged to a ninety-year-old.

Her pulse pounded. She slid over to the next body, another one of the children, and rolled it over. Similar wrinkled skin. Dark liver spots on one cheek. Curled arthritic fingers. Milky white cataracts filled both eyes.

She muttered, "This can't be." She moved from one body to the next.

John stepped closer as she examined the father. "What do you think did this?"

She rummaged through her bag for the sample kits. "I have no idea, but I need to collect samples of tissue and blood. Also, can you get some of the food and maybe some of their clothing? We need to see if we can determine how they were exposed."

John bent down over one of the children. "But they look so...old."

"It's like some form of Hutchinson-Gilford syndrome. But that's genetic and not contagious. And it's not this fast. We'll have to wait until we get back to your lab."

"I'm afraid that won't be possible. We have something else in mind for you," a familiar voice said.

Ames looked up to see Dan standing in the doorway in a snug-fitting black hazmat suit. Four of the black-armband guards slid past him and fanned out in the room, guns leveled at Ames and John.

Only it wasn't Dan.

She took a step back. "You're his twin. Cain, right? What do you want?"

Cain nudged the guard to his right. "Finally, someone smart enough to ask the right question," Cain said.

John removed his hazmat helmet and tossed it on the floor. "You know, I've always wondered how many Neanderthals I could beat the crap out of at the same time." In a fury, he ripped the gloves from his hands. "Now, why don't you boys put down those weapons, and let's see what you're made of."

Cain laughed. "This isn't the movies, old man. Does that kind of talk ever work in the real world?"

John flashed him a pirate's smile. "Probably not, but you never know how stupid the hired help may be. I, on the other hand, like to rely on sleight of hand. Have you ever seen this trick?" He held up his empty hand, snapped his fingers, and a grenade appeared in it, seemingly out of thin air. "Catch," he yelled and tossed it at the nearest gunman.

John spun and drove Ames to the ground. Gunfire erupted from the guards. She felt two rounds hit John as he landed on top of her. A blinding flash and a deafening concussion followed as the grenade detonated. She fought to draw a breath. Bright pulsating orbs filled her vision.

Rough hands pulled her up. She wanted to stop and vomit, but the hands propelled her forward. She stumbled and fell. The hands lost their hold, and she rolled onto her back. Her vision began to clear, and she realized that the hands belonged to John. He hauled Ames to her feet and pushed her onto the porch. His mouth was moving, probably shouting, but all she heard was the ringing of a thousand bells.

As John hurried her down the steps, she saw Cain in the doorway behind them. He had blood on his forehead and held a weapon of some kind—a boxy-looking rifle. Her mind swam. She wanted to tell John, to warn him. But she did not find the words before Cain raised the weapon and fired. Two oversized darts connected to wires planted themselves in John's neck. Ames felt his body tense as an electric shock surged through him. His face spasmed, and he toppled over on her. She fell backward onto the hard pavement. The weight of John's rigid body pinned her to the ground.

Cain stepped forward. He smiled down at her. "As I said—I have something planned for you. Something extraordinary."

She struggled and failed to get out from under John. After a moment, she relaxed and glared up at Cain. "They will come for me. Dan won't give up until he finds me."

Cain laughed. "You believe that? But it won't even be necessary." He bent down close to her face and whispered, "I'm going to take you to him." He paused and gave her cheek a gentle touch. "But first." Cain straightened and gave John a hard kick to the ribs. "I need to help this one learn to *not* interfere with my plans."

CHAPTER TWENTY-SIX

Dan looked out the driver's window of their parked Tahoe and drummed his fingers on the steering wheel. A quick check of his watch revealed what he already felt.

7:42 p.m.

Four hours earlier, he had eased the white vehicle into the side parking lot of a building across the street from their target. He rubbed the back of his neck. Four hours of watching the steady trickle of personnel and materials coming and going from the warehouse made him restless.

Like John's other vehicles, this one had a premium sound system. Dan had found a Johnny Cash–Willie Nelson playlist, and it had shuffled through a series of tunes for the last hour. Willie began "Always on My Mind," and Dan's thoughts drifted away from the op.

And back to Ames.

She filled an empty space inside of him. That dark hole he pretended did not exist. He wondered how things might have turned out if he had not left.

Reid cleared his throat. "I think we should move before any night shift shows up."

Dan gave a start and looked out his window. The people had vanished along with the sunlight, and security lights in the parking lot now illuminated the area. All of the cars had left. Only two security guards remained at their post near the front door. A glance at his watch gave him another surprise. *8:27 p.m.*

Need to stay focused.

He used his surveillance scope to observe the guards. "They look bored. The bright security lights are killing their night vision. I think we can approach from the shadows on the left."

With the cabin lights disabled, they slipped out of the Tahoe and stole across the dark street. Each carried a high-power air rifle loaded with John's version of a hippo tranquilizer. Dan led as they maneuvered up the side of the warehouse and approached the front corner. He risked a quick peek to ensure their targets remained unaware.

"Looks good," Dan said. He checked the chamber for the dart. "I'll take the far one."

Reid took his turn for a quick look. "How about I take the far one. We both know I'm a better shot."

Dan suppressed his reply but allowed himself a shake of the head. "Fine, you take the far one." He crouched down on one knee and aimed around the corner. Reid leaned around above him and sighted in on his target.

"Ready," Reid whispered.

"On three," Dan said and counted, "One, two, three."

On three, both weapons sounded with a soft spurt. The nearest guard grabbed his arm and cried out. He staggered a step and crumpled to the ground. The other man drew his weapon and spun in their direction. The guard held a hand above his eyes and tried to peer into the shadows. He started their way.

Both agents withdrew back around the corner. Dan dug a second dart from his pouch, pulled the plastic tip off the needle with his teeth, and dropped it into his gun. He slid the bolt action in and looked at Reid.

"Better shot, my ass," Dan whispered.

Reid drew his pistol. "I know I hit him."

Dan risked a quick look around the corner. The man lay sprawled out on the pavement. "Guess he needed the elephant version," Dan said. "I'll get them out of sight. You check the door."

While Reid examined the doors, Dan dragged the men to the Tahoe and zip-tied their hands and feet. John had promised they would be out for a couple of hours, but Dan had seen too many strange things in the last thirty-six hours to take chances. He fished the bag of explosives out of the SUV and headed back to Reid.

As Dan approached, Reid pushed the door open. "This one wasn't even locked. Inside's a different story."

Dan moved past Reid into the dark interior. The dim illumination of the security lights outlined another building. It occupied the center of the large warehouse, surrounded by twenty feet of open space on each side. Dan clicked on his flashlight for a better look at the house-sized structure. White walls with narrow windows at the top. At the end of six wooden steps, a metal door sat three feet above the warehouse floor.

The lab.

Reid took the steps two at a time and tried the door. He turned the latch and gave it a firm pull with an extra shake. "Locked." After a moment's careful examination, he added, "Looks biometric. I don't think I can hack it."

Dan looked up at the small dark windows. "That's okay. No lights on. Looks empty." He ran his hand down the wall. "I don't need access to demolish this baby."

He withdrew a can of spray paint and began shaking it. The loud clack, clack, clack echoed from the far walls. "I'll need about forty-five minutes to plan the placement and get the C4 set." He slipped his comms into his ear. "Why don't you keep watch outside with our sleeping friends? I'm on channel two if anyone shows up." Dan ran his hand along the wall again and paused to paint an orange X six inches from the corner.

"Will you have enough C4?" Reid asked.

Dan smiled and painted his next X to the right of the door. "Oh yeah. We'll flatten the lab and bring down the whole warehouse right on top of the rubble. Reminds me of an op we ran in Syria. Did I ever tell you about the one when we had to take out this radar installation?" He turned to look back at his partner only to see Reid going out the door. Dan shook his head with a chuckle and painted the next X.

Yep, Syria was awesome.

———

Dan stood next to the exterior wall of the lab. He mopped his brow with his shirt sleeve and took a steadying breath. He pressed the blasting cap into his last brick of C4 and used a long strip of duct tape to fasten it to the wall, right on top of the X. He gave the explosive a once-over, nodded with satisfaction, and then reached up and flipped the toggle on the radio trigger to armed.

He loaded the remaining supplies back into the duffel and headed out. With a quick glance around the warehouse, Dan paused by the exterior door and scratched his head. It had almost been too easy.

Maybe they aren't as smart as John thinks.

Dan exited the building and hurried across the parking lot to their vehicle. Just visible in the shadows, Reid stood behind the car.

"They're all set," Dan said. "Thirteen bricks. Ready to blow."

Reid nodded his approval. "All quiet out here. The guards are still out. I'd say we are good to go. I'll get the detonator ready."

The burner phone in Dan's pocket started buzzing. He glanced at the screen for the caller-ID.

Ames.

Dan stepped to the front of the car and answered the call. "Ames, we're about to blow the lab. Is everything okay?" He heard her take a deep breath.

"They have me, Dan. They took me," Ames said.

His chest tightened. He tried to take a breath but failed. A memory gripped him—one of his mom saying almost the exact same words. *Someone has him, Dan. Someone took your brother.*

Her voice broke when she continued, "Oh God, Dan. They hurt him. They hurt John." She took in a sharp breath. Her voice slipped to a whisper. "They forced me to watch."

His mom's voice echoed in his thoughts. *Oh God, Dan, what if they hurt him?*

"Where...where are you?" Dan stammered.

He heard her anger. "I'm not sure. They drugged me, and I just came to a little while ago. I'm in a lab, but there's no one here, and the only door is locked. I thought I heard someone outside a few minutes ago, but it's all quiet now. And the idiots left my phone. Hold on a sec."

She paused, and Dan heard the sound of metal scraping on metal. He pictured her pushing something around.

With exertion in her voice, she said, "There's a small window, kind of high up. Let me climb up." Another pause. "That's odd."

"Can you see out?" Dan asked. "Can you tell where you are?"

"I can see a little. It's like the lab is inside another building. A large warehouse of some kind. There are some security lights on, but I don't see anyone."

Dan's head snapped around toward the building across the parking lot. Time seemed to slow down. He saw Reid activate the power switch on the detonator and flip up the safety cap. Ice formed in the pit of Dan's stomach. The phone slipped from his grasp. His field of vision narrowed until his entire world became just the one thing—the detonator.

"For God's sake, stop!" Dan yelled.

Startled, Reid looked at his partner. "What the hell?"

"All this talk of God and hell. Did you guys get religion or something?" a voice asked from the shadows behind them.

The two agents spun toward the voice and drew their weapons. Five men stepped out of the shadows and spread out facing Dan and Reid. Four wore black tactical gear and carried automatic weapons. They had the strong, muscular builds of trained fighters. The fifth man wore jeans, expensive-looking shoes, and a long-sleeved white shirt. His gold watch glinted in the pale light. He stood at the left end of the line with nothing in his hands and a wicked smile on his face.

Cain.

"Hello, Brother," Cain said. He gestured toward the warehouse and chuckled. "Man, I thought the good doctor might not wake up before you guys set off all of the fireworks. That was close." He began a slow stroll down his line of hired muscle. "But you know. It always makes me happy when the new staff excels at their assignment. I mean, Tomlinson really came through for me." He picked up a pebble and tossed it across the lot.

Dan shot Reid a look.

"And they walked right into it," Cain said to one of his men. The man smiled, and they shared a laugh.

"Cain," Dan growled. "If you hurt her, I'll—"

"I know, I know," Cain said. He resumed his stroll down the line. "You won't have me over for Christmas this year." He reached the end of the line and turned to face them. Anger moved the smile off his face. "Now drop those weapons."

"I don't think we—" Reid began.

Cain bellowed, "That's right. You don't think!" In three strides, Cain closed the gap to stand face to face with Reid. Reid planted the barrel of his gun in the middle of Cain's chest.

A smile spread across Cain's lips. And a large knife appeared in his hand. Cain glanced at Dan, winked, and rammed the knife upward into Reid's chest until only the hilt remained exposed.

A look of surprise flashed across Reid's face, and he fired into Cain's chest. Dan saw the red spray of blood exit Cain's back as both men toppled in opposite directions.

"No!" Dan screamed. He fired two quick shots at the closest thugs, hitting one high in the shoulder and the other in the chest. Both men went down.

Instead of returning fire, the remaining two men charged him. The first slammed into Dan, lifted him from his feet, and drove him into the hard pavement. Pinned to the ground, Dan cried out as the second man stomped on his gun hand. His weapon sprang free, and the man kicked it away.

The man on top of Dan punched him hard in the face and then sprang back to his feet. He bounced on the balls of his feet like a prize-fighter ready for the next round. He motioned for Dan to get up and said, "Remember me, mate?"

Dan's vision swam. He rolled to his side and spat blood from his busted lip. Reid lay next to him, staring at him with lifeless eyes. A dark pool grew from under his partner and crept toward Dan like it had something to share with him but was a little shy. "No," Dan whispered. He stood slowly, ready to beat someone, anyone, to death.

But Dan froze. He watched as Cain rolled to his feet. His brother rubbed at the bloody front of his shirt, fingered the hole the bullet had made in the middle of his chest, and turned to look at Dan with cold eyes.

Dan stared in disbelief. He realized his mouth was gaping open and snapped his jaw shut. He shook his head, trying to clear his thoughts. *Just like John. But how?*

Cain bent down to retrieve Dan's gun and gave it a critical once-over. "Now, Daniel." Cain sauntered over to him. He tapped the barrel of the pistol on Dan's chest. "I know you may be a little troubled by this." Cain gestured toward Reid's body with a sweep of his hand. "Or you might even have a few questions about me." He wiped his bloody hand on Dan's shirt. "But let's not forget the good doctor. I think she might be wondering what is going on out here. Maybe, why you *abandoned* her." Cain glanced back toward the warehouse. "And there's that little problem of you almost blowing her up. I mean, I think she might even thank me for rescuing her from you morons."

Cain forced out a laugh, took a step to the side, and gave Reid's body a hard kick. "Morons," he repeated with a shake of his head.

Anger surged through Dan. He grabbed Cain by the arm and spun him around.

Cain met his stare. "Tell me, Brother," Cain asked just above a whisper. "Did you get this angry when they took me? Did you even miss me?"

Dan froze. Cain took the opportunity to club him on the side of the head with the butt of the gun. Dan staggered back, hand to his temple. He felt the warm ooze of blood from the wound.

Cain shook his head. "Weren't you supposed to be watching out for her? Wasn't the good doctor *your* assignment? I guess some people never change." He stepped close and rammed his fist into Dan's gut.

Dan bent forward, hands on his knees. His head swam. He tried to catch his breath. But Cain's accusations hit the hardest. His mind replayed an image from fifteen years earlier.

He and his friends in the convertible, racing out of the mall parking lot. Them laughing and pointing as Cain ran after them. The look of anger and betrayal that clouded his brother's face as he stood there—all alone.

Dan could only watch as Cain stepped over Reid and picked up the detonator. "Should I still blow it up?" Cain said. He began flipping it on and off as he said, "One potato, two potato, three potato, four."

Dan staggered forward. "No!"

Cain put his thumb on the red button at the top of the detonator. A smile crept onto his face. "Oh, Brother, you look so miserable. You want a chance to save her?"

Dan stood straight, slowed his breathing, and tried to show no emotion. He nodded his agreement.

"Fine, let's see if you can get her out before I run out of potatoes," Cane said. He flipped the safety cap closed. "Where was I...one potato—"

"The lab is locked. You know I can't get to her," Dan said in a flat tone.

Cain let his hand fall to his side. "Wow, not letting me have any fun with this, are you? Marco, what's the code to the interior door?"

"Eight seven five two six seven, sir," one of the men called out.

Without hesitating, Dan burst into a sprint. With each stride, he demanded his success.

Got to get to her.

I can save her.

Won't leave her again.

But as he neared the door, his mind replayed one more image—the one from fifteen years ago. Of his mom, dying in the hospital. Her last words to him, her final accusation, echoed in his mind.

Why did you ever leave him?

"Too late," Cain shouted.

The building disintegrated in a blinding light. Dan felt himself lifted by the shock wave, and darkness filled his world.

CHAPTER TWENTY-SEVEN

Images floated across his consciousness. He tried to remember. He knew something important, something urgent, depended on him. He drifted on past an image. One of burning white-hot pain as the fingers on his right hand disintegrated in the blast. But there was something he needed to remember. Something he needed to do.

He considered opening his eyes but could not recall why he wanted to. He needed to remember the other thing first.

Breathe.

He drew in a sharp breath and opened his eyes. A light shone from somewhere ahead, far away.

Am I dead?

He blinked his eyes and forced them to focus. The bright light became one of the security lights at the top of a pole in the parking lot.

A soft *clink* made him roll his head to the right. A piece of rebar leaned against his chest. A drop of blood held to its tip for a lingering moment before it fell onto his shirt. Dan took a slow breath, held up his hands, and rotated them back and forth to examine both sides. He stared at his right hand for a long moment and then wiped the dust from his face. He paused as it crossed his lips. The busted and bloodied lower lip now felt smooth.

Dan sat up, and a hundred shards of glass tumbled from his chest. They hit the pavement, playing him a sweet melody like his backyard wind chime. Several small pieces of jagged metal and splintered wood clung to the remains of his shirt. He stood and gave himself a quick check, searching for the severe injuries he knew he must find. His blood-soaked shirt hung in tatters down his chest, but he discovered no gaping wounds. He found no injuries at all.

What in the world?

His mind reeled—spun out of control. A wave of nausea coursed through him, and he bent forward with his hands on his knees. He struggled to breathe.

Then, his thoughts came together so fast he thought he almost heard the *click* of understanding, and he jerked upright. One by one, events of the last day played out in his mind.

The fight at the diner.

The attack on the town.

Getting the intel from Tomlinson.

Planting the C4.

Cain springing his trap.

Reid lay at the end of the line of memories with the knife in his chest. Dead. And Cain, Dan's identical twin, shot through the heart but standing over his partner. Alive.

"I'm one of them," he whispered. One more memory barged through the line and tried to suck the life back out of him.

Ames.

He took in the scene across the parking lot. The blast had thrown him at least fifty feet. Wreckage lay scattered in all directions. The explosion had vaporized three of the exterior walls. Three-quarters of the back wall still stood, but all of the glass had disappeared. Several small fires burned in the pile of rubble. The remains of the collapsed roof entombed the interior lab.

Dan started running before he realized he had been blown out of his shoes by the explosion. The glass crunched underfoot, and he almost pulled up. Although it still hurt as it ground into his feet, he felt the cuts close as fast as they appeared. Dan felt light-headed but kept going and sprinted faster across the debris-filled pavement.

He stumbled into the wreckage of the warehouse and surveyed the destruction of the lab. A large roof joist blocked any access to the lab. He grabbed the steel beam and yelled as he tried to lift it. The beam failed to notice his efforts and remained in his path. His blood boiled with rage. A secondary explosion rocked the area, and more flames erupted on the far side of the pile. Tears streamed down his face as he staggered back.

"Ames!" His hands fell to his side.

Why did I ever leave you?

A bright light panned across the remains of the warehouse, and Dan noticed the *thrump, thrump* of the helicopter blades for the first time. The oval of light kept moving. Searching. Sirens wailed in the distance. He took one last look around and shook his head. His hands balled into fists.

He turned and hurried across the parking lot toward their vehicle. He had to get to Reid. He did not want to leave his partner's body to some no-name cop who might think he was just another perp. But when he rounded the Tahoe, only the dark pool remained. Cain had taken everything.

Dan looked up into the night sky. His heart pounded in his chest, full of newfound energy. His skin tingled as a night breeze brushed past him. His body seemed more whole than it ever had—but he still felt fractured like a broken mirror with the shattered pieces still clinging to the frame. Dan hung his head and swallowed hard.

The spotlight from the helicopter panned his way. Dan moved to the SUV and slid into the driver's seat. He pressed the ignition, and the playlist resumed. "Hurt" by Johnny Cash flooded the cabin. He drove into the night as darkness enveloped his soul.

CHAPTER TWENTY-EIGHT

The blare of a horn caused Dan to look up at the streetlight. The green light beckoned him forward, and he let his foot slide from the brake. The Tahoe started a slow roll through the intersection. The impatient horn yelled at him again. He looked in the mirror and considered killing the man.

The insistent driver sped around his vehicle. As the car passed, Dan made eye contact with the driver and saw a look of fear grow on the man's face.

Someone was going to die. Dan might need a little time, but he would find them. He would kill them all.

Even Cain?

He pulled the Tahoe to the curb and rested his head forward on the wheel. The playlist moved to the next song. Willie Nelson's smooth voice began "Georgia on My Mind." Dan's pulse pounded. Adrenaline surged through him. He had other things on his mind.

Dan punched the audio system so hard he felt the bones in his hand break along with the console display. Silence replaced Willie. He stared at his hand as he felt the tingling sensation of the bones knitting back together. He flexed his fingers and leaned back into the seat.

His thoughts shouted at him. He needed weapons. He needed to find them. He needed to make them pay. But one realization forced its way through the angry crowd.

He needed John.

———

Dan eased the Tahoe into the parking garage at Georgia Tech. Cain had tracked them somehow, but he saw no evidence of surveillance. He wound down to the lower level and parked against the far wall, away from the elevator to John's facility. The Rubicon was missing, but the elevator door had a large arrow painted on it with dark-red paint.

Or maybe blood.

Dan stepped out of the SUV and left the door open. He moved through the garage with the practiced silence of a trained killer. The painted arrow pointed to his left, and he made his way to the end of the row of cars before he heard a soft moan. A large panel van sat parked parallel to the wall across three parking spaces. Dan slid further to his left. He wanted a clear view of behind the vehicle before he approached. What he saw froze him in his tracks.

John hung from the wall—arms spread wide with his wrists nailed to the wall by metal spikes driven into the concrete. Another spike pinned both feet together against the wall about a foot above the floor. John's head drooped forward. He looked unconscious, but a soft murmur reached Dan's ears, and he dashed to John's side.

"John. It's me. Can you hear me?" Dan asked. His eyes made a frantic survey of John and the spikes. "What do I do?"

John raised his head and looked at Dan with bloodshot eyes. "Amelia?"

"Dead."

"Reid?"

"Gone too."

John tilted his head back and loosed a scream of rage at the ceiling. He let his head drop back down with a loud sob. After a moment, he whispered, "Please, get me down."

Dan grabbed the spike hammered through John's feet and strained to pull it free, but it failed to budge. With a yell, he tried a second time. "I can't," he said in failure.

John stirred again and forced himself up to draw a breath. "In the arsenal...get a machete. Cut me down."

Dan hesitated, and John raised his head again. "It's okay," John whispered. "They'll grow back."

———

While overseas, Dan had done some pretty terrible things in the name of his country. None came close to severing the hands and feet of a friend, even if they did grow back. John blacked out from the pain, and Dan watched the bones, muscles, and tendons reform.

Until Dan puked.

He hefted John's limp form over his shoulder and headed for the elevator. Dan breathed a soft thanks as he placed his hand on the sensor, and the door opened with a *ding*. He lowered John into a corner and selected the "B" button.

The door scraped closed, and he squatted next to John. Dan grabbed the lapels of John's jacket and pulled him straighter. "Hey, John, you with me?"

"Yes," John replied without opening his eyes.

"Good," Dan said. "Don't *ever* make me do that again."

Eyes still closed, John rubbed his wrists and took a deep, shuddering breath.

The loss of Reid and Ames washed back over Dan like a cold downpour. He leaned back against the wall and slid to the floor next to John. The elevator stopped, and the door opened, but neither man moved. The door waited for them like an unsympathetic bystander but finally gave up and slid back closed.

John rested his head back against the wall with a thump. He banged it into the wall twice more, each time with a deeper, louder thud. "They were waiting for us. I let my guard down. They took me by surprise."

Dan had trouble drawing his next breath.

John raised his right hand and looked at his wrist. "I think I killed two of them with a grenade, but they had a weapon made to stop me.

Tied me up, threw me on a stretcher, and marched us right past your FBI buddies at the scene." John kicked the closest wall.

Dan shook his head. "It was a trap. Cain planned it all along. He guessed exactly what I would do. Seemed to know right where we were." He paused. His throat felt tight. He swallowed twice. "They brought her into the lab right under our noses. Cleared everyone else out." Dan rubbed his temples. "He killed Reid right in front of me." He squeezed his eyes shut. "Then he blew the lab up before I could get Ames out."

Silence filled the elevator.

Dan took a deep breath and continued, "But, John, there's more. Cain's one of you. Reid shot him in the heart, and he just got back up." Dan met John's knowing stare. He thought of the explosion and ran his hand across his chest. "And so am I."

———

They remained in the elevator for over an hour, reliving the finer details of what Cain had done to them. Finally, Dan forced himself to stand and held out his hand to John. John looked at it for a long moment and then grabbed it and hauled himself to his feet. Dan punched the door-open button and stepped into the round entryway. He stopped and turned to John. "But one thing still bothers me."

"Only one?" John replied.

"How does he know where we are? I'm sure Reid and I weren't tailed. They might have expected you would go to Buford, but how did he know where I was? Or, for that matter, how did he find Ames at the diner?"

John rubbed his chin. "It's not trackers on the vehicle. I have them scanned daily. The cell phones are burners, so it's not them."

A memory from Dan's action overseas surfaced. One of sitting in a dim room watching a nerd at a console as they tracked a convoy in the desert. Dan smacked his forehead with his palm. "Drones. Like the military uses. He must have access to advanced drones."

John headed down the long hall. "Well, now, I've got just the thing for that." John glanced over at Dan. "When you're like *us*, avoiding detection is a top priority. For some time, I've worried the government might begin using military drones to track civilians." John paused at the corner. "I invented a nifty countermeasure just in case. We can use it when the time is right. But first, we need to check my lab."

They made their way to the long white room. John hurried down the lab table to the computer surrounded by Ames's notes.

Dan followed and scanned the neat block letters of her printing. "Can you make anything out?"

John ran a finger down two of the pages. "Looks like she had made progress on combining her enzyme with the carrier bacteria from the plague."

At the mention of the bubonic plague, Dan took an involuntary step back.

Without looking up, John said, "Don't worry. You're immune to all diseases. Don't even have to get a COVID shot anymore."

Dan felt the urge to grin but lost it with a thought of Cain. "Okay, how do we use it on them?"

"Well, from what I can make out from her notes, we have to inject each one of them with the serum. The plague's bacteria will spread through their body fast, but to make it nonlethal, it's no longer contagious."

"Okay, we break out your air rifles and load up some darts."

"Well, we have a big problem," John said. He opened a small refrigerator and withdrew a rack with a single test tube. "She only managed to make one sample so far. Only enough for one of them."

Dan's hands balled into tight fists. "So, what are we going to do?"

"We need a few hours of sleep. Then we can decide," John said.

Dan shook his head. He did not want to sleep. He wanted to kill someone.

John placed a hand on Dan's shoulder. "But first, we need to remember them. I'll have Petros bring us something from the wine cellar."

Dan sighed and rubbed the back of his neck. "I need something stronger."

John nodded. "My liquor cabinet is full."

John led them into his study. He opened a cabinet, filled two glasses with a dark liquid from a large decanter, and handed Dan a glass. John raised his glass. "To lost friends."

Dan clinked the glasses together. A lump in his throat prevented any reply.

John picked up the bottle of liquor and motioned for Dan to follow him down the hall. John entered the large meeting room and moved a comfortable chair by the couch. Dan downed half his glass in one gulp. The smooth liquid spread warmth through his chest, and he slumped onto the sofa. John refilled Dan's glass without asking.

"Tell me about Reid," John said. "He must have been a good man."

"He was." Dan sank lower into the cushions. "I met him my first day at Quantico. He lectured in a few of my classes. I requested the Atlanta field office, hoping to work around him. Never expected to get to be his partner." Dan took another swallow and stared down into his glass. "I can still hear him running through the details of techniques and procedures. Man, he knew how to be FBI." He drained the rest of his drink.

John poured more dark liquid into Dan's glass. "When did you meet Amelia?"

"That was a long time ago." Dan swirled the contents of his glass. "We dated for a while." He took another sip. "I almost proposed." The glass trembled in his hand. "But something came up." He emptied his glass and lapsed into a long moment of silence. But rage boiled in his gut. "How did we let them do this to them, John?" Dan asked. He stared at his hand, willing the shaking to cease. Failing, he hurtled the empty glass across the room. "To her."

John had no answer, and they fell back into a dismal silence.

CHAPTER TWENTY-NINE

Dan blinked his eyes open. Somewhere, not far away, someone played a piano—some abrupt classical piece in a minor key. It sounded awful. He squeezed his eyes shut and willed the horrible sonnet to cease. And it did. Dan sighed a thank-you and relaxed.

Until it began again.

His head pounded with each discordant strain. His tongue felt like sand. He sat up, rubbed his temples, and scanned the room for the source of his torture.

With his back to Dan, John sat at a grand piano that Dan did not remember seeing the previous evening. John hammered out more of the brutal melody, paused, grabbed a pencil from behind his ear, and leaned forward to scribble on a sheet of music. Seconds later, the pounding resumed.

"Are you trying to kill me?" Dan demanded over a rapid string of notes.

John continued to play. "It calms me down to write music, and anyway, it's time you got up."

Dan opened his mouth to yell at John, but a ring from his burner phone silenced them both. Dan stumbled around the couch, stubbed his toe, and cursed under his breath. He snatched the telephone from the table and looked at the caller-ID.

His mind snapped into sharp focus. He sucked in a quick breath and placed a steadying hand on the back of the couch. The cracked screen displayed both a promising flicker of hope and a damning accusation in four haunting letters.

Ames.

He stared at the screen. The phone rang again. Then the display threw out a simple indictment.

Missed call.

John rotated on the piano stool to face Dan. "Who was it?"

Dan tried to answer, but nothing came out. He hesitated, sucked in another breath, and pressed the callback button. Dan began pacing as he waited for the call to connect. The next twenty seconds seemed to take hours, but finally, he heard a ring. His chest tightened as he counted them, one…two…three, before someone picked up.

Silence greeted him.

Dan halted midstride and squeezed his eyes shut. "Ames?"

He heard a soft chuckle in reply. "No, Agent Alexander," a man with a slight accent replied. "I'm afraid that Doctor Cranford is no longer able to take your calls."

Dan's eyes snapped open. They had taken so much, and now they came back for more? He wanted to be alone, to be away from what he had done, and he almost hung up. But he knew too much. Too many people still needed them.

Instead of jumping into the abyss, he let his training take hold. He could almost hear Reid's running commentary on the situation. *The target needs to feel dominant, in control. He is formal and probably European. Make him take the next step and draw him in.*

John closed the lid to the piano keyboard and moved to stand opposite Dan, a questioning look on his face. Dan held his index finger to his lips, shifted the call to speaker mode, and set the phone down.

They waited.

After several seconds, a small huff sounded from the other end of the call. Reid's monologue continued in Dan's mind. *You will likely need to provoke the target at your first opportunity. Focus on undermining his feelings of importance.*

"It is past the time we should have been introduced and—" the voice began.

"I'm sure you're just another one of Cain's lackeys," Dan interrupted. "I want to speak to someone in charge."

John stiffened, and his face darkened as he appeared to recognize the voice. He opened his mouth to speak, but Dan motioned for him to remain silent.

"Now, now, Daniel." The voice sounded irritated. The man asked, "Can I call you Daniel?" but continued without waiting for a reply. "I can assure you that I am the person in charge."

Dan looked at John and received a nod of confirmation. *Keep the target talking.*

"Now, as I was saying, it is past the time we are introduced. My old colleague John may have mentioned me. I've gone by many names through the centuries, but my friends just call me Professor."

Dan imagined he saw Reid smile. *Provoke the target again, and then give them something.* Dan let his anger creep into his voice. "So, what do your enemies call you?" He waited for a beat; then he sighed and added, "But yes, Dan will be just fine."

After a moment of silence, the Professor cleared his throat. "Well, *Daniel*, I told your brother we should administer the test to you, but I must apologize. I am afraid he was a little extreme in his implementation. However, you will have to agree that the results were most positive. I am happy that you have now crossed over into our ranks."

Dan fought to control his anger. He pictured Reid at the front of a class. *You must set your feelings aside. Control yourself, and you have a chance to control the situation.* Dan took a deep breath and remained silent.

The Professor continued his monologue. "You have been granted the most special of gifts. You will find that you have transcended the mere mortals around you. I want to offer you a chance to join us, to become a part of the future."

Dan stared across the table at John. "What about your old friend John? Is he a part of your future?"

"John is too attached to the transients of this world," the Professor said. "He lost his way, trying to stay true to the Carpenter all these years." With amusement in his voice, the Professor continued, "Cain mentioned he even gave John a little reminder of that way of life when he took the doctor from him. Just one more failure. Why, I'd even wager John's listening right now."

John looked at his hands and rubbed his wrist. But he held his tongue.

Push the target along. Dan put a hard edge in his voice for his next line. "But how could I trust you after what Cain did to Reid…and to Dr. Cranford?"

Dan heard a sigh through the phone. "Cain needs someone to teach him how to be subtler, more civilized. He will benefit from the company of his brother. And perhaps you can even atone for your past sins."

Dan felt his chest tighten, but he concentrated on his training. He let his voice become softer. "But he will never forgive me."

The Professor responded with a deep laugh. "They say time heals all wounds, and now you have all the time in the world."

Create an opening, and set the hook. Dan nodded to himself. "But if my history is correct, you used to help people too. Even cared for them. John told me some stories. How you and John were friends once, back when you both followed Jesus. When you went by a different name."

John's gaze returned to Dan, and they locked eyes. John's face clouded, and he seemed to almost plead with a slight shake of his head.

"I never followed him," the Professor said.

Dan ignored the reply and asked, "No…I'm sure I've read your stuff. What did you go by back then? Did they call you Doctor Luke or just Luke?"

"It seems our mutual friend has been most talkative. But no matter," the Professor said. "I've grown so much since then. My god is genetics, and with it, I will remake the world in my image. You will see."

Dan remembered Reid finishing the lesson at Quantico. *Once they're hooked, keep it moving along, and…*

"Well, maybe I can talk my friends at the FBI into getting involved. What if we found some evidence of Cain and your boys at the warehouse?" Dan said. "A security feed from the next building. Paints a nice picture—going to restore my credibility with HQ." Dan paused to allow it to sink in. He let his voice sound angry as he delivered the final piece. "And man, will they be pissed over what Cain did to Reid."

"Oh, Daniel, what a mundane ploy." The Professor coughed out a laugh. "Cain said I would find you boring. There were no security cameras. But it wouldn't even matter because, my young simpleton…"

…*they will tell you everything you need to know.* Dan smiled in satisfaction as the Professor continued. This was the moment when the target always revealed something useful.

"…in twenty-four hours, they will all be dead."

Dan struggled to stay calm. Thoughts of his training evaporated. "What do you mean? Are you going to attack the FBI again?"

The complete silence on the line caused Dan to check to see if the call remained active. "Answer me!" Dan demanded.

"No, Daniel, I have much bigger plans than just the FBI."

Dan looked to John for some insight. John only shrugged.

"You mean another town?" Dan asked.

The Professor chuckled again. "No, my new friend. I mean everyone."

The call disconnected. John sank back into the chair, head in his hands. It was Dan's turn to stare up at the ceiling.

Only twenty-four hours? What do we do now?

Dan began pacing. "John, we have until tomorrow to stop them from releasing the virus, or millions, maybe billions, will die. With Ames gone, there is no hope of developing a cure for the virus in time. And we only have one dose of the serum."

At the mention of Ames, John looked up and scrubbed his hand across his face. His eyebrows gathered in as his eyes dulled. He hung his head. "There's only two of us. We can't stop them."

Dan stepped over and put a hand on John's shoulder. "No, we can't. But I might know how I can make them stop themselves. If only we knew how to find them."

John raised his head and dug through his coat pocket. He pulled out his phone. "You told me they took everything, including Reid's body, correct?" He unlocked the screen and began scrolling through its apps.

Not sure where John was heading, Dan nodded his reply.

John said, "We know he was using the phone I gave to Ames. And Reid had his, right?" John held his phone out and pressed the screen to launch a program.

"Yes," Dan replied.

"Well then," John said. A wicked grin spread across his face, and he pointed to two side-by-side flashing blue dots on the map. "I'd say they are right there."

With excitement in his voice, Dan whispered a prolonged, "Yes." He clapped John on the back hard enough to almost knock him out of the chair.

Time to make them pay.

———

Dan led the way to the arsenal. "Here's how I see it. We have about twenty-four hours. Let's hustle to the location your tracker has for us. We'll set up a stakeout and run surveillance long enough to make sure we have the right location."

They stopped in front of the door. John pressed his hand into the biometric reader and said, "I'll need about fifteen minutes to get the drone jammer online. They're about to lose some expensive hardware."

Dan walked into the weapons room. "We'll take lots of C4 this time. And some incendiaries to burn the crap out of that virus. Now, where are those dart guns?"

John pointed to a row. "Pneumatic weapons on aisle five."

"We need to eliminate the Professor. He's driving this whole thing, and I think he's the key to stopping them," Dan said as they walked down the aisle.

"That's not going to be easy. How will we even get inside their compound?" John asked. He stopped and grabbed Dan by the arm. "And we can take him, but I won't let you kill him."

Dan glared at him. "He's behind what they did to Ames and Reid. And the virus."

John hung his head. "I know, but I failed him before, and that's what led to all this. I can't kill him. I need to save him." John looked back up and met Dan's gaze. "And there's your brother."

At the mention of Cain, Dan had to put a hand on the wall. "I'm just as responsible for Cain. I left him the day the Professor took him. Gave him up for dead too soon. At least you were able to find your friend." Dan hung his head and sighed. "At least you went looking."

"So, we're a couple of losers," John said. "But we're the only ones in the game that can do anything."

Dan picked up a pistol version of the dart guns and checked the chamber. "Okay, let's take them if we can, but we only have one dose of the serum. We have to do whatever it takes to stop the virus from being released."

"But how will we get in?" John asked again.

Dan set the weapons back down and rubbed his chin. "Did you see the Star Wars movies? The first one with Luke, Han, and Leia?"

With a perplexed look on his face, John nodded.

Dan smiled. "I've got an idea, but you're going to think this is crazy. All we need is a long black coat, a white shirt, and a Wookie."

———

The drone pilot yawned and cracked open another energy drink—his fourth one. He kept his drone in a low orbit above the parking structure to avoid detection by airport radar. Target number two had returned to the parking garage ten hours ago and remained somewhere inside the building. He had to sit and stare at the monitors. He could not afford to miss them. Not even for a pee break.

To pass the time, he zoomed the camera in and out on the exit to the garage. On one of these rotations, he jumped as a black Ford pickup pulled out of the garage. He yelped as his hand slipped from the camera control, and he lost sight of the truck for a moment.

The woman at the next station looked up from her book. With the targets all at one location, her drone was at their refueling station. "Problem?" she asked.

"Possible contact," the pilot replied. He zoomed out and panned to follow the truck. It parked in the nearby surface lot, and two men got out. He zoomed in and did not need to use the facial recognition software. He keyed the priority channel on his comms. "Cain, sir. They're on the move."

While he waited for Cain to reply, the pilot adjusted the screen to watch the men. One climbed into the back of the truck and opened the top of a large plastic crate. The other man held a tablet out at arm's length. The man began to turn as he held the tablet skyward. He stopped when it pointed directly at the drone.

"What are they doing?" Cain asked in his earpiece.

"I don't know, sir. They have exited the parking garage, but they stopped just outside. Let me zoom in and..." The pilot trailed off as the clear image of the men and the truck began to fade, and the screen filled with meaningless snow.

"And what?" Cain said.

The man's hand began to tremble. "Sir, I don't know, sir. There is some malfunction with the drone. I've lost the image."

"Well, get it back."

"Might be some localized interference. I'll move the drone to a higher..." The man looked at his instruments and struggled to catch his breath. He leaned forward and flipped two switches. Then he flipped two more. "Sir, I don't understand what has happened. But, sir, it appears that we've lost the drone."

"How can you lose a drone?" Cain shouted back.

"It's gone, sir. Just gone."

—

"We'll have to leave the truck here," John said. He still held the iPad pointed up at the night sky, and a broad smile spread across his face.

Dan followed his gaze but saw nothing. "Did it work?"

"Yep," John said. "That bird is now headed north to Charlotte. No other ones are in the air, so I'd say we are good to go. Let's take the Bronco."

Dan grabbed the duffel bag with their gear and followed John across the lot. "Out of curiosity," Dan asked, "how many cars do you own?"

"Here in Atlanta or Georgia or altogether?" John said.

Dan shook his head. "Never mind."

John tossed him the keys. "You drive. I can access the jammer remotely. I'll continue to monitor for other drones that come poking around. Might bag me another one."

Dan slid into the driver's seat and fired up the car. John pulled out his phone and selected a song. "Born to Be Wild" by Steppenwolf blasted from the speakers. Dan pressed down hard on the accelerator, and the Bronco fishtailed as they sped out of the lot.

CHAPTER THIRTY

Dan and John sat in the Bronco in an alleyway in West Atlanta. Dan checked his watch. *2:12 p.m.* They had watched the front of the four-story building across the busy street for three hours. The complex occupied the entire block but only seemed to have one entrance. As people came and went through the dark double doors, Dan caught a glimpse of the security station just on the other side of the opening. He counted at least three security guards and observed an X-ray station.

John continued to focus on the iPad and its remote connection to the drone jammer. He had snagged another drone and had sent it out toward Birmingham.

A familiar face exited the building. Dan tapped John on the arm and pointed. "Cain."

John raised his binoculars and watched as Dan's brother entered a black sports car and sped off down the street. "He wasn't wearing the same black coat as at the diner. Your disguise may not work."

Dan ran his hand through his hair. "Then, I'll just have to make it work."

"How long do we give him?"

Dan turned in his seat and hauled the equipment duffel close. "I say we wait ten minutes." He rummaged through the contents of the bag, extracted a pair of handcuffs, and tossed them to John. "You'll need these."

John frowned at him. "And?"

Dan smiled and held up the small key.

John snatched it from his hand. "You use hand sanitizer?"

"What?"

"Never mind." John popped the key into his mouth. "Nothing like a little something between your cheek and gum. Reminds me of when I played pro ball."

Dan checked his pistol and settled back in his seat with a sideways glance at John. "You played professional baseball?"

John chuckled and shook his head. "Never made it out of Triple-A."

They lapsed into silence and watched the trickle of people entering the building. Dan's thoughts drifted back to Ames. There were so many things he should have done differently. His heart began to pound, and he gripped the wheel with both hands.

"They're gone, and I know it hurts," John said. "But we have to stay focused to pull this off. You have to be Cain."

Dan blew out the breath he held and nodded. "Let's do this."

He stepped from the car and pulled on the long black coat of his disguise. John grabbed his brown duster and circled the back of the Bronco. Dan lifted the duffel from the back seat, and John reached into the bag, withdrew the eighteen-inch weapon he called "the spear," and slipped it into a scabbard inside his jacket.

He faced Dan with a smile. "Hit me. In the face." Dan only hesitated a second before he punched John square in the nose.

John grabbed his face. "Ow. I think you enjoyed that." Blood poured down his face for a few seconds. He wiped most of it away but left some for the guards to see. John clicked the handcuffs onto his wrists and took a bow.

"Your Wookie is ready."

———

Dan marched John up the steps. He kept his gun pointed at John's back for all to see and carried their duffel in his other hand. He shouldered his way through the doors and shoved John forward like a high school principal who just caught a kid selling drugs on campus.

Three guards manned the checkpoint. Alert and professional-looking, they still paled a little as they took in the murderous look on Dan's face.

To his credit, guard number one still stepped forward and held up his hand. "Cain, sir. What has happened? Who is this?"

"This piece of crap was looking for a way in," Dan said. "And did any of you notice?" He swept his gun hand across the room. "Anyone?"

"Sir, we saw nothing on the cameras," guard number two said. "I didn't even see you take him."

Dan felt John tense—ready for action if their disguise fell apart. Dan whirled on the man. "Then you should pay closer attention, you moron." Dan glared back at guard number one. "And you. Get the hell out of my way. This is a high-value target. The Professor will want to see him right away."

Guard number three drew his weapon. "Do you need assistance with him?"

Dan put a sneer on his face and made eye contact with the man. "Do I look like I need assistance?" Dan poked John with his pistol.

"No, sir. Sorry, sir," the man said and holstered his gun.

"Keep up the great work, boys," Dan said.

The guards mumbled their acknowledgment, and Dan and John strode across the foyer to the interior door. Dan was feeling more confident until he saw the biometric reader attached to the door. He might look like Cain, but even identical twins have different fingerprints.

And fingerprints don't lie.

A small bead of sweat formed on Dan's forehead and began a meticulous march toward his nose. He glanced back at the guards. "Hey, morons. Can't you see my hands are full? Buzz me in."

"Sir?" guard number one asked. All three men turned in their direction.

"Get the damn door for me!" Dan yelled at the man.

The guard hurried to the door and placed his hand in the reader. The lock gave a satisfying click, and the guard pulled it open for Dan.

"Idiots," Dan said with a shake of his head and pushed John forward across the threshold.

The overhead fluorescents cast a bright, sterile light down the twenty-foot hall. The beige walls ended at an intersection with corridors extending to the right and left. The door closed behind them with the loud metallic *clack* of the lock.

"What now?" John whispered.

Before Dan had time to think of a reply, the sharp *click, click, click* of hurried heels on the tile floor announced unwanted company. A tall woman in her early thirties rounded the corner from the left and approached. Black-rimmed glasses highlighted bright-blue eyes on a smooth face that would have been pretty if it found a smile. Her blond hair sat tucked in a small bun at the nape of her neck. She smoothed her short black skirt as she approached. Dan kept his gun pointed at his friend's back.

She gave Dan an icy stare. "Cain, why are you back so soon? You're supposed to be overseeing the security details for the transfer of the infants." The woman gave John a quick look and then checked her watch. "And who is this? We're under three hours, and you're still messing around?"

"High-value target," Dan said. "The Professor will want to speak with him right away."

"Now?" She placed her hands on her hips. "You think he wants to do a test today?"

He had no idea what she meant. "Where is he?" Dan asked in a level voice.

"In his study, of course." Her gaze intensified, and she looked him up and down.

Dan's mind raced. *Where the hell is his study?*

Her forehead wrinkled, and she looked back down the hall. "Has the timetable changed?"

Dan ran with an idea. "I need to see him right away. And bring me some coffee."

A frown tightened her face. "Bring you some coffee?" she said. "And will you need anything else, *sir?*" Her eyes tried to bore a hole through his head.

"Maybe. Come with me, and we'll see if I think of anything else along the way."

She huffed, spun on her heel, and clicked off down the corridor. They followed and wound through a series of identical hallways ending at a smooth metal door with no handle. She paused, and her hands returned to her hips.

"Shall I join you, *sir?*"

"No, and you can forget the coffee," Dan said. He met her gaze with his best predatory look. "I don't think I want to see you again today."

Startled, the anger on her face melted into fear. She stepped close and placed a familiar hand on Dan's arm. "I'm sorry, love. I didn't mean to anger you."

He shook her hand away. "I'm your love now?" he asked softly. He leaned in as if to kiss her cheek. "Not today, I think," he whispered in her ear. She shuddered and backed away.

"Now, be on your way," Dan said with a wave of his gun. "You and I are done here."

She vanished down the hall as quick as her three-inch heels would carry her.

"That was risky," John said in a low voice.

"But it got us here," Dan said. He closed his eyes for a moment to center himself and slipped his gun into a coat pocket. John spat out the key and unlocked the handcuff.

Dan extended his hand. "For those we've lost."

John clasped his hand. "And for those who still need us."

Dan took a step closer to the door and was rewarded by the soft pneumatic swoosh as it opened. Warm light and cool air spilled out from the Professor's sanctuary. Grabbing John by his arm, Dan resumed his role of Cain-the-Captor, and they walked through the door.

———

Dan took in the room with a glance. More of a laboratory than just a simple study. Two rows of computers and technical equipment occupied the space to his right. It reminded him of Ames's lab at Stanford. But that was where the similarities ended. A macabre-looking chair dominated the center of the room, like a dentist chair with restraints. A massive mural stretched across the opposite wall filled with an intricate pattern of hundreds of small circles and connecting lines. Dan dismissed it all and focused on his target.

In front of the mural, the Professor sat behind a mahogany desk filled with two curved computer monitors and stacks of papers with spreadsheets and charts. He held an iPad in one hand and tapped on a keyboard with the other. The man's eyes never left the computer screens.

"You're back early," the Professor said in a distracted voice. "Is something wrong?"

Dan pushed John forward. "No, boss. Just found this for you."

The Professor's fingers paused above the keyboard. He did not turn his head, but his gaze slid from the screen and onto Dan. "My, my," the Professor said with humor in his voice. "You are a clever one."

Dan propelled John a few steps closer. "Not sure what you mean, boss. But I found this guy trying to break in, and I knew you'd want to see him."

"Oh, I am sure you did," the Professor said. His hands remained perched above the keyboard. A smile played at the corners of his mouth. "I'm afraid you've overestimated your chances, Agent Alexander. You should have brought more help."

The Professor resumed typing for a few seconds before he paused again. "Oh wait," he said. "There isn't anyone else. You're responsible for the deaths of your friends." He hesitated for another moment. His eyes looked up as if he were recalling a memory. "All of them." The smile took hold and spread across the man's face.

Dan advanced three more steps, dropped the duffel, and drew his Glock.

"Really, Daniel? There is nothing either of you can do that will cause me lasting harm," the Professor said. "And a gunshot will bring security in a matter of seconds."

John stepped forward to the desk, withdrew the spear from inside his duster, and used the tip to push a stack of papers off the mahogany surface. "This can," John said.

"Hello, old friend," the Professor said. "Did you bring me a gift?"

"More of an encouragement," John said. He used the sharp edge of the spear to carve a six-inch scratch into the top of the desk. "Your boy took Dr. Cranford from me, and it made me angry. You're going to come with me, and we will see what we can do to make this right."

The Professor pushed back from the desk and stood. "John, John, still stuck in your ways." He turned and moved to look up at the tapestry on the wall behind his desk. His hand traced along the gold-threaded line between the circles. "Technology has aided me, and I've found many of our brethren. Where we once thought it was just the two of us, I've found hundreds. And I've discovered it—a way to repopulate the world with our kind once we are rid of all of the Normals."

John rounded the desk, grabbed the Professor's arm, and spun him around. He thrust the tip of the spear under the man's chin and pressed up, making the Professor tiptoe to keep the spear from cutting him.

"I don't care," John said through gritted teeth.

"Be careful with that, old friend," the Professor whispered. "We both remember what you did with the spear last time. You won't want to break your vow."

"I'll do what I have to." John waved his hand at the lab. "One way or another, you have a different future now. A life away from all of this. I will not let you harm the innocents." John lowered the spear and pointed at the door. "Now move!"

The Professor sighed and shuffled across the room.

John caught the Professor's arm to hurry him along. John said, "Dan, I'll take him back and find somewhere to stash him. You stay here and do whatever it takes to stop the release of that virus."

As they passed him, the Professor jerked free and spun to face Dan. "Do you know your Bible, Daniel?"

When Dan said nothing, the Professor continued, "Genesis 4 tells an interesting tale. A story of two brothers. Do you know how it ends, Daniel?" He paused as if expecting Dan might know. Unwilling to play his game, Dan held his tongue. The Professor smiled and quoted the text from memory in a soft, almost reverent voice. "Genesis chapter 4, verse 8 reads, 'Cain spoke to his brother. And when they were in the field, Cain rose up against his brother…'"

John lowered the spear and touched it to the Professor's chest. The Professor glared at John but moved out the door. The Professor finished the quote from the hallway as the door slid closed.

"…and killed him."

CHAPTER THIRTY-ONE

John led the Professor down the hallway toward the exit and pulled up as they reached the last door before the security station. He pressed the tip of the spear into the man's sternum. "One wrong word, Luke, and you will see how fast I can put this through your heart."

The man stared at him with cold eyes. "I don't use that name anymore."

John met his stare. "You're still Luke to me."

"And you're still the same misguided fool," Luke replied.

John pulled him close. "I wasn't the one with the bone saw in his hand at Auschwitz."

Luke sighed. "It was necessary research at the time. Technology had not advanced far enough to allow me to access the workings of DNA."

"Well, don't make it *necessary* for me to end you. Remember, one wrong word…" John said. He slipped the spear into its sheath and pushed the door open. They strolled into the lobby.

One of the guards looked up from his security station and jumped to his feet. "Professor, sir, we weren't aware that you were leaving. I'll call your security detail."

"No, that won't be necessary," Luke said with a wave of his hand. "I'm just going with my friend here to his car."

John winked at the guard. Another guard rose, hand resting on his holstered weapon.

The guard pointed at John. "But, sir, Cain said he was a high-value target."

Luke looked back at John and smiled. "A high-value target? That sounds just like Cain, doesn't it? Always the flair for the dramatic." His smile faded as his focus shifted back to the guard. "This is a high-value *friend*. Step aside before I ask him to hurt you."

John gave the guard a feral grin, and the man backed away. Luke led the way, and they exited the building.

"To the left," John said. "I have a vehicle waiting. And you know I don't need the spear to beat the crap out of you."

John's backup vehicle, a black Camaro, sat three blocks down the street at a local grocery store. He stopped them by the passenger door and said, "Hold out your hands."

Luke sighed and held his arms out, wrists together. "Is this necessary?"

John withdrew a white heavy-duty zip tie, circled it around Luke's wrists, and pulled it tight without comment. He opened the passenger door and gestured with his hand.

Luke shook his head and chuckled. "I predicted you would come. The odds peaked at 88 percent following Cain's exploits yesterday." He slid into the seat.

"Always a nerd. How's that prediction working out for you?" John said and slammed the door.

The Camaro's deep-throated mufflers rumbled as they accelerated onto the freeway. John's mind raced. Now that he had Luke, what was he going to do with him?

"We don't have to be enemies, you and I," Luke said.

John shot him a glare and pulled up a playlist in the car's audio system. The staccato drumbeat of "Sympathy for the Devil" by the Rolling Stones began, and John turned up the volume.

"Their kind is finished, John," Luke called out over the music.

John frowned and turned the music up louder.

"I've found a way to replace them all," Luke shouted.

John heaved a sigh and turned the music down. "I won't let you do it. You can't just kill innocent people."

"They're not innocent, and you know it. And you're not one of them, even as much as you pretend to be. We both know what they will do when we are exposed."

"I've lived with them. Many have the capacity for greatness."

"Don't delude yourself. You're smarter than that. To them, we're freaks in a sideshow. They're all accepting when they need you. But as soon as they don't, they'll chain you up and see what entertainment you can provide. And just wait. You'll see how good they are as soon as things start falling apart on them. They'll carve you up looking for the cure."

John gripped the wheel and ground his teeth. "That's not going to happen. Dan will stop the virus."

"You're still the naive one," Luke said with another chuckle. "Daniel's no match for his brother. His feelings for Cain will betray him. No, my old friend, things will proceed as I have planned. And in the end, you'll join me."

—

John pulled the Camaro into the garage. He parked near his entrance, and they exited the car. With a nod of his head, John urged Luke into the elevator.

While they descended, John fished a knife out of a pocket. He snapped the blade open and motioned with his fingers for Luke to raise his wrists.

"Decided I'm not much of a threat?" Luke asked as he held out his hands. John cut through the plastic without comment, and Luke rubbed his wrists.

The elevator doors opened with a *ding*. They crossed the rotunda, and John paused to look down the long hall as the lights clicked on. His mouth went dry. He felt exposed. His unfinished research sat on the writing table, and each of the glass displays held his treasures—pieces of his life. He did not want to share any of it with Luke. John's pulse pounded. He withdrew the spear and held it at his side. "You will not comment as we pass through this area."

A smile played at the edges of Luke's mouth as John marched his captive down the corridor. Luke glanced at each display but held his tongue.

Until they reached the display with the rose and the ring.

Luke's face darkened, and he jerked to a stop. After a moment, Luke reached out and gently touched the glass. He whispered, "She was the best of them."

John left Luke to his memories. He crossed to the last display and pressed the hidden button. After the glass retracted, John placed the spear on its stand and stepped back. The glass slid closed with a soft hiss.

Luke remained frozen with his gaze fixated on the rose.

"Come with me," John said.

When Luke hesitated, John reached out to take his arm. Without looking, Luke caught John's wrist, and John felt the slightest of pricks. He grabbed Luke's hand and forced his arm up. A simple silver band encircled Luke's ring finger. A small needle glinted in the light from the display—a drop of red glowed on its tip.

John backhanded him, and Luke staggered back. John launched himself forward. His roundhouse kick connected with the side of Luke's head. The man fell to his knees. John moved in with a right cross to Luke's jaw that sent him sprawling to the floor, unconscious.

John felt the effects of some toxin spreading through his system. Winded, he leaned forward with his hands on his knees. He needed time for his body to win the war with the unknown chemicals. But Luke already stirred, and John felt the icy grip of dread fill his stomach.

I can't let him escape.

John straightened and lurched forward. As Luke pushed himself up onto his hands and knees, John kicked him in the midsection but without the same strength. Luke rolled to his side, placed a steadying hand on the wall, and climbed to his feet.

John advanced with two punches. Luke blocked both and landed a blow to John's stomach. The air rushed from John's lungs, and he lurched back. He shook his head, trying to fight off a growing dizziness.

And desperation.

With a yell, John charged back forward, lifted Luke from the floor, and slammed him down on the writing desk. Books flew across the corridor. A groan escaped from John as the desk collapsed, and both men landed on the hard floor. They rolled away in opposite directions.

Luke got to his feet first. He balanced on the balls of his feet in a way that revealed more training than John expected. John used the wall to help himself get upright and raised his arms defensively as Luke advanced. John managed to block three quick jabs, but an uppercut rocked him. Luke pressed his attack and swept John's legs out from under him.

John landed flat on his back. Stars swam across his vision. He had trouble breathing.

Luke loomed above him. "Nasty little toxin, wouldn't you say?" Luke stepped back and kicked him again.

John stifled a moan and rolled to his side. He lay about halfway down the hall—just across from the display of his Japanese artifacts. Trying to stall for time, he said, "You can't leave. And Dan will still come."

"Oh please, John. We've tracked your every move. Do you think my men don't know where I am? All we needed was the spear to prevent any others from duplicating her work."

The spear!

"What do you mean?" John asked. He rubbed his forehead. The effects of the drug began to fade.

"I know all about the doctor's research. Cain delivered her to me," Luke said and glanced back over his shoulder at the display with the rose. "She reminded me of someone you and I used to know." Luke turned back to John. "Before the end, she told me everything."

John's breath caught. He rolled over and struggled to rise. "I'll make you pay for what you did to her." Anger surged within him. John pressed his hand to the wall and managed to get his feet under him. With his head clearing a little more, he retreated up the hall away from Luke and stopped next to the display of the American historical items.

"Looking for something?" Luke called out as he stalked after John.

John pressed the button to open the display. He reached past the card with "*For Doc*" written on it and grabbed one of his western-style revolvers. He spun back—only to find Luke right in his face.

"Think that will help?" Luke asked and punched John in the face.

John reeled back. He fought to remain conscious. His vision cleared in time to see Luke lean back out of the display with the other pistol. He turned toward John and brought the weapon up. John raised his revolver.

A loud boom echoed down the hall as both guns fired simultaneously. The bullet impacted the right side of John's chest, and it threw him from his feet. He landed hard on his side only to see Luke topple to the ground in front of him with a bullet hole in the middle of his forehead. Luke's dead eyes gazed at him as John struggled for a breath.

John felt the slug pushing out between his ribs and his breathing return to normal. He levered himself up onto his hands and knees. A tiny *plink* made him glance at Luke. A flattened bullet lay on the floor next to Luke's face.

With a blink, the spark of life returned to Luke's eyes, and he smiled. Luke rolled onto his side, swung the pistol around to point at John, and pulled the trigger three quick times. A *click-click-click* was only his only reward. Luke snarled and threw the gun at John, but it sailed wide and clattered down the hallway.

John took a deep breath and jumped to his feet in time to give the still prone Luke a hard kick. Luke coughed in pain as he rolled away.

An unexpected wave of nausea roiled through John. He staggered several steps past Luke before he had to lean into the wall for support.

Behind him, he heard Luke get to his feet. A deep laugh filled the corridor.

"That little virus is very tricky. I developed it just for you. Mutates every ninety seconds," Luke said.

John slowed his breathing and leaned hard against the wall. He heard the soft scrape of a shoe on the tile floor and spun with a high kick that connected with Luke's temple. Luke's eyes rolled up, and he collapsed to the floor.

Fighting the effects of the virus, John took a few halting steps further down the hall. Dizzy, he leaned against the wall and then slid down to sit on the floor and waited.

Waited for Luke.

Sweat poured off his forehead. He only got a few seconds before Luke's eyes fluttered open. John forced himself back to his feet.

The virus can't last forever. Just need to immobilize him.

With a glare on his face, Luke rose to his feet.

John stood next to the display of Japanese artifacts. It held several items: an ancient tea set, a set of samurai armor, a silk robe.

And his katana.

As Luke charged down the hall at him, John opened the display and withdrew the weapon. Luke leaped into the air to deliver a tae-kwon-do-style flying kick. John countered with a kenpo one-arm block that sent Luke spinning past.

John turned to face his opponent and slid the thirty inches of cold steel from its sheath.

Luke stood about twelve feet away. He glanced into the display to his right, and a smile worked its way onto the corners of his mouth. With a shout, Luke shattered the glass with a swift punch and reached into the display of Crusade items to withdraw a short sword. He held the weapon up, feeling its balance. His smile broadened.

John swung the katana in an arc to loosen his muscles. He took a deep breath and relaxed.

Luke advanced on him with a series of rapid overhead strokes. John parried with his katana but retreated under the onslaught. Steel rang against steel. John backed into the wall as Luke closed in on him. One of Luke's strokes went wide, and John managed to force the sword down with his katana. He delivered a quick punch to Luke's stomach, and Luke stumbled back.

A fresh wave of viral dizziness consumed John. He had to buy some time, or Luke might chop him to pieces. He slid further back down the hall to stop by the display with the rose, resting a hand on the wall. "Who taught you how to fight?"

Luke advanced on him slowly. "I found Achilles about thirty years ago. He says I'm one of his best students in the last millennium."

John straightened and said, "I'm sure it has something to do with how *smart* you think you are."

"No," Luke replied and swept his sword back and forth in a series of controlled arcs. "He said I had the most single-minded approach he had ever seen."

"Then stop all of this," John said with a wave of his hand. "Return to the man you once were. Use that single-minded approach for good. We can save them from themselves. Teach them a better way."

"I'm afraid we are long past that, my old friend."

John looked at his blade. It glimmered in the soft light. "I saved you once using this. Don't make me use it to end you."

A savage look filled Luke's face. With a snarl, he charged forward with sword held high to rain blow after blow against John's katana. Luke danced to his left and thrust his sword at John's chest. John parried, forcing Luke's blade wide with his katana, and stepped in close, intending to slice through Luke's throat.

With lightning speed, Luke ducked and spun to his left with his sword extended. John cried out as Luke's sword sliced across his leg, cutting through his quadriceps and severing the femoral artery. On instinct, John brought his blade down hard and made contact. Luke's hand plopped onto the floor, and his short sword clattered to the side. Both men stumbled back, blood spurting from the gaping wounds, and waited.

The blood flow ebbed, and John felt his strength returning. He watched as Luke's hand reformed even as John felt the muscles of his leg knitting back together. "I only want to save you again, Luke."

Luke flexed his regrown fingers and retrieved his sword. "I don't need saving. You know they must pay for what they did to me. Before they do it again. And once they're gone, I will fill the world with clones of Immortals. I will build Eden again."

They locked eyes. John saw only the madness of revenge.

Time to end this.

Luke surged forward and renewed his attack. John parried an overhead blow. The steel grated together as he let his blade slide down Luke's, and he slammed his shoulder into Luke's chest. Stunned, Luke stumbled back into the wall. John lunged forward and drove his katana through Luke's chest, burying the steel tip deep into the wall behind the man.

Luke's eyes flared in surprise. He dropped his sword, gasped for a breath, and grabbed John by the shirt with both hands. John struggled back, but Luke's iron grip held him firm. With a choking sound in his throat, Luke slid along the katana. Blood poured from the wound in Luke's chest, but he just pulled harder. In an instant, they were face to face.

"I'm afraid it is you that will need saving," Luke whispered. He extended his arms, pushing John away, and then pulled back hard and delivered a powerful head-butt.

Pain exploded in John's head as stars swam across his vision. He felt himself slip from Luke's grasp as he lost consciousness and tumbled to the floor.

—

John heard glass crunching under someone's feet. Another bout of weakness gripped him, and he shuddered as the toxin assaulted his systems one more time.

How long have I been out?

He slowly opened one eye. Luke stood in front of one of the oldest displays—the one with the rose and the ring. The sword and John's katana lay abandoned to the side.

Confused, John called out to his once-friend, "Luke?"

Luke stared at the rose. After a long moment, Luke spoke but just above a whisper. "You didn't deserve her."

A memory of Amelia, the woman they both had loved, flashed through John's mind. "None of us did."

John shook his head. He had to prevent Luke from escaping. He placed a hand on the wall and managed to get to his knees. "We both know your poison won't kill me. I will eventually beat it. There is nowhere to hide, Luke. I will hunt you down."

Luke turned back and softly said, "I believe you, my old friend." He picked up the chair from the writing desk and walked over to the last display case, the one holding the spear. "And you're correct. There's

"Why do you care so much about them? You don't even know them," Cain said. He pointed an accusing finger at Dan. "And the ones you know, you always abandon. Like you did with your doctor friend."

Dan's breath caught.

And you.

Dan let his hands drop to his side. "I won't leave you again, Cain. But please, you have to help me stop this."

Cain's face reddened. "I don't care if you leave me. I never cared!" He lunged forward and delivered a barrage of jabs and kicks. Dan retreated under the onslaught. Cain landed a solid uppercut that staggered his brother. Trying to clear the fog from his mind, Dan backed away and bumped into the front of the desk.

"Feeling it yet, Brother?" Cain said. "We're just getting started."

Dan glanced at the timer.

Six minutes and twelve seconds.

"Cain—" Dan began, but Cain's renewed attack silenced him. Dan managed to land a straight jab as Cain stepped in, but the blow did not slow him and Dan took one to his body. He blocked the next two punches but only saw the sidekick just before Cain's heel connected with his jaw. Dan flew across the desk. The air whooshed from his lungs as he landed hard on his back. The knife clattered to the floor just to his right.

"They're not even like us!" Cain yelled. Then he added softly, "The Professor helped me see."

"But he's wrong. They're worth saving," Dan managed to reply.

Cain moved to stand over Dan and glared down at him. "So, your mission is to save them." Cain kicked him hard. "Well, mine is to destroy everything you care about. Just like you did Mom." He delivered another vicious kick that doubled Dan back up. He bent down close and added, "I'll *take* them all."

Cain turned, pulled the key from around his neck, and headed to the desk. "This is working out just fine for one of us. Let's not wait any longer. I say we get this party started now!"

"Stop," Dan said, anguish in his voice. "Don't make me kill you."

Cain spun back toward him but stopped when he saw Dan had managed to stand and now aimed the tranquilizer gun at him. Cain barked out a laugh. "Kill me! Haven't you learned anything yet? What are you going to do, knock me out? Poison me? None of that works on us, you fool."

Dan took a labored breath. "Ames figured it out. Just before you took her. John helped her understand the essence of the Spear of Destiny. She found its secret. It let her make a…a serum. It will make you mortal again."

Uncertainty passed across Cain's face. He looked at a bank of monitors on a far wall. "The Professor thought she might try that. She didn't tell us she succeeded."

Dan followed his gaze to the security feeds. Most displayed empty labs or server rooms. But in one, a woman sat at a table, head in her hands. *Ames.*

"How?" Dan whispered.

Cain's sneer returned. "You're so gullible, you idiot. It was all part of my plan. The Old Man wanted to see if she had discovered uses for the spear, but I couldn't pass up the chance to have some fun with you first. You should have seen the *extraordinary* look on your face when you thought she was in that building. But now, you'll get to watch her die for real, along with the rest of the trash." With the key in hand, Cain moved around the desk toward the inlay.

"Forgive me, Brother," Dan said and fired the dart.

Cain flinched as it stuck high on his shoulder. He whirled on Dan, snatched the dart from his arm, and threw it. "This changes nothing! I'll never stop taking them from you," he bellowed. But a spasm shuddered through him. Swaying, Cain shook his head and placed a hand on the desk. He glared at Dan with hate-filled eyes, took the final step, and moved to insert the key.

Dan's heart hammered in his chest. He looked around the room, desperate for help, and saw his one hope—the knife. Dan grabbed it from the floor. "Cain, stop!"

Cain slid the key into the inlay. He smiled and whispered, "I'll take them all."

Dan straightened and raised his hand with the knife to a throwing position, all the while willing Cain to stop. But Cain's hand tensed on the key.

And Dan let the knife fly.

It spun through the air, end over end. Each time the tip rotated toward Cain, a glimmer of light reflected from the blade like a warning light on some tower.

Until it found its target.

Cain looked down at the blade protruding from his chest. Shock, then fear, cascaded across his face. He clutched the knife with both hands to pull it out, but his knees buckled, and he toppled forward, bouncing off the desk to sprawl on the floor. His eyes found Dan as he struggled for a breath.

Dan raced to his side and took his hand. Tears began streaking down Dan's face. "Cain, I'm here. I've got you."

Cain gripped his hand tight and pulled him closer. "Mom never forgave you, did she?"

Dan rocked back as if Cain had delivered one final blow, but his brother's grip tightened again and pulled him even closer. Cain's eyes held his gaze for an accusing moment. "He will finish this for me," he managed to whisper. And with his last breath, he spit in Dan's face.

For a long moment, Dan just stared at his dead brother. He wiped the spittle from his face and looked at the bloodstained streak it made on his hand. Rage and guilt boiled within him, and he yelled a defiant "Why?"

But no answer came.

He took a deep, pained breath and closed his eyes. He wanted to stay with his brother. But in his heart, he knew he had to finish the mission.

With Cain's blood still on his hands, Dan rounded the desk and turned the key to the standby position. The timer stopped at five minutes and four seconds. He pounded on the computer keyboard and squeezed his eyes shut, but relief did not make it past his pain.

Dan leaned back in the chair and glanced at the display with the twelve small feeds of the target cities. The deadly virus still had to be collected. Dan withdrew his phone and snapped off several pictures of the screen. He attached them to a hastily composed email to the Director's office in DC and hit send. He wanted to do more, but there was no time.

With a quick look around the lab, Dan set three charges of C4 at strategic locations. He grabbed his duffel and made for the exit but stopped for one last look at his brother. A shuddering breath escaped him. Dan glanced at the video feed of Ames.

She's still the mission.

Jaw clenched, he headed out the door.

CHAPTER THIRTY-THREE

As he wandered the corridors, Dan wondered how much time he had before someone found Cain. Various people passed him, most dressed in white lab coats. All in a hurry. He checked another door, found it locked, and moved on with a frown.

He had no idea how to find Ames.

As he rounded a corner, Dan saw two guards stationed outside a door. No other door had security posted. Without hesitation, he strode up to the guards. "Open the door. I want to interrogate the prisoner."

"Sir?" one asked. "This is the Server Control. The prisoner is in Lab C."

A bead of sweat ran down Dan's spine. "I know that, you idiot." Dan held up the duffel bag. "I want to drop this off and then go see the prisoner."

The guard exchanged a worried glance with his partner. "Okay, sir," he said, and they stepped aside.

Dan stared at another biometric lock. His mind raced. He reached into his pocket, pulled out his cell, and looked at the screen. With a look of annoyance, Dan pretended he had a call. He motioned to the man. "Get the door for me." Then he said, "What?" into the phone.

"But, sir," the guard said. "You know we can't do that."

Dan smiled at the man as he fake-listened to his call and nodded toward the door. "*It's okay*," he mouthed silently.

The guard's worried look deepened into a suspicious frown.

Dan turned slightly to his right and set down his bag. "Yes, yes," he said into the phone and casually stepped closer to the man. He made eye contact with the guard and raised his eyebrows with a smirk as if annoyed by the call. "Okay, we will just have to—"

Dan hit the guard square in the face. The man reeled back against the door. Dan leaped at the other guard and drove him into the wall. They grappled for a moment before Dan delivered a head-butt that collapsed the man to the floor.

The other guard pulled his weapon and yelled, "Freeze."

Dan straightened and glared at the man. "Holster your weapon, you fool."

The guard's eyes shifted from Dan to his partner on the floor and back. "I don't understand, sir." The guard did not lower his weapon.

Dan smiled. "Just having a little fun. Seeing what you guys can handle." Dan ignored the weapon and moved to retrieve the duffel. He pushed past the guard as if he meant to open the door and then elbowed the man hard in his stomach. The guard grunted and bent forward, but his weapon hand came up and fired point-blank at Dan.

Pain exploded in Dan's leg as the round hit him in the upper thigh. Dan cursed under his breath and finished the guard with a powerful uppercut to his jaw.

With a deep breath, Dan straightened and closed his eyes. The pain faded, and he heard a metallic *plink*, like the sound a quarter makes when you drop it on a hard floor. With a smile, he looked down to find the bullet lying on the smooth tile.

It took a few awkward tries to get the unconscious man's hand onto the biometric read, but the lock clicked happily, and Dan pulled the door open. A long, rectangular room stretched out for about forty feet. Rows of server racks filled the room. A table with six monitors occupied the left wall with a nerd wearing headphones sitting at a keyboard.

The man jumped up when he saw Dan and pulled the earbuds from his ears. "Cain, sir. I was not expecting anyone. Is something wrong?"

Dan sensed an opportunity he had not expected. "I just received word of a breach at the external hosting facility." Confusion swam across the man's face. Dan ran with his idea. "Didn't you complete the off-site backup of the formulas?"

"Sir?" the man stammered. "We have the external drives ready for transport as the Professor directed." The nerd pointed at two briefcases. "But I was not made aware of any cloud storage. I mean, given the Professor's paranoia regarding security, I don't see how we will ever—"

Dan interrupted him with a quick jab to the face, and he crumpled to the floor. Dan hauled him to one side and returned to the desk. The displays crowded the small workstation. One labeled "Environmental Systems" caught his eye. With a little green and red light in each room, it presented a layout of the complex. He clicked on the floor plan, and it expanded, displaying more details of each room with the room's name flashing in bold.

A quick search through the plans revealed the location of Lab C. Dan shouted, "Yes!" and tapped the screen. The lab sat in the middle of his floor, just a few doors away.

He armed four blocks of C4 and hid them in key positions. Dan hurried from the room, dragging the nerd out, and piled him onto the unconscious guards. Only one thing remained.

Getting Ames.

———

Dan planted more explosives on the structural support columns along the way to Lab C. With his firearm at his side, he rounded the final corner. Another guard stood outside a door on the left, and Dan marched up with concern on his face.

Dan held his gun at the ready as if he expected an attack at any moment. "There's been a breach. We have to get the prisoner to a more secure location."

The guard took one look at Dan and drew his weapon. He glanced up and down the hall for any threats. "Yes, sir, Cain, sir. But why has no one sounded the alarm?"

"There's been some confusion. I think someone is impersonating me. I'll secure this position," Dan said. He nodded at the door. "You get the prisoner."

"Will do, sir." With a press of his hand on the reader, the guard unlocked the door. Dan clubbed him on the back of his head as the man pulled the door open, and the guard sagged to the floor.

"Sorry," Dan said.

Ames looked up as he entered. She sat at a metal table with a computer and some lab equipment arrayed in front of her. She glared at him. "I told you. I won't help you."

When he took a step in her direction, she grabbed the computer keyboard and hurled it at him. Dan deflected the keyboard with his left hand and blocked the mouse with his right as he rounded the end of the table. She stood defiantly. Only then did he see her ankle handcuffed to the bench.

He raised both hands. "Ames, it's me, Dan."

Arm raised, ready to throw a coffee cup, she hesitated. Hope flashed in her eyes, but they narrowed back into an angry glare. "You showed me the video of the explosion, you bastard. I saw him die!" She let the cup fly, and it glanced off his forehead.

He staggered back a little and rubbed his brow. "Ames, it's really me," he said. "I can prove it."

She paused in her search for the next projectile. "How?"

Dan knew what he had to tell her.

"I left you once. Just left. Never even told you why." He put a hand on the cold metal table. "My mom called that day. I hadn't spoken to her in five years." He breathed deep and forced himself to continue. "You see, it was my fault. My fault that they took Cain." Dan ran his hand through his hair. "She blamed me. And she was right. Wouldn't forgive me. And I didn't deserve it, anyway. But when she called and said we needed to talk, I thought she might give me another chance." His gaze fell to the floor. "I couldn't tell you without having to explain about Cain. So I flew out to see her, thinking I'd call you after I talked with her."

Ames's eyes softened. She took a step in his direction, but the metal cuffs clanked against the bar.

Dan moved closer to her. "She was dying. That's what she wanted to tell me."

Ames held out her hand. But Dan did not take it. Instead, he bent down to unlock the restraints. He finished without looking up. "She died the day I arrived. She never forgave me. Told me that with her last words."

He stood and faced Ames. "I don't deserve your forgiveness either, Ames. But I'm going to get you out of this."

She placed a hand on each side of his face and stared into his eyes. "You've finally come back. It took you long enough," she said in a tender voice.

And she kissed him.

———

After getting some much-needed instructions from Ames on virus disposal, Dan planted enough incendiaries to roast the remaining virus in its canisters, followed by the careful placement of the rest of the C4, enough to bring down the whole complex, on the interior support columns. Satisfied, Dan motioned for Ames to wait and stepped out into the hall.

Outside the door, he rolled the guard over and tapped his face a couple of times. The man started coming around, and his eyes fluttered open. Dan pulled him up into a sitting position.

"What…what happened?" the man stammered.

Dan rubbed the back of his own head. "They ambushed us. We've lost containment in the lab. We've got to get everyone out."

The man's eyes opened wide, and he struggled to rise. "How?"

Dan helped him up. "Don't know for sure. I need you to sound the alarm, then check on the men down there." Dan pointed down the hall in the direction of his other casualties.

With confusion in his eyes, the man looked both ways and opened his mouth to object.

"Move!" Dan ordered. "They've set explosives. You've only got a couple of minutes before this place blows."

The guard's mouth snapped shut, and he ran down the hall in Dan's specified direction. He slid to a stop at the corner, pulled the plastic cover from an alarm, and pounded the button. A loud klaxon sounded, and the man hurried on around the corner.

Dan turned back and held out his hand to Ames. "I suggest I continue my performance as my brother with you as the prisoner."

As he turned to go, the two guards from the server room came charging around the corner with their weapons drawn. They pulled up and leveled their gun at Dan and Ames.

Dan stepped in front of Ames. "Hey, boys."

"Down on your knees," one guard yelled.

Hands raised, Dan took another step closer. "It's okay, men. There's been a breach in the lab. We've got to get out."

"Don't come any closer," the other guard shouted.

"We just—" Dan began and took another step. Both guards opened fire, and Dan took a round high in the chest. He staggered back.

"Dan!" Ames screamed.

Dan spun to face her, smiled, and drew his weapon. With a quick turn, he fired two times and dropped both guards.

Ames rushed to his side. "Oh, Dan. Let me help you."

He bent forward, hands on his knees. "I'm okay. I just need a minute."

"But how?" she asked.

Dan straightened with a grin. "I've had some upgrades."

———

By the time they were approaching the lobby, Dan felt fully recovered. They joined the tide of those seeking to escape from whatever impending doom the alarms foretold. The anxious crowd surrounded them like a school of fish, and they flowed through the doors and out into the street. Dan took Ames by the arm and led her across to the waiting Bronco.

Once seated, Dan pulled out the detonator and flipped off the safety cap. They watched as the river of evacuees slowed to a trickle.

"Where's John?" Ames asked.

"He's back at the compound. We kidnapped the Professor, and John's got him locked up," Dan replied. "Probably has Petros cooking him some Greek dish by now."

Ames's smile was fleeting. "And Reid?"

Dan's breath caught. "Didn't make it."

A stillness filled their small space.

"And your brother?" she whispered.

Several beats of silence passed.

"Dead," Dan said and flipped the switch on the detonator.

CHAPTER THIRTY-FOUR

They headed back toward Georgia Tech. Silence filled the car like a rising tide on a moonless night. The lab was gone, but so was Cain.

Dan glanced at Ames. As she stared out the side window, she bit her lip and ran her hand through her hair. He put his hand on her shoulder. She turned to him, and her eyes sought the reassurance he hoped she found.

"We're safe now, Ames. Everyone is."

She offered him a tight smile and relaxed a little. Her gaze returned to the front.

He had saved her. *But not Cain.* Dan heaved a sigh and shook his head.

He pulled the Bronco into the garage of John's building and parked. Ames did not reach for the door but stared out the front.

"What happens now, Dan?" she asked softly. "Do we just go back to our old lives? Knowing what we do now?" Her green eyes met his. "And what about us, now that you're, you know…one of them?"

"I don't know. But I'm not leaving you. We'll figure out the rest. John will know what to do," he said and then exited the vehicle.

After a moment, Ames joined him at the elevator. They rode down in silence and stepped into the round room. Dan froze and raised a wary hand. The four paintings on the walls hung in tatters. A knife lay discarded in the center of the room.

"Stay behind me," Dan said. He stared into the shadows of the long hallway. "John?"

Silence filled the complex.

They moved into the gloom of the hallway, and the lights began to flicker on. Soft light filled the corridor from the sconces spaced down the walls, except for one at the far end. Broken pieces of glass lay scattered just at the edge of the light. Halfway down the hall, the shattered pieces of the small writing desk littered the floor.

Ames grabbed his hand and whispered, "What happened?"

"I don't know." He gently removed his hand from hers and started down the hall. "But wait here."

She jerked him back around by his arm. "Like hell. I'm in this with you, Dan. We stay together."

He met her gaze. The look in her eyes convinced him that any argument would be long and probably lost. "Okay, just stay behind me," he said. She frowned but nodded her agreement.

They edged down the corridor. Glass crunched under their feet as they neared the end of the hallway. Blood coated the floor and a large section of one wall. A few of the displays were open. Others had the glass smashed. Items appeared to be missing, but Dan was unsure what might have been taken.

As he approached the last two, Dan paused and held up a warning hand to Ames. The display with the rose and the ring sat empty. The rose lay in the middle of the floor, pulverized as if ground under someone's heel. The remains of the last display were strewn about the hallway with apparent disregard for their heritage.

But the spear was missing.

"What happened?" Ames whispered again.

Dan held his finger to his lips. He tilted his head as he strained to pick up any sounds. The hall that continued to the right toward the arsenal was dark, but the door to the meeting room stood open to the left.

A small thud came from somewhere to his left. He motioned for Ames to remain behind him, and they entered the meeting room. A dim light came from a single lamp on the far side. Dan surveyed the area, trying to piece together what had happened. The couch lay on its back. The long table that occupied the middle of the room had found its way to the opposite wall. Overturned chairs and a smashed lamp littered the floor—all evidence of a vicious fight.

A soft, pained whisper escaped the shadows to their left. "Dan."

They spun toward the voice. Dan saw someone lying in the gloom near the wall.

John.

"Ames, get the lights on," Dan called as he rushed to where John lay.

Ames hurried to the control panel behind the desk and pressed a button. Light filled the room.

Dan knelt by John, and his breath caught. *Jesus, what happened?* Multiple bruises, a busted and bleeding lip, and a swollen eye—all shouted at Dan that John had changed. But the moist, dark patch on his ripped shirt told a more urgent story.

"Ames, get the med-kit!" Dan shouted.

John's eyes blinked open, and he grabbed Dan's hand. "I failed you," he said. "I'm sorry, Dan. I let my guard down. He took it." John paused and struggled for a breath. "But I don't have much time. Get the Bible."

Dan pried his hand free of John's grip. "It's okay, John. We stopped them. Everyone is safe. Now, lie still. Ames is here. She'll help you." He ripped open the man's blood-soaked shirt. A small red stream ran from a jagged wound in his chest. Dan looked about, desperate to find something to staunch the flow. "Ames, where are you? He's hurt bad," Dan shouted again.

"Dan, listen to me," John pleaded. "I can feel it…I don't have much time. You must get me the Bible." He managed to lift one arm to point at the desk. "Hurry."

Dan looked from John to the desk and back. Ames rounded the corner and rushed to John's side. She opened the kit, ripped the packaging from a large gauze pad, and pressed the white bandage onto the chest wound.

"Apply pressure here," she ordered. Dan placed his hands over the already red cloth. Ames said, "We need to stabilize him here and get him to a—"

"No!" John shouted and then moaned in pain. "There is so much I didn't tell you. You must get the Bible." A wet cough erupted from John, and blood trickled from his lips.

Dan nodded at the bandage for Ames to take over. He made a frantic dash to the desk, yanking open three drawers before he found an old, tattered Bible, grabbed it, and hurried back to John's side. Ames's tear-filled eyes met his as he knelt. With a soft sob, she shook her head.

Dan thought the man sought some final comfort. "Here it is, John. Is there some passage I'm supposed to read?"

"No," John hissed through clenched teeth. "Just open it."

Dan hesitated, not understanding what the dying man wanted, but opened the old book and stared at the pages. A pair of light-brown tinted sunglasses sat in a carved-out section in the center of the book. He pulled glasses free and held them up for John to see.

"It gives it to you," John said with an effort. "John-21-23 is the activation code. Say it."

"Gives what to us?" Dan asked.

"Everything. Everything I have. Say it!" John said and then lapsed into a spasming cough.

Dan's mind raced. Confusion filled his thoughts. But seeing the look of distress on John's face, he held up the glasses and repeated, "John-21-23." The glasses seemed to flicker to life. Dan caught a glimpse of something displayed on the interior of the lenses.

John sighed. "You will..." he said. Dan dropped the glasses back into the book and leaned in to hear the rest. "You will need it all to stop him. Luke has the spear and will find a way to use it." He continued in a halting voice, "He's not done. It may take time, but he will try again. You need Ames. Don't lose her."

"She's right here, John. We'll stop him," Dan looked up at Ames. "And I'll never lose her again."

John's eyes sought out Ames, and he breathed a soft, "Amelia." With desperation, John struggled to say more but failed. Ames's hand went to her chest, and she leaned forward to kiss him softly on the cheek. A small smile edged onto John's lips.

"It's okay," he managed with a sigh. "I'll finally be back with him. It's been so long." His smile faded, and he gasped for breath. His eyes locked onto Dan's again. "You must promise me..." John began, but he lapsed into silence. His eyes fluttered closed.

Dan took John's hand. "Promise you what?"

John struggled for another breath. "Promise me…that you will succeed where I failed."

"Of course, John. We'll stop him. I promise," Dan said.

Although his eyes stayed closed, John's grip tightened on Dan's hand like a vise and pulled him close. "No, not that," John said. "Promise me… that you'll save him. That you'll save Luke." He shuddered and exhaled his last breath.

Dan held John's hand for a long moment. With the weight of the dead man's last request heavy on his heart, he eased John's hand gently onto his friend's chest. Dan gazed up at Ames. The fierce look of determination on her face matched his feelings. He reached out and took her hand, and she gave him a firm, single nod.

Together.

CPSIA information can be obtained
at www.ICGtesting.com
Printed in the USA
BVHW040831240122
627016BV00015B/427/J